Awakening

Also by J. Ross

Awoken

The Adanya Saga Book 1

Awakening

J. Ross

J. Ross, LLC

jrossauthor.net

First edition 2025

Book Cover by Kozakura

Edited by Kelly Scriven

Library of Congress Number: TXU002498554

ISBN: 979-8-218-61626-7

For Jack – the Rashidi to my Adanya

HARRUN
RYDELL
OKEFE
DAHO

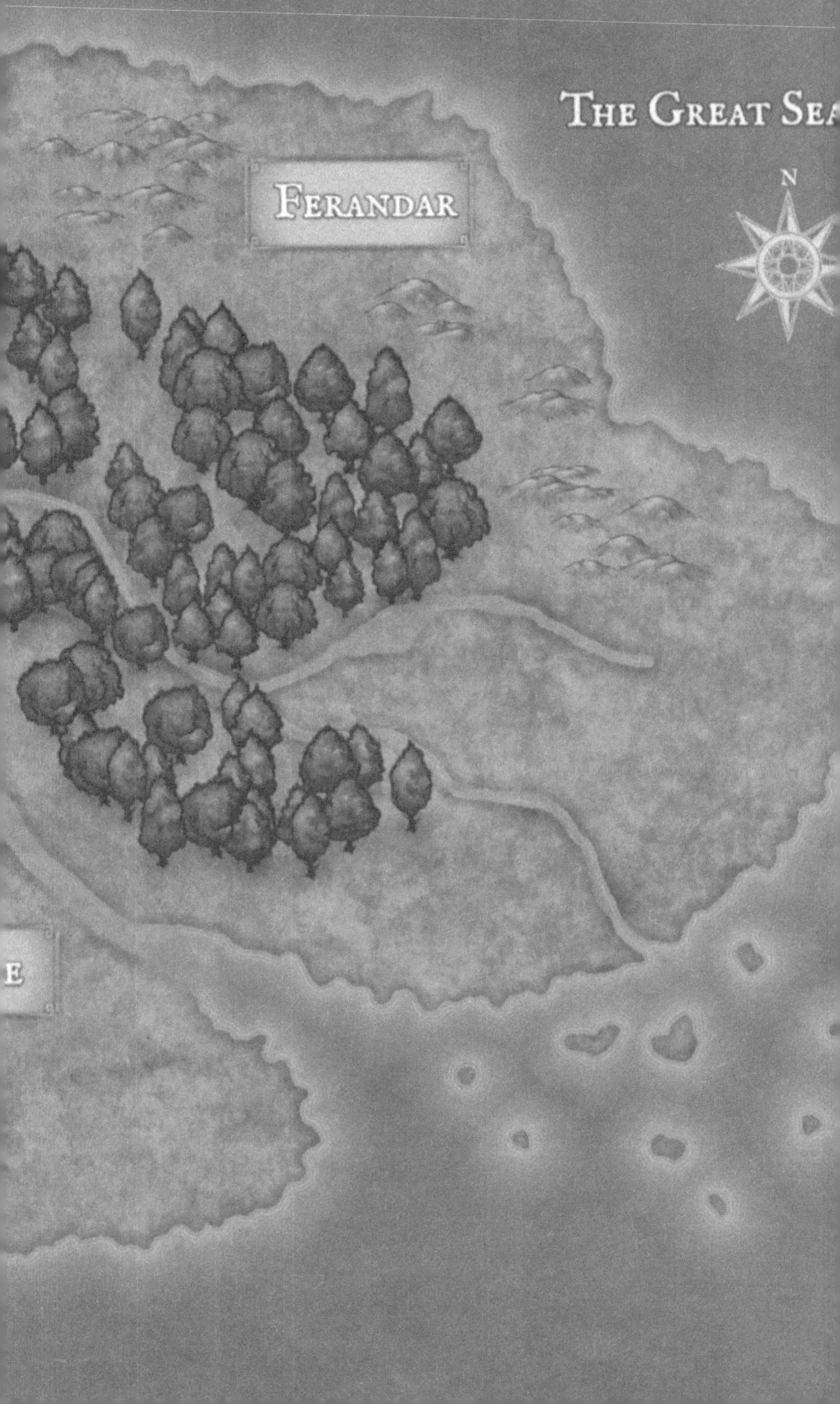

THE GREAT SEA
FERANDAR
N
E

Chapter One

I'll see you when you wake up. I love you.

Adanya's eyes fluttered open, slowly focusing on her surroundings through her waking haze. Something was wrong. This was not her room at the palace; that would be brightly lit in the morning, with sunlight streaming in through gauzy curtains and morning breezes carrying the fresh scents of honeysuckle and lilac into her simple, cozy space.

This? This place was dark. Dismal. Lacking any warmth. The only light came through a square window, roughly hewn from the stone walls around her. Instead of her soft sheets, she lay upon a hard cot barely off the floor. A wooden table and chair stood in the corner, but these were coated with dust and in brittle stages of disrepair. As she attempted to sit up, she jolted in surprise, discovering a netting over her that protected her from that same dust.

She cast the netting aside, shaking out her waist-long black braids and her gray robes as she continued trying to figure out what was going on. The stiffness in her limbs puzzled her; the magic that had caused her slumber should have warded against that. Her eyes, brown except for the ring of gray around the irises, spotted her wooden staff leaning against the single door to the room, and she moved over to take hold of it.

Suddenly, everything came rushing back. The magic slumber. Nehanda's promise. The enemy invasion. Rashidi.

If she was awake, it must mean the kingdom was saved. The invading army had been destroyed, the people were safe, and it was time to get back to business as normal.

Then why did everything feel so wrong?

Adanya closed her eyes, tightening her grip on her staff to ground herself as she called upon her magic. As a Sage, blessed with the powers of telepathy and empathy, she could sense the presence of every living thing, especially those with personal connections to her—like the people of Rydell. If she chose, she could sense what they were doing, even what emotions they were feeling at the moment. In some cases, she could see them as if through a mirror.

But reaching out now? She felt nothing. No one. She should have been able to feel them all slumbering, waiting for her to awaken them. Something was terribly wrong.

Gathering herself, she reached for the door latch and pushed down, fighting against what seemed to be the rust of time before it finally moved. The door swung open on creaky hinges.

Adanya froze. As they had planned, Nehanda had found a simple cottage some distance from the palace where Adanya would slumber, waiting for Rashidi to awaken her when everything was safe. When she entered the cottage, the woods around it had been pushed back, and there was even a small flower garden out front. Now the garden and woods were overgrown, vines and roots creeping back into the yard and beginning to overtake the house. It was clear no one had approached the cottage in quite some time. But the slumber had not been meant to last beyond a few months, a year at most.

Her mind raced. Had Harrun attacked the capital before Nehanda and the others were able to enact their part of the plan? Had something gone wrong with the magic? She had to get to the palace and find out what was happening.

She only made it a few steps from the cottage door, however, when an ear-shattering roar split the air. She tensed. She knew that sound. An *Ugwe*. The monsters she had worked so hard to protect the kingdom from. If they had broken the magical barriers she created to keep them out...

The sorceress's thoughts were cut short by a series of crashes and the earth shaking. The monster was approaching.. She took a stance, bracing herself and gripping tighter to her staff as she reached out with her magic to pinpoint where the creature was. *There.* She could not see all of its bulk, but flashes of razor-sharp teeth and claws darted through her mind. She was powerful, but not powerful enough to fight it on her own. She focused her thoughts, directing the creature in a different direction with all her willpower.

She felt the creature respond, altering its course and thundering away from her, back into the woods. She paused, waiting for the crashing to die away into the distance before relaxing her stance.

She struggled to collect her thoughts, trying to decide her next steps. Should she go to the palace? Or should she go to Rashidi's resting place and find out if something had prevented him from waking?

Her fingers twisted the engagement ring on her hand, a simple golden band with a single amethyst set into it, which she wore next to the ring of office that showed her rank as the head of the magical council.

Rashidi it was.

Adanya set out through the woods, using her staff to push through the underbrush. She reviewed the plan in her mind, attempting to reassure herself that there were safeguards, that the worst couldn't have happened.

But the fact that she had awoken alone, and that she could not feel the presence of her people, gave her a sinking feeling things had not gone to plan.

After nearly twenty minutes, she found the road leading to Rashidi's waiting place. Even here, things seemed amiss. The roads in Rydell had always been meticulously maintained, making travel through the country easy. But now the dirt road was filled with holes, and several parts seemed to have been washed away by floods.

She closed her eyes again, searching this time for animals instead of people. Soon, she felt the presence of a horse, and she used her power to call out to him. After a few moments, a whinny sounded from her right. A beautiful dapple-gray horse trotted over, resting his head on her shoulder in greeting before standing alongside her to allow her to mount. She gripped his mane and swung herself onto his back, holding her staff in her left hand.

"Thank you, friend," she murmured, patting his neck. "I don't know what's going on, but I'm glad of your company."

They galloped off down the road. Adanya kept reaching out with her magic, trying to connect with someone, anyone; she encountered nothing but the animals who now seemed to roam freely across the land.

As they drew closer to Rashidi's resting place, she felt her heart nearly stop in her chest. Nestled in another clearing, the cottage that should have been his hiding place was in ruins, the roof caved in and overgrown with vines, a tree growing inside it.

The horse cantered to a stop, allowing her to slide from its back and slowly approach the cottage. She took hesitant steps, anxious to know if he was inside but unsure what she would do if he was. Then she noticed something she had not seen from afar: what looked like a gravestone in front of the house.

Rashidi - Devoted soldier, husband, and father

Adanya's staff clattered to the ground, her hands shaking. What did this mean? Not only was there a gravestone dedicated to him in the place he should have been, alive and well, but ... husband? Father? None of this made any sense.

A crackle of branches nearby snapped her back to the present. Reaching for her staff, she looked to see where the horse had gone. He was nearby, but he was not the source of the noise.

Stepping out of the trees was a man in a brown cloak who looked exactly like Rashidi, from the bald, scarred head to the black beard and muscular stature.

They stared at each other for a moment. Clearly, he had not been expecting to find anyone there, as evidenced by his hand at his sword.

Adanya's throat was suddenly dry, her mind trying to make sense of what she was seeing. She cleared it and croaked, "Rashidi?"

He tilted his head. "No ... Who are you? How did you find this place?"

"You ... you look like my Rashidi." She subconsciously examined him with her magic, her heart sinking when she sensed this young man's energy was not that of her fiancé.

He took a hesitant step forward, hand still on his sword but his grip loosened. "Who are you?" he asked again.

"I am the Head of the Council of Sorcerers, Adanya." She couldn't fathom why he didn't know who she was.

He gasped. "It can't be."

"Please. Please tell me what's going on. Where am I?"

Now his hand left his sword, and he took another step toward her. "The stories were true. You never did awaken, until now."

"Please," she begged in a half-whisper, tears springing to her eyes with the overwhelming emotions swirling in her. "Please tell me."

He hesitated. "This ... This is not the time in which you went to sleep. The legends said that you were still slumbering somewhere, but your magic protected you from outside eyes, so no one was able to find you or wake you. It's been nearly seventy years since you went to sleep."

"But ... how?"

"I am Rashidi's great-great-grandson. And things did not go to plan."

Chapter Two

"The numbers that we have are not great enough to defend the people. Even if we brought in more soldiers, we would still be no match for their forces. The soldiers kill with no rhyme or reason, attacking at random and killing everyone in the towns they approach. Harrun is determined to destroy everyone in the kingdom, not just overtake us.'" The echoes of King Keon's booming voice faded into the recesses of the empty throne room as he finished reading. He folded the correspondence back up, falling into silence.

Adanya looked over at the king from her seat beside his throne, sensing his troubled thoughts. This man was the closest thing she had to a father. She admired his control in hard situations and his calm temperament no matter what was happening. Even now, he was still calm, but his furrowed eyebrows let her know he was deep in thought. Though she could easily have looked into his mind, she chose instead to wait for him to share his thoughts with her, knowing it would be an invasion of his privacy.

She remained silent to let him think, her own thoughts racing. If the army could not defend the kingdom, it would be up to the council to use magic to do so—but none of them were strong enough, even together, to defeat an entire army. It would take coordinated efforts, perhaps striking at leadership to weaken the enemy's morale. And if what they had seen from the enemy thus far was any indicator, even morale wouldn't slow them down.

"To the best of our knowledge," King Keon rumbled, turning to look at her, "does Harrun have any sorcerers that would be able to counter you and the council?"

She shook her head. "They have no formalized magical council. There may be other undiscovered sorcerers like I was, but they would not be trained or organized enough to aid him. From what I understand, their King doesn't care much for magic anyway. He prefers to make things happen with brute strength."

The king nodded. "Take this information back to the council. I'm sure that you all can come up with a plan to help the people."

"Of course, Your Majesty." She rose to go, straightening her robes.

"Adanya." He caught her hand, squeezing it comfortingly. "Don't be scared. I have every confidence in you and the council. Everything will be alright."

Adanya smiled at him, then bowed and left the throne room for the council chambers. Though the king did not have Sage magic, he was always very in tune with her thoughts and feelings. Normally, such reassurances from the king would instantly put her at ease, but there was something about this situation—the reports of Harrun's soldiers killing all who crossed their path—that would not leave her mind. The feeling of something being ripped from her heart hours before reports of another massacre arrived only strengthened them; her Sage powers made her especially attuned to the loss.

She cleared her mind long enough to reach out to the council, requesting their presence in their chambers in an upper room of the palace.

Once there, she paced back and forth beside the long table that housed their discussions, waiting for the members to arrive. They were not long in coming. The six of them greeted her respectfully as their leader and took their places at the table, sensing from Adanya's summons that it was no time for pleasantries.

They watched her as they waited for her to speak, their eyes all carrying the outward sign of their kind of magic, a colored band around their irises. She finally sat down at the head of the table, her hand fidgeting with her staff and looking around at all of them. They were the youngest council in Rydell's history, no one past middle age, but the room was full of wisdom and experience. So though she was the head of the order, as the youngest of them, there were still times she did not feel as if she were ready for the position.

Nehanda, her mentor who sat to her right, fixed her with an icy glare. *Get ahold of yourself,* Adanya read in her look.

"I take it there isn't good news," Adio said, his light-skinned cheeks rosy despite the seriousness of the situation.

"There's really nothing the army can do," Adanya reported. "We may be the only chance that the country has. The question is, what do *we* do?"

"It's going to have to be a concentrated effort," Gabir mused, dusting a stray leaf from his pant leg. "The seven of us are powerful together, but something of this magnitude won't be as simple as flexing our magical muscles."

"What motivates their king?" Naeemah asked in her musical voice. "Why is he so dead set on destroying us? Is it resources? Riches?"

"We are the only country standing between him and the other kingdoms," Kamaria pointed out, eyes flaring slightly as she spoke. "Whether he wants to conquer or he wants to trade, he has to go through us. I'll remind everyone that Harrun is one of the few countries that have been openly hostile to magical folk, likely because we're not easily controlled."

"His soldiers aren't motivated in the same way that ours are," Adanya said. "Our soldiers fight to protect families, loved ones, and the country that they care about. But Harrun's soldiers ... It's as if fear drives them to the most violent versions of themselves. Destroying their leaders would likely do nothing to dissuade them if they are still afraid. It's so strong I would almost think it magical influence if we did not know of Harrun's aversion to magic."

"It's the king's influence, nothing more," Nehanda cut in matter-of-factly. "They know that if they fail him, a far worse fate than dying in battle awaits them and their families at home. Based on what I know of the history of their kingdom, fear and control and violence is what built it in the first place."

"So if we destroy the king, will it truly end this?" Adanya asked.

"It is likely," Nehanda replied.

Jabari shifted, the hawk on his shoulder shifting as well to keep its balance. "He doesn't have an heir? Or some council member that would take over if he's gone?" he asked.

Nehanda shook her head. "He never married, and he does not keep council."

"A bold move for a king looking to expand his borders," Kamaria said.

"I have an idea, though it will be up to the council to decide if we think it is plausible," Nehanda said. Everyone looked at her, one of the oldest members of the council though she was only fifty-one. "What if you were to put everyone to sleep? The whole kingdom."

"So everyone is more easily slaughtered?" Kamaria snorted derisively. "Brilliant idea."

"Kamaria," Adanya scolded gently. "Let's hear her out." The two women had never been able to get along; Adanya suspected their fiery natures caused them to clash.

Nehanda scowled at Kamaria before continuing. "I've been doing some research, looking at some of the notes your predecessor left behind." She reached into her pocket for her ever-present notebook.

The energy in the room grew tense as everyone reacted to Nehanda's use of 'predecessor' instead of Ziyad's name. Adanya used her power subtly to relax and calm them as they listened to Nehanda's explanation.

"In the records, it says that a powerful enough Sage can use their magic to slow others' minds and bodies—in effect, putting them into a coma. Because it is magical, it can last for years, centuries even, and the people's bodies won't age or wither away. Once they wake up, it will seem as if no time has passed for them."

"I don't see how this helps," Adanya frowned. "As Kamaria said, if everyone is asleep, doesn't that just mean Harrun's armies can kill everyone without any resistance?"

"That's the other amazing piece. With everyone asleep, you can use the strength pulled from your connection with everyone in the kingdom to create a barrier, much like the one we use against the Ugwe, to make the kingdom invisible and inaccessible to Harrun. That way, the council will be able to focus on finding out how to kill their king without worrying about the people's safety."

"So we just ... keep everyone asleep while we figure out how to kill Harrun?" Gabir asked. "That's a massive undertaking."

"Adanya's magic is strong enough to do it," Nehanda said confidently. Adanya was silent, sensing that, somehow, Nehanda had put a lot of thought into this plan.

"But you're proposing putting thousands of people to sleep. This includes the king? The army?" Naeemah asked.

"Everyone. Including Adanya herself."

Adanya's eyebrows raised in surprise. "Me? But how would the barrier be maintained if I were also asleep?"

"Your magic is the most powerful kind in the kingdom," Nehanda said. "Your slumber would be the piece that makes everything work, channeling the magic into the barrier."

Adanya considered. "How do we know I'll be able to *keep* everyone asleep? For that matter, how would someone wake me up once things were safe?"

"Since the council isn't going to sleep, one of us can wake you. Your Sage magic will be active in your sleep; someone close to you will be able to connect with you and bring you out of it—though your actual hiding place will be invisible to everyone except those with a connection to you."

"As a safeguard, it should be someone who isn't on the council," Jabari said, though not without some trepidation. "If things go wrong, then we can work to defend the people while that person wakes you."

Everyone was silent, contemplating.

"I see no better plan," Adio finally said. "It buys us time to hit him while stopping the massacres. We know the barriers work because of our experiences with the Ugwe."

There were nods around the table, and then everyone turned to look at Adanya for her decision as the Head of Council. She was about to respond when the world around her blurred. Cries and feelings of terror filled her head. She squeezed her eyes shut and pressed a hand to her heart to steady herself, tears brimming at the corners of them. "Another village," she breathed.

The council's faces were troubled, knowing immediately what she meant.

When the voices and emotions finally subsided and she was able to bring herself back into the room, tears were streaming down her face and her eyes were red. "How soon can we do this?"

"Who will we choose to wake you?" Nehanda asked, seemingly unfazed by her mentee's tears.

"Rashidi. He is the only person I would trust with this."

"It's settled then. I'll start putting things in motion."

Adanya rose, wiping tears from her face and clearing her throat. "I will inform the king and Rashidi. The king trusts our judgement, so I'm sure there will be no objections. Nehanda, I place you in charge of preparations. Everyone else, please follow her lead on this."

Without waiting for anything else, Adanya hurried from the room.

She spoke to no one, only briefly reaching out to Rashidi to ask him to meet her in her chambers as soon as he could.

Sometimes, her gift was incredibly useful; other times, it was a burden she wished she did not have to bear. She could still feel the dull ache the kingdom's latest loss had imparted to her, the sudden cutting off of hundreds of lives. She wished that pain would not be so present.

#

Once in her room, Adanya went over to the window and stared out at the treetops of the forest gently waving like a green ocean. The breeze made her braids float about her face, and she felt the warmth of the setting sun on her skin. She needed some separation, some time to get away from all that was upsetting and disorienting her. Slowly, she released her consciousness, dissociating and letting her mind focus on nothing.

She was never fully aware of how long she was dissociating. It was only when she felt a gentle hand running down her back and a bearded kiss on her cheek that she pulled herself back into awareness, inhaling sharply before breathing out slowly to reorient herself to her surroundings and the fact that any time had passed at all. Outside was now night, illuminated by the stars and moon, the room filled with the yellow-orange light from the fireplace.

She turned to look at Rashidi, his deep voice whispering in her ear, "Come back, my love."

A smile of pure joy lit up her face as he smiled at her, the warmth of his love surrounding her and chasing away her confusion and stress. "There you are."

He took her in his arms and kissed her sweetly. "You say it like I've been gone forever; I just saw you this morning."

"A lot has changed since then." She pulled him by the hand over to her table, sitting him down in the chair and perching herself on the edge of the table as they had done many times before. "I know I made the decision, but I cannot help doubting this plan." She outlined Nehanda's plan to him, including the part he was to play.

When she finished her explanation, his brow was lowered. "I'm not going to pretend I understand all of the complexities of this plan and the magic involved," he said. "And I'm more than willing to do whatever you need me to to make this plan work. But I'm getting the feeling you're not quite confident in it yourself."

She sighed, crossing her arms and looking away from him. "I feel like I'm stuck in the middle of everything. The council has to act, and there was no other alternative that presented itself to us." She pressed her hand to her heart again, still feeling the dull ache of loss. "We lost another village today. I know I can't live through more losses like this without them destroying my mind. But I can't shake this feeling that there's something we're overlooking."

Rashidi paused before saying, "And you said this was Nehanda's idea?"

"Don't do that. Don't put it on her."

"I'm not accusing her of anything. I'm just saying that, when it comes to you, I don't feel her motives are always coming from the purest place. Especially now that you've mostly separated from her."

"It isn't just about me!" She rose from the table and began pacing. "It's the entire kingdom! We know that the barriers can work; this is just a larger scale."

"I just want you to be sure. Any doubt from you will rattle everyone else." He rose as well and took her shoulders, stopping her pacing. "And my priority is making sure that you are okay."

She heaved a heavy sigh, dropping her head forward so it rested on his chest. "I wish this was not up to me. But everything about this plan makes sense. It's more fear of the unknown that is troubling me."

He kissed the top of her head, then drew her into his arms. "We know that we can't let fear stop us."

"I know." She inhaled deeply, savoring the smell of sandalwood that always lingered about him. In his arms was one of the few places she found peace, the troubles of the people around her fading away until there was only his energy connecting with hers. "I need to tell the king," she sighed into his chest.

"The plan will be enacted tonight?"

"Likely tomorrow."

"Tell him, then come back. I'll be waiting for you." He squeezed her tightly before releasing her from his arms.

Adanya gave him an admiring look, retrieved her staff, and went to tell the king.

#

She found King Keon rocking a sleeping toddler in his arms. He looked up at her approach, then smiled back down at his only child. "I take it a plan has been made?"

"Yes, Your Majesty." She outlined the plan as before, then waited with bated breath to hear his response.

"Tell me truthfully, Adanya," he said after a few minutes of contemplative silence. "Do you have faith in this plan?"

She considered his question. He would take her word as gospel, and she was not sure if she truly believed in the plan. But there was no other plan forthcoming, and the longer they waited, the more people perished. This was all that they had.

"Yes. This is the best thing to do," she said with more confidence than she felt.

"Then I trust you. I'll give orders to follow your directions."

"Thank you, Your Majesty."

He stroked his son's head. "I'm sure Rashidi is waiting for you."

She could not help but smile. "You know us too well, Your Majesty."

"I know true love when I see it. That man would walk through fire for you; I'm happy that you found each other. It's about time you had someone taking care of you, for once."

She returned to her chambers after briefly conferring with Nehanda about their plans. There, Rashidi sat by the fireplace, his armor hung neatly by the door. He hummed softly as he watched the fire crackle.

"Always humming, yet never an actual song," Adanya said, resting her staff against the wall beside his armor and coming to stand beside him.

"Maybe one day I'll have time to sit down and write one for you." He held out one arm and patted his lap with the other, inviting her over.

She sat, wrapping her arms around his neck and planting a kiss on his scarred head. "Did you ever consider growing your hair out to hide these, once you made rank?"

He chuckled as she traced some of them with her fingers. "I think my hair pattern would make them more obvious."

"Only five years and you made captain. You worked so hard to get to where you are." She sighed and rested her head on top of his. "I'm sorry that I'm reducing you to a babysitter."

"Hey." He pulled back to look up at her. "Don't do that. You are the most important person in my world, Adanya. I would do anything for you, I hope you know that."

She smiled at him, unable to think of anything to say.

He gently reached up and pulled her neck down to him, kissing her softly. "You may still not see it, but you were voted to be the Head of Council for a reason. Even though you're doubting yourself about this decision, you've got to believe that you're doing the right thing." Rashidi rose, holding her hand and drawing her toward the bed. "But tonight isn't about anyone but us."

He stopped just beside the bed, first kissing her before helping her out of her outer robes. As if sensing she needed the distraction, he was slow in removing the rest of her clothes. First, he kissed her neck, gently nibbling and sucking as she cradled his head. He pulled her long shirt over her head, moving to kiss up and down her shoulders as he gently undid her binder, freeing her breasts for him to move his attention to.

Unintentionally, her mind began to wander back to her troubles. He put an end to that by sucking her nipple into his mouth, grazing it with his teeth and drawing a gasp from her lips. "None of that, now," he scolded with a smile. "You're here with me."

"I am," she replied as he kissed a trail down from her belly button to her waistband, getting on his knees to undo the tie. No matter how many times they made love, she was always amazed at the care and attention he gave her body. She had never thought herself much to look at, but Rashidi showed her time and time again that he loved every inch of her. Though he was the first man that she'd slept with—and that only when she was nearly thirty—she knew she'd never be able to bare herself to anyone the way she did with him. He had such a way of understanding her, even without magic, that he was able to calm and counsel her like no one else could.

She drew in a breath as her pants fell to the ground and the cold air touched her skin. But this lasted only a moment, replaced by the warmth of Rashidi's hands and lips.

Eventually, they fell into the bed, kissing, touching, moaning. Her magic made their connection stronger, her releases more powerful and meaningful. After several releases had passed, they lay in each other's arms, allowing their breathing to return to normal. Rashidi toyed with her braids, and she ran her hand back and forth across his chest as she listened to his heartbeat.

"We should get some sleep," he murmured, kissing the top of her head. "A lot to do tomorrow."

"Hm," she hummed absently.

"Adanya."

She pushed herself up on one arm so she could look at his face. "Yes, my love?"

"I have faith in you," he said seriously. "This will work."

"I hope so."

He put a hand on her cheek and turned her head so they were looking into one another's eyes. "This will work," he repeated firmly.

"This will work," she echoed, sounding more confident than she felt.

He pulled her down for a kiss, then they settled in to sleep.

#

The next afternoon, they stood inside a small cottage hidden in the depths of the woods surrounding the palace–Adanya, Rashidi, and Nehanda. "Everything is ready," Nehanda was saying. "As soon as we get you settled, I'll take Rashidi to the other cottage that I've prepared. He'll stay there, out of sight, until it's safe to wake you."

Adanya nodded her understanding. Rashidi noticed her hands shaking, and he took one of them and squeezed it.

Nehanda glanced at them both and cleared her throat. "I'll give you both a moment." She strode outside, leaving them alone.

Adanya took a deep breath, eyes fixed on the small bed against the wall.

"My love. Look at me." Rashidi turned her by her shoulders, then cupped her face in his hands and bent a little to meet her gaze. "Everything is going to be fine."

Adanya could sense his support and love radiating toward her, and she leaned forward to kiss him. He kissed her back, wrapping her in his arms and squeezing her tightly.

Then he helped her into the bed, resting her staff against the wall and arranging her robes and hair around her to make sure that she was comfortable. He leaned over to kiss her again, and she wrapped her arms around his neck to kiss him for as long as she possibly could. Then she lay her head back on the pillow, allowing him to drape the netting around her.

"I love you, Rashidi."

He smiled at her. "I'll see you when you wake up. I love you."

She smiled back, then closed her eyes and focused on using her magic.

Chapter Three

The young man—for truly, compared to her, he was young—held up his hands as if to show he did not want to harm her. "My name is Sefu," he said. "Please, let me take you back to my cabin. It's not safe here."

Adanya was still struggling to understand what was happening. "Not safe?" she repeated.

"Besides the Ugwe, there are also spies loyal to Nehanda roaming about. I fear that learning you've awakened could make life a lot more difficult for everyone."

Adanya's eyes hardened. "Nehanda is still alive?"

He nodded. "She is the reason that the original plan failed." His hand snapped back to his sword as a bird soared into the air, knocking a few stray leaves to the earth. "Please," he tried again. "Let us go."

Adanya hesitated. All of this could be a lie, or a fanciful dream brought on by the elongated slumber. But something about the young man's presence made her doubt ... well, everything. She could sense nothing but earnestness from him. "Alright."

"Please, follow me." He turned and led the way back into the undergrowth.

She hesitated a moment more before following him.

They traveled in silence, him showing her the way and her trying to process everything. She could not recognize any of her surroundings, though she knew she had to have come this way before. She knew if she tried to think about everything without all the facts, she would only drive herself crazy. So instead she focused on following Sefu, the ghost of the man she had loved.

After some time in silence, they emerged onto a road slightly more well kept than the one she had first traveled. Adanya stopped dead in her tracks as she saw a statue by the side of the road that was unmistakably her, posed with her staff raised and looking intently at something in the distance. Though it must have been raised long after she went to sleep, the statue was nearly covered with mold and weathered from years of exposure to sun and rain.

Noticing her staring, Sefu returned to stand beside her. "I couldn't believe it when I first saw you. But I've passed this statue for years, and there was no mistaking you."

"When was this raised?" she asked, still staring.

"After Rashidi died. Everyone knew then that the last hope for finding you was gone, so laborers erected this in secret to honor you. I'm sure they never imagined you'd actually get to see it."

People saw her as history. A figure from the distant past. Adanya couldn't even begin to know how to feel about that, not with all of the other emotions battling for dominance over the confusion in her mind.

After staring at it a moment more, she turned away. "Let's go."

An hour later, they arrived at a run-down cottage. From the outside, it seemed as if it had been abandoned, much like the rest of the land. The only sign anyone was within was a wisp of smoke curling lazily from the brick chimney. To her surprise, Sefu pushed open the door and escorted her into a warm, cozy room. There were basic living necessities: a picnic-style table that could sit at least ten, a simple kitchen, chairs arranged around a higher table covered with maps and papers, and a doorway doubtless leading to the sleeping quarters.

Sefu ushered her to a chair, quickly bringing her a cup of water before sitting down across from her. "Where would you like me to start?"

She considered, her mind racing until she settled on the most pressing question. "Do you know what happened after I went to sleep?"

He nodded. "After you went to sleep, Rashidi and Nehanda headed to his hiding place. They had barely made it there when Harrun's soldiers overtook them and Rashidi was badly wounded. When he finally recovered, he went in search of Nehanda.

"It was then he discovered that she had deceived everyone. Your power had put everyone to sleep and hidden them, but she used Sage magic and everyone awoke—and the barrier vanished. She had been controlling Harrun and his soldiers, and all of the people of Rydell were slaughtered. Rashidi had only been spared because he nursed himself back to health in the woods and no one knew he had survived. He sought to find and awaken you, but your magic was strong enough to keep you both asleep and hidden from the world.

"He then dedicated his life to fighting Nehanda. As her power grew, she took over more kingdoms until she ruled over all of them. Anything else magical she either controlled or destroyed; the Ugwe are the only magical creatures left. Rashidi searched for you for years until his advisors told him there was no way to find you without magic. From the tales my parents told me, he resisted remarrying for many years after, focusing on the fight. But he eventually married and had children, though the woman he married was more friend than lover.

"He continued working with refugees from the different kingdoms, trying to find some way to free them from her control. But without magic, defeating her is impossible. The other sorcerers on the council were never heard from again, and generations have passed fighting against her as we can, with my family serving as leaders of the resistance."

Adanya wasn't sure which revelation was hitting her the hardest; she could feel emotions bubbling up inside of her, and she struggled to contain them as Nehanda had taught her for the protection of those around her.

Nehanda.

Everything that had happened was because of her.

Sefu looked up to the window as a sudden storm burst overhead, pounding the cottage with rain and illuminating the room with lighting. A boom of thunder seemed to shake the very timbers.

"What else would you like to know?" he asked.

Adanya took a deep breath, her magic and emotions swirling within her and making it even more difficult to focus on the young man before her. She could feel his concern and sympathy radiating toward her, which made things worse. "She rules over all of the kingdoms?" she finally managed.

"Everyone on this side of the Great Sea," he replied with a grave nod. "It took her years, but every kingdom was eventually conquered. The other kingdoms put up more resistance, since she hadn't infiltrated their governments, but she got them all in the end. Now she has an army that spans the continent."

"And no one has been able to counter her?"

"A few have tried. But without magic, there's nothing that we can do against her. We haven't seen any magic from anyone but her since she took over."

Suddenly, everything was just too overwhelming. She didn't know how to even begin thinking about what was happening, and she found herself longing to just slip into dissociation. She needed an escape, some time to make everything stop moving.

She needed the King to smile at her and encourage her, bolstering her with his faith in her ability to figure things out.

She needed the council members, her friends and colleagues, to work together to use their magic to solve the issues.

She needed Rashidi to hold her and tell her everything was going to be alright, to remind her of her strength and lend her some of his own.

But she wasn't going to get any of that. Because Nehanda had killed everyone.

She vaguely became aware of Sefu shifting awkwardly in the seat across from her. With effort, she pulled herself out of her own thoughts and focused her eyes back on him, still unable to say anything.

"I know I've revealed a lot, and you need some time to process it," he said, standing and extending his hand. "Please, take my room. The others should be back in a couple of hours, so you have time before anything else happens."

Dumbly, she allowed him to take her hand and help her from the chair, guiding her through the doorway into his bedroom.

She barely registered her surroundings as he closed the door behind her. She walked over to the bed and sat down, letting her staff clatter to the floor.

How long had Nehanda been planning this betrayal?

Chapter Four

A teenaged Adanya caught the eye of the deer that crossed her path. It was a young deer, barely out of its first year. She could feel its immediate concern at the sight of her, and she extended herself to convince it she was not a threat as she continued walking past.

The deer watched her go, seemingly reassured.

She was most at peace in the woods. There, she had spent most of her childhood alone before Nehanda found her and brought her to live and train in the capital. Her mother had died when she was eight, and she had never known her father; with no living relatives to care for her, she was taken in at the orphanage.

But after several incidences of her magic manifesting—unintentionally influencing other children to do what she wanted—she was kicked out of the orphanage and forced to survive on her own at eleven.

She had learned some measure of control over her gift, learning the land from the animals and befriending them. In return, they kept her safe and would come when she called.

When Nehanda found her, explaining that she wished to train her to use her magic, Adanya was at first skeptical. But Nehanda shared a similar upbringing, living alone because her magic had inadvertently hurt someone, and she decided it was okay to take the chance. After all, Nehanda was now a member of the Council of Sorcerers. Surely that meant there was a better future for her.

She paused in her walk alongside the river, spotting a fallen tree crossing the river from bank to bank. The bridge was only a mile farther down the river, but...

A mischievous smile crossed her face, knowing Nehanda would not know what she had done and therefore would not scold her for impropriety. Tying her robes high enough over her knees to give her freedom of movement, she leapt from the riverbank to the tree trunk, easily hopping across it before landing lightly on the other side. She laughed with exhilaration. This was the life she missed, free of the rules and expectations that came from being in training. There was no one to judge her or expect anything from her; it was just a calm place where she was once again a child of the woods.

She glanced up at the sun through the tree branches and sighed. Nehanda would be expecting her back for her daily lessons. They were her least favorite part of the day, as learning how far to extend her powers before reaching a dangerous limit could be both taxing and confusing. But, she reckoned as she untied her robes and rearranged her braids, it was better than fearing she'd accidentally hurt someone.

Nehanda was waiting for her in the Arena, a dirt circle at the edge of the compound where other sorcerers-in-training lived. It had been magically fortified by Ziyad (the Head of Council and most powerful sorcerer in the land) for young magic folk to learn how to use and control their magic. The older woman was tapping her foot impatiently, and she crossed her arms as Adanya hurried over and dipped her head respectfully.

"I'm sorry that I'm late," Adanya said. "I lost track of time while I was on my walk."

Nehanda didn't respond, instead reaching for the staff she was teaching Adanya to use to focus her powers. "Let's get started."

Adanya took the staff and moved to the center of the circle, closing her eyes and willing herself to be absolutely still.

"Clear every connection," Nehanda said, pacing slowly around her mentee. "The only one you should be able to sense is me."

Adanya tried to do as she was told, focusing on Nehanda's voice and the feel of the staff in her hand. She had almost completely focused when she felt someone's distress: a frazzled horse, a mother's panic, a child's fear.

Without a second thought, she reached out to the horse to calm it. She felt it soothe as it connected with her, and she could sense the mother and child's relief. She smiled to herself, happy she'd been able to avert some kind of crisis. The smile vanished, however, as she opened her eyes and saw Nehanda glowering at her.

"What did you just do?" she demanded.

"There was a child," Adanya stammered, a flush rising to her cheeks. "They were in danger; I think they were about to be trampled by a horse. I calmed the horse."

Nehanda scowled. "How many times do I have to tell you? You can't solve everyone's problems, Adanya. Sometimes getting hurt is the natural order of things. It's how children learn. You deciding to save them may have kept them from learning the important lesson of staying out of the way of horses."

"It was a very young child, Nehanda," Adanya protested. "Not old enough to really understand."

"All of that in two minutes? Your powers are strong, Adanya, but you're being reckless. There may come a time when you have to use your powers to help the kingdom, but if you're distracted by every minor problem, you'll miss the larger picture."

"You make it sound like I overlooked the kingdom to save a child," Adanya muttered under her breath.

Nehanda's eyes flared, and Adanya could instantly feel a wave of heat emanating from her mentor. "You'd do well to remember that without me, you'd still be living in the woods as an outcast. Most people in your position would be grateful rather than showing disrespect at every turn!"

"That was not my intention," Adanya said, lowering her head again. "I just ... sometimes I get frustrated."

Nehanda paused, almost visibly calming herself down. "You have to trust me," she said finally, unclenching her fists. "The world is quick to turn against magical folk if they see us as a threat. The only way we are safe in this world is if we prove our usefulness to them. We have to show them that having us around is a benefit, not a danger. That's why we have to be one step ahead of them, foresee things that might happen and act to protect them before they're even aware of what could harm them. That is how we gain their trust; that is how we protect ourselves. Do you understand?"

Adanya nodded quickly. This was a side of her mentor she was unused to seeing. Nehanda kept her feelings buried, as she was trying to teach Adanya to do. But there was a slight quiver in her voice as she spoke, and the teenager could sense the sincerity behind her words.

"I'm sorry. I know that you're trying to help."

"Just ... let's get back to work."

Chapter Five

Adanya didn't know how long she had been sitting on the bed, dissociating. She couldn't confront these emotions now. There were too many; she needed time.

And everyone she would once go to for counsel was now dead.

She slowly came back to the present, heaving a heavy sigh. For now, the emotions were buried deep enough that she could focus. She needed to talk to Sefu, to get a better understanding of what Nehanda was doing.

Before she could finish the thought, he cracked open the door as if making sure she was decent before stepping fully into the room, his eyes wide.

"I've never really experienced magic before," he said in awe. "But I felt you drawing me to you."

"Forgive me," she said, heat rising to her cheeks. "I try not to use my magic to call those who are not used to it."

"Don't apologize. I know there is a lot for you to take in, but you've no idea how excited I am that there might be some magic that can counter Nehanda."

Adanya didn't answer. She wasn't sure if she was powerful enough to counter Nehanda, especially now that her former mentor had dozens of years of strength under her belt, but she kept that to herself for now.

"My lieutenant has returned with fresh news. He can help me explain where everything stands." He extended his hand to her, and she took it after retrieving her staff. She was barely able to suppress a shudder, his resemblance to Rashidi momentarily far too strong for comfort.

Sefu led her back to the main room, where an older man was hunched over the map table, scribbling notes and muttering to himself. His eyes, too, widened as he saw Adanya, and he made a hurried bow of respect.

"So it's true," he said. "You really have awakened."

She nodded, feeling his hopes rising just as Sefu's had. She quickly glanced him over, observing his strong arms and his cocoa butter skin, hardened to leather from days spent in the sun and weather.

"This is Waed," Sefu said as introduction. "My right-hand man. I trust him with my life."

"It's a pleasure," she said politely.

"Lady Adanya—" Sefu began, but she interrupted.

"Please, just Adanya. My title doesn't matter anymore."

Sefu nodded apologetically. "Adanya knows everything that happened since she went to sleep, but I think it would be helpful for her to know where everything stands today."

"Of course." Waed stood to the side to allow her a clear look at the map upon which he had been scribbling. "Rydell was the first kingdom that she dominated; it's also the only one she completely destroyed. Only roaming bands like ours live here." He pointed out four other capitals located south of Rydell. "All of the southern kingdoms were taken over soon after, without much resistance."

"Did other members of the council aid her?" she asked. "Or was it all her magic?"

"Her by herself. It's hard to tell from what little record was kept during her first take over, but it seems as if the other sorcerers just ... vanished."

"It's likely they feared she would try to force them to use their magic to take over. She only had Ember magic; there's no way she could have used that on her own to defeat the other kingdoms."

"Maybe she only used Ember magic initially, but she's shown a range in the years since." Sefu scowled.

"A sorcerer developing powers after adulthood?" Adanya said in surprise. "I've never heard of it. Unless..."

Unless she had them all along and hid them.

The two men waited to hear her finish her thought. When she didn't, they glanced at each other and continued the briefing.

"Nehanda keeps the kingdoms in check using stewards charged with doing her bidding," Waed said. "The people in each kingdom are all enslaved, working to improve the capitals to her liking and fortifying against any attack, in case anyone should try to rise against her."

"Is anyone fighting her?"

"Besides us? No. She's extremely paranoid that someone is going to take away everything that she's built, even though no one has been strong enough to challenge her." Sefu grew somber. "I lost both of my parents to the resistance. Everything we've tried has failed; we've been trying to come up with new tactics, but we're running out of options." The hopeful look returned to his face. "That's why finding you may be the turning point that we need."

"By myself, I'm not strong enough to counter her if she has that much magical power," she cautioned. "But perhaps we can use my magic to find a way," she added quickly, seeing both men wilt with disappointment. "Where is she?"

"She rotates between the kingdoms; it's hard to pinpoint where she is," Waed answered. "She never stays in one place for long, though. Like I said, she's paranoid."

Adanya was quiet for a moment, processing everything they had told her. She could not help but feel like they were missing a piece of the puzzle.

"Is the palace still standing?" she asked finally.

"After a fashion," Sefu answered. "Some of it has crumbled away with time, but many of the rooms inside are still there."

"I need to go there. There may be a clue, something that would give us an idea to defeat her."

"So you'll help us?" Sefu said, unable to keep the excitement from his voice.

She sighed. "I'm not doing anyone, including myself, any good by just sitting around. At the very least, maybe I can get some answers at the palace."

"It will be safer if just the two of you go," Waed said. "Draw less attention."

"You're probably right," Sefu said with a nod. "Though I doubt she's keeping a watch on it. We should leave at dusk. Gives us a few hours." He turned to Adanya. "Are you hungry at all?"

"No, I..." She stopped herself, tears springing to her eyes. Rashidi always used to fuss at her about eating regularly. "Yes. I should eat something."

Waed went to the kitchen to prepare something, while Sefu gave her a sympathetic pat on the arm. "I know that I'll never be able to understand what you're going through right now. Just know that I'm here if you need to talk."

She nodded her thanks, then went to sit by the fireplace and wait, idly twisting her engagement and Head of Council rings on her fingers as she thought.

How had Nehanda managed to hide other magic? All magical people manifested their powers at puberty, and she'd never known of anyone gaining more later in life. But Adanya's Sage powers should have been able to sense other types of magic, especially in a person she had once been extremely close with. She vaguely remembered someone discussing a kind of Sage that was able to possess all of the different types of magic ... but Nehanda was an Ember. How had she been able to not only gain other powers but both hide them from everyone and use them to control Harrun? Nehanda had never taught her how to use Sage powers to control others, only to subtly influence them. Had she found something in her research that revealed this knowledge?

And when did she decide power was more important to her than proving the necessity of sorcerers?

There were so many unanswered questions, and no answers seemed to be coming quickly. She could only hope they would find something in the palace that would help to clarify things. Her eyes glanced back to Sefu as he bustled about in the kitchen, and another pang of grief made her heart ache for Rashidi.

She twisted her engagement ring again, and part of her wanted to take it off given that the man she was engaged to was both married and dead. But she couldn't face that change, not yet. Not when his ghost was only feet from her, believing in her in the same way he had.

The ghosts of her past were not going to let things be easy.

Chapter Six

"A guard?" Adanya repeated, looking at King Keon incredulously. "Why do I need a guard?"

The king chuckled at her. "You're the Head of Council. As such, you must be protected."

"I'm fully capable of taking care of myself, Your Majesty. I've been Head of Council for three days. Why is this an issue now?"

"You also haven't left the palace for three days," he pointed out. "Understandable, since you've been trying to put things back in order since we lost Ziyad."

"Ziyad didn't have a guard."

The King paused from sharpening his sword, and Adanya could sense a wave of sadness emanating from him. "He did, actually. He just chose not to take them with him while he worked on the barrier."

Adanya was taken aback. "I ... I never saw him with a guard."

"He treated them as very optional. Because he was older and his magic was strong—and he was most often away from the palace in my company, with my guards—I didn't press the issue. But I wish that I did. Maybe ... maybe he would still be with us."

Adanya fell silent, remembering how excited Ziyad had been to begin erecting the barriers to keep out the Ugwe once she'd shared her idea with him. It had taken him months, but he kept her updated on his progress and had promised to bring her with him to finish sealing the barrier. In their last conversation, he'd praised her again for her forward thinking. It wasn't until the king got worried and sent out soldiers to find him that Ziyad's body was discovered.

"I know that you value your solitude, Adanya, but we have to make sure that you're protected." The king's voice cut into her thoughts as he resumed sharpening the sword. "They won't be around you every waking minute. Just the times when you go out of the palace, much like me. You're a leader now, Adanya. Things have to work differently than before."

"I didn't ask for this! I don't know why the council voted for me to be the Head of Council instead of Nehanda. She's far more experienced and wiser than I'll ever be."

"Ziyad supported you," King Keon said with a shrug. "Perhaps he, and the council, saw something in you more worthy of the leadership position." He wiped his hands on a cloth before placing a hand on her shoulder. "If something happens to a leader, whether a royal or a sorcerer, things can be set into chaos. We have to have processes to prevent that from happening."

She sighed heavily. "What if they made a mistake?" she said quietly. "What if I can't do this?"

He placed a gentle finger under her chin and lifted her head so he could look her in the eye. "I believe in you, Adanya. And I can assure you that you have many people who agree with me, even if you don't want to see it."

He had told her this many times before, but she still found it hard to believe. Instead of leaning into her doubt, however, she smiled at him. He kissed her forehead, then returned to his sword.

"Your guard should be waiting for you outside. As I recall, there is one last area where a barrier is needed?"

"The Ashanti Forest, yes. After that, we shouldn't have any more issues with the Ugwe."

King Keon smiled again. "I'm so proud of you, Adanya. You've grown so much in the time that I've known you."

A warm flush rose to her cheeks, and she ducked her head so her braids covered her face. "Thank you, Your Majesty." She bowed, then turned to go outside, where her horse and guard were waiting for her.

Four men awaited her on horseback. All wore their heads shaved, as was traditional for lower-ranking members of the army, but the fourth stood out to Adanya, drawing her eye as she came to the top of the steps leading to the courtyard.

The dark skin of his head was crisscrossed with scars, and one cut across his cheek and disappeared into his neatly trimmed beard. He wore a captain's cloak—curious, since most upper ranking soldiers grew their hair out as soon as they were promoted, excited to express themselves with their hair. But his eyes...

He was clearly a hardened soldier, but his brown eyes carried a kindness and compassion at odds with his rough exterior.

He nodded respectfully as he saw her, and his soldiers stood to attention at his movement. "Lady Adanya, my name is Captain Rashidi. I've been placed in charge of your personal guard."

Adanya tried not to make a face as he used her proper title; after her ascension three days prior, she was still getting used to it. "A pleasure to meet you, Captain." She swung easily into her horse's saddle, gripping the reins with her left hand while holding her staff in her right. "This should not take us long. With all of the other barriers raised, this will be a simple task."

"We serve at your pleasure, ma'am."

She managed an awkward smile, then spurred her horse on.

The small company galloped out of the courtyard and onto the main road into the capital city. The city was, as always, bustling with life, traders selling their wares by the side of the road, the sizzle of meat over fire, children running to and fro, their mothers calling after them to be careful. When Adanya was younger, the city was a challenge to her. All of the people going about their own business unconsciously sent their thoughts and feelings into the air—thoughts and feelings that would assault the young sorceress's Sage abilities. Now older and in control of her powers, the thoughts and feelings of the people were only dull prickles at the edge of her consciousness, allowing her to focus on her own tasks.

She did notice, however, the curious stares as she and her guard passed. Doubtless they had heard of her elevation, and the guards around her made it quite clear she was much more important to the kingdom than she had been previously. She hated every bit of the attention, and she spurred her horse into a trot to get through the city quicker.

After nearly half an hour, they veered off onto a narrower road leading out of the city and into the flatlands. The open countryside was breathtaking, gentle wind blowing through fields of wheat and corn, with the occasional shepherd and their flock passing along the side of the road. In the distance, forests bordered the fields.

Adanya closed her eyes and breathed in deeply, enjoying the ride. Life had been tense as the council fought off the Ugwe, but it had finally seemed to settle. This ride, guarded though it was, was the first time she had been out of the palace in nearly a week. Out of the city, she allowed herself to feel the energy of everything around her: the horses, the men, the birds that fluttered by them. She could especially feel Rashidi's energy. It was strange to feel his energy so strongly; after all, they'd never met before, and though he may have seen her during his work, there was nothing to suggest a connection. But she pushed the thought from her mind, remembering Nehanda's frequent reminders to stay focused on the task at hand.

They slowed their horses as the road turned into the forest. A snap of the captain's fingers, and the other soldiers moved their horses to better surround Adanya while staying out of her way. Despite her annoyance at having the guard, she was impressed at their efficiency.

The forest was even more alive with energy, animals and insects going about their business while hidden in the trees and underbrush. Adanya was alert, feeling for anything amiss. She expected no trouble, but Nehanda had taught her to be hyper-vigilant.

The road reached a clearing. Running through the road itself was a shimmering, translucent wall, which looked as if it were made of a bubble and reached so far into the sky that the end couldn't be seen. Birds flitted freely through it, and the trees it cut through were undisturbed. The wall stopped a little past the road; here was the last piece of the border to keep out the Ugwe.

Adanya dismounted, gently patting her horse's nose before approaching the wall. "Won't be ten minutes," she said over her shoulder, seeing the captain nod in response.

Standing before the empty space, she closed her eyes and breathed in deeply to center herself. She used her Sage magic to draw power from the energy of the people, weaving their emotions and thoughts together to create the magical barrier that would destroy any magical creature trying to pass through with evil intentions. She could feel the energy of her magic flowing through her, directed through her body like water rushing through a funnel.

A quick thought and the energy flew to attach to the existing wall, manifesting as the same shimmering magic that made up the rest of the wall, beginning to close the gap. A smile of satisfaction crossed her face, knowing the threat to the people was nearly gone.

But suddenly, something felt wrong. Her eyes flew open with a gasp, the magic vanishing as she felt the threat of oncoming danger in the animals fleeing the woods. She whirled around, seeing Rashidi tense as he saw her face. "Ugwe!" She gasped. "At least ten of them."

"Back on your horse, my lady," Rashidi ordered. "Surround the lady!" he told the other soldiers.

She did as she was told, swinging into the saddle and gripping her staff tighter. "I can slow them," she called. "Give you a chance to take them down before they attack."

"We'll follow your lead," he replied.

She closed her eyes again, struggling to think over the anxious beating of her heart. She reached out to the energy of the approaching Ugwe, willing them to slow in their thunderous approach.

They slowed, but only slightly. She had never used her magic on any Ugwe before, and they fought against her influence. Changing tactics, she focused on the nearest one. She knew from Ziyad that it would push back against her, its violent instincts drowning out any calming influence she might have. If she could turn it away, then it would be one less for Rashidi and his men to have to fend off...

The first Ugwe burst through the trees into the clearing, trailing leaves and broken tree branches in its wake. This was not the first time Adanya had seen one of the beasts, but she could not contain a squeak of terror as it snarled at the small group, thirsting for blood.

It was nearly as tall as the trees, with fangs that curved like a tiger's but ten times as long. Its body resembled an emaciated panther, muscles and sinews straining beneath almost translucent skin. It moved on its hind legs, leaving its long talons free to slash and tear at prey. Making it even more difficult to attack was the long tail, lined with spikes, that twitched back and forth as if it had a mind of its own.

Rashidi didn't hesitate, directing his men into an attack pattern. Two of them drew its attention while he and the third circled around it from behind. To Adanya's surprise, they were able to quickly dispatch it in this way; the two behind it sliced through the animal's neck on either side, sending the massive corpse crashing to the ground. They didn't waste an instant over their victory, immediately turning to the next creature coming at them.

Adanya felt her powers straining as she tried to focus her energy on the remaining beasts. She knew the odds of the Ugwe continuing to attack one at a time were very low. She needed some way to help her guard.

Then it dawned on her.

"Keep them busy!" she cried, spurring her horse toward the opening in the barrier.

"Where are you going?" Rashidi asked incredulously, dodging an Ugwe tail.

"If they touch the barrier, they die! I have to finish it and then draw them in!"

He considered for a split second, then nodded as he slashed the tail cleanly off. "Do it!"

Adanya pushed her horse to leap over the underbrush in the opening. Dropping from the saddle, she planted herself in a solid stance before focusing all of her energy on the barrier as she had done before. To her surprise, her focus returned quicker this time, and with more power and intensity. The gap continued to close.

One of the Ugwe noticed her and thundered in her direction. Rashidi broke off from his attack and followed the creature, slashing at its back to get its attention away from her. He succeeded, but not before the creature's tail slashed deeply into her shoulder.

Adanya felt the pain but willed herself to keep her focus on the barrier. It was nearly closed now, though she could see four Ugwe on the other side being fought off by her guard. Just a few moments more...

There!

The barrier met the other side, shimmering brilliantly as the border was completed. "Captain!" she cried. "Drive them to me!"

He gave the order, and the guard worked together to push the creatures toward the barrier. As Adanya knew would happen, the instant the monsters touched the barrier, their skin began to sizzle and burn like meat on a fire. They were consumed, engulfed in shimmering magic until they seemed to melt into puddles of skin, bone, and teeth before completely vanishing into nothingness.

Everyone stood in breathless silence after the monsters' remnants disappeared, staring at each other. The men were spattered in the creatures' blood, and Adanya herself could feel wetness soaking through her robes.

Finally, Rashidi nodded. "It was a good plan, my lady."

"I only wish I would have thought of it earlier," she replied, wincing as she placed a hand on her wounded shoulder.

"It was just in time. Here, let me bind that before we return. It looks deep."

She climbed through the underbrush, the barrier shimmering as she passed through but causing no damage. "I don't think it's that bad."

He cleaned his hands on a clear space on his pant legs before touching her. Then he gently pulled the ripped fabric from around the jagged wound, making a face. "It's going to leave a nasty scar. Can you move it at all?"

Adanya flexed her arm, tears springing to her eyes as pain radiated through it. "Maybe it's deeper than I thought."

He reached into his pack and brought out a roll of bandages. "You took it like a true warrior. Perhaps you don't need a guard after all."

She winced at his touch, though belatedly reflected how gentle it was. "I don't know if I'd go quite that far."

He finished wrapping her shoulder. "Avoiding wounds isn't what makes you a warrior. It's how you react when things go wrong." He held her gaze for a moment, and the warmth she had sensed in him earlier seemed to radiate through his eyes. "We should get back and make our report," he said. "And you should get that looked at by a physician."

"Yes, of course."

Once he saw her mounted, the small party returned to the palace. They were met in the courtyard by Nehanda, who had an unreadable expression on her face as she hurried directly to Adanya.

"What happened?"

Adanya winced as she dismounted, putting a hand to her shoulder. "We were attacked," she said calmly. "My guard was able to defend me as I finished closing the barrier, and the Ugwe were destroyed."

"But you were wounded?"

"It's not bad. A few stitches and I should be fine."

Nehanda turned to the guards and Rashidi, who had remained on their horses. "Thank you, gentlemen, for protecting our leader."

"No need for thanks, ma'am," Rashidi said. "We were simply doing our jobs."

Nehanda's eyes studied Rashidi for a moment, and Adanya could tell she was thinking rapidly. Adanya could not help but try sensing Nehanda's emotions, but she could sense nothing. Nehanda nodded to the captain before guiding Adanya inside.

"You've got to be more careful," she scolded. "If anything happens to you, so soon after Ziyad's death and your ascension, then the council will be thrown into chaos."

"It's not like there aren't other sorcerers who could take my place," Adanya said, a touch of annoyance in her voice.

"That isn't the point, and you know it. There are processes, orders to leadership. Just ... be more careful next time."

Now Adanya scowled. "Because I threw myself into danger," she said sarcastically. "Wanted to get a war wound so I'd have a scar and worry you."

Nehanda grabbed her uninjured arm and spun her around, pointing a finger in her face. "Just because you've become the Head of Council doesn't mean you have the right to disrespect me. If it wasn't for me, you never would have learned to control your powers enough for others to see your potential. Never forget that."

Adanya ducked her head at the scolding from her mentor. She should have known better than to mouth off to her, even now that she was Head of Council. To Nehanda, she would always be a child.

"I'm sorry. I didn't mean to be disrespectful," she said quietly.

Nehanda seemed to suddenly remember herself, and she straightened and continued walking. "Come, let's get that arm looked at."

Chapter Seven

As darkness fell, Adanya and Sefu slipped from the cottage and walked through the woods toward the palace, avoiding the main road. Adanya now wore a rough brown cloak over her robes, helping her to better blend in with their surroundings.

"What are you hoping that we'll find?" Sefu asked as they walked. "A spell or something?"

She shook her head. "Magic doesn't work that way." Then, realizing the only magic Sefu likely knew was Nehanda's, she explained further. "Every sorcerer born has a connection to a natural element: fire, water, weather, animals, plants, and life. The most powerful sorcerers were those like me, Sages. We have a telepathic and empathic connection to every living being we come in contact with, and some that we may have never met, as was the case with myself and the kingdom. We can sense their energy and, sometimes, influence them to do things. Sages had to be specially trained so we would not use our magic to influence people and nature without considering the impacts of using that influence. Our magic depends on the energy—the connection—with others."

"Did any sorcerer ever have more than one elemental connection?"

"Not any that I had ever heard of, except in legends buried in history books. Though Nehanda must have found some way if she has been able to take and keep control of all these kingdoms."

"Does magic just ... spontaneously appear in a person?"

Adanya was grateful for the distraction and launched into an explanation, similar to how she would teach young sorcerers at the palace. "When a magical child reaches puberty, their eyes develop rings around their irises representative of their magical ability. Green is for Flora, dark blue for Aqua, teal for Clime, yellow for Fauna, red for Ember, and grey for Sages. I was taught that magic runs through royal bloodlines, though it won't manifest in everyone, sometimes even for several generations. All of the sorcerers I trained with were not royals, but magic was still present in them. Ziyad, my predecessor, once told me that those sorcerers were likely very distant relatives of the first King of Rydell. He and his family were able to use magic to repel beasts like the Ugwe, as well as to defend against roving groups of barbarians, in order to create a unified kingdom. Similar stories happened in other kingdoms. For a few generations after him, magic was strong in all of the royal family. But as they married and had children of their own, the magic was diluted and became less and less common. King Keon—he was king before I went to sleep—was the third king in a row to have no magic powers. We theorized that his son Kayode might have had magic, but...” She bit her lip, realizing the little boy must have been slaughtered along with the king. “I suppose we'll never know now,” she finished quickly.

Sefu seemed to sense her pain and fell silent.

Soon what was left of the capital city came into view. Crumbling remains of houses, broken carts, and stalls were settled within an eerie silence. Adanya suppressed a shudder as she pulled her hood farther over her head, attempting to shut out the chill that seemed to seep into her very bones. It carried a sense of foreboding for what she would find—and feel—once they reached the palace.

Once past the city, they left the woods and edged along the crumbling walls until they reached the courtyard. There they found the familiar gates hanging off of rusted hinges, and grass and trees growing through the pavement stones, rendering it worlds away from the place she had left. Many of the walls of the palace itself had crumbled, leaving gaping holes that opened rooms to the elements.

Adanya placed a shaky hand on the wall, looking up at the broken-down palace that once was her home. Her heart felt like it was being squeezed; she could hear the dying screams of those who had once lived there echoing within her head. No one here had died peacefully.

"Adanya?" Sefu's voice brought her back to the present. "Are you alright?"

She wiped stray tears from her eyes and cleared her throat. "I'm fine. Let's go."

She took the lead, moving up the stairs and through the open doorway where the wood had long since rotted away. The place was chaos, evident even under the layers of dust and more plants growing inside. Rotting chairs were thrown about; the rich tapestries that once hung from the walls were moth eaten and torn into shreds. Here and there were telltale red stains, though the bodies that bled there had long since crumbled into dust.

Moonlight streamed in through the windows, allowing them to see as they continued.

"What are we looking for?" Sefu asked in a hushed voice, as if he were afraid to upset the spirits around them.

"I ... I don't know. Maybe Nehanda will have left something behind that can help me piece things together."

Though she knew she should go upstairs to Nehanda's chambers, something was pulling her toward the throne room. She stopped walking for a moment, trying to resist the pull. Sefu stopped as well, watching her expectantly.

"Can you go upstairs?" she asked. "The council room and Nehanda's chambers are there. See if she's left something ... she used to always carry a journal with her. Maybe she left it behind."

"Of course. Where will you be?"

"Down here, somewhere. I can't explain it, but something is pulling on my magic."

He nodded. "Alright, then. But be careful. I don't know how sturdy the walls are."

Adanya nodded back, then turned to the throne room as Sefu headed for the stairs.

His footsteps faded, and she found herself hearing echoes of laughter and conversation from her days spent in the palace. Rashidi had kissed her in that alcove. Naeemah had walked hand in hand with her down that hallway. Memory after memory assaulted her as she walked, and she found herself struggling to hold back tears.

The pull grew stronger the closer she got to the throne room, the chaos and destruction around her failing to catch her attention.

Once she reached the doorway to the throne room, she paused, suddenly thrust back to the present as she came face to face with the last place she had seen the king.

Now she cried openly, sobbing softly to herself as she surveyed the room.

The throne itself, along with the chair where she often sat beside him as his counsel, still stood as a ghostly visage at the far end of the room. The once-rich carpet that led the way to them was now threadbare and stained. As she slowly drew nearer, she stumbled on something metallic. She bent to pick it up, only to realize it was the king's prized sword. He must have died here, taking his last stand.

She clutched the sword to her chest, stumbling over to her chair and dropping into it heavily as tears streamed down her face. Outside, thunder boomed, another storm blocking out the moonlight and sending sheets of rain blasting through the windows. But Adanya was oblivious to it all, her grief at losing the king and everyone she loved overtaking her. She closed her eyes.

When she opened them a moment later, she was shocked to see the throne room returned to its former glory, with sunlight shining brightly through the windows and guards posted by the door. She slowly turned, gasping when she saw King Keon sitting beside her, smiling broadly.

"There you are, sweet girl," he said. "I was wondering when you'd make it down here."

"Is ... is this a dream?" she stammered.

"In a sense," he replied. "Nehanda always kept this from you, but your Sage abilities make you sensitive to souls who have passed from life. Especially if you had a personal connection with them."

Adanya was silent, trying to process all of this new information while also overwhelmed by everything she wanted to say.

"I'm so sorry," she finally blurted. "I should have seen through her. I should have known that she was going to betray us."

"There's no way you could have known. She deceived all of us, Adanya."

"But I was closest to her! I should have been able to realize she was tricking us the whole time!"

He took her hand, and she could feel the warmth of his touch. "It's because you were closest to her that she knew how to manipulate you. You can't blame yourself for that. If anything, you should blame the rest of us for not seeing it and protecting you."

Adanya's eyes grew misty again as she thought of the conversation she'd had with Rashidi the night before her slumber began. "Rashidi saw it. He may not have known exactly what she was up to, but he was doubtful. I should have listened to him. I should have asked more questions, looked into things for myself…"

"Adanya. Look at me."

When she hesitated, he gently turned her head with a finger under her chin, as he always had in life. "You can't blame yourself for this. You're a leader, and leaders often have to make difficult decisions quickly. We had to stop them from destroying the kingdom."

"And my bad decision accomplished that anyway!" she cried, tears streaming down her face. "Now I'm all alone."

He pulled her to his chest and allowed her to sob, gently stroking her hair.

"Your heart is so big, Adanya. Nehanda knew that you would do anything to save the people, and she set things up to back you into a corner. You couldn't have done any better if you tried." He pulled her back and looked into her tear-stained face. "I'm so proud of you. And I know that whatever happens next, you'll be just fine. You have people who are looking to you to help; without you, Nehanda has won. I know you don't want that to be the case."

"But how? She's more powerful than I could ever dream of being."

"Only because she and you limited your powers."

"What?"

"You'll find the answers you need here. I have faith in you, sweet girl. I know the challenge may seem impossible, but I know that you can do this."

Adanya closed her eyes as he kissed her forehead. When she opened them again, she had returned to the decrepit room in semi-darkness. The storm had calmed; now the rain fell gently and soothingly outside.

She rose, reverently laying the king's sword across the arms of his throne before backing away. Waves of emotion washed over her, but she knew it wasn't the time to fully process them. So she took a deep breath, forcing her emotions back beneath the surface and drying her tears. Then she reached for Sefu's energy and followed it up the stairs.

She found him in what was left of Nehanda's room, struggling to open a locked drawer in the nightstand. The elements, it seemed, had been kinder to the inner rooms upstairs. Though everything was covered in dust and spiderwebs, and some of the finer fabrics of the curtains and bedsheets had rotted away, the room was, for the most part, just as Adanya remembered it. *Likely because they didn't come here to kill her,* she thought bitterly.

Sefu deftly pulled a knife from his belt, pushing it between the space above the drawer and jiggling it around. It clicked open, and he reached in carefully, pulling out a small book tied shut with a length of leather. "Do you think this might be something important?"

Adanya caught her breath. It was Nehanda's journal, where she'd recorded her research about the slumber. She'd told Adanya that thoughts could be dangerous if left unexplored, so she would write things down and examine her own stream-of-consciousness writing. The book rarely left her side, except, apparently, when she went to bed—or when she had betrayed the kingdom and decided privacy was no longer needed.

"It might be," she finally answered. "But I won't know for sure until I read it. I don't think she'd write down anything obviously treasonous." She tore her gaze away from the journal and looked around the room. "Did you find anything else?"

"There are lots of maps and old records in the council chambers. I pulled a few out and looked at them as best I could, but there didn't seem to be anything directly linked to Nehanda."

Adanya could not help but think there was still something missing, though she couldn't put her finger on it. Her mind replayed the king's words over and over: *Only because she and you limited your powers.*

What could that mean? Could it be that she, too, could wield all of the powers? But how had she not known, not felt that she could use them?

Then again, maybe she had.

As there were so few Sages, it was difficult to pin down exactly what nuances she'd experienced were common among Sages and what were her own unique experiences. Could it be that her connection to animals and the way storms seemed to appear whenever she was sad or upset were early signs of the other magical powers? It wasn't a wholly unreasonable assumption.

She suddenly realized that she'd been sitting there thinking in silence for several minutes while Sefu stood by patiently.

I'm sorry, she thought before catching herself.

He started slightly, then answered aloud, "It's fine. I imagine that this was a lot to take in."

"I shouldn't keep using my magic to speak to you like that." Her cheeks reddened.

"It's fine. I should probably get used to it."

Adanya stopped herself from making a face. There was her awkwardness and introversion again, almost as if she'd never learned to overcome them in her time as Head of Council.

He nodded toward the door. "We should probably be getting back soon; the sun will be coming up."

"Of course."

"Is there anything else here that you wanted to see?"

Her thoughts immediately went to her bedroom, but the thought of the last place she had intimately shared with Rashidi colliding with his doppelgänger descendant caused an uncontrollable shiver of horror to run down her spine.

"No," she answered. "Let's go."

He picked up the journal and tucked it into his belt, then followed her from the room.

Adanya paused as they left the gate, another wave of emotions struggling to swallow her. She took a deep breath, turned back to the ruins, and said aloud, "She will pay for what she did to you. I promise ... I will help you be at peace."

As the words left her lips, she could feel the relief emanating from the ruins, the souls of the dead receiving her promise. A breeze seemed to blow from the ruins, pushing her hood from her face and allowing her tears to mingle with the rain.

She turned back to Sefu as the breeze settled. "Lead the way."

Chapter Eight

"For the hundredth time, Adanya!" Nehanda snapped. "You have to focus!"

The teenager pouted. "We've done this a hundred times!" she complained. "Can't we just accept that I can't do this?"

Nehanda scowled, and Adanya could sense she was trying to keep her temper even. "Every Sage has the ability to use the energy of the people around them to create barriers, whether temporary or permanent. You need to be able to tap into that ability."

"Just like that?" She waved a hand in frustration. "'Oh, I feel like keeping people away from me today. Guess I'll just pull some energy and make a barrier!'"

Nehanda's eyes flared red even as she began measuring her breathing. "If you're not going to take this seriously, you're not going to make any progress."

"Maybe I don't want to. How is this important to my training? What possible difference could this one little thing make in the course of my life?"

"We don't always know what the things we learn can do to help us in the future. That's why it is important for us to learn as much as we possibly can."

"She has a point." They both turned at the new voice, bowing when they saw King Keon and Ziyad walking into the circle. "There are many things I learned as a young man that have been valuable to me as an old one." Ziyad continued.

"Old might be an understatement, my friend," King Keon chuckled.

Ziyad smiled, then came over and took Adanya's hand. "This is Adanya, Your Majesty. The child I was telling you about."

Adanya always found herself overwhelmed by Ziyad's presence in the few times she'd met him; he was a Sage, like she was, but far more experienced and in control of himself. He periodically came to see the progress of her training, and she never quite adjusted to her feelings of awe. But when she saw the King, she felt a different kind of energy from him. She was drawn to him, as if there was some part of her that knew him though they had never met.

King Keon seemed to feel the same way; he came directly over to her and took her hand from Ziyad. "It's a pleasure to meet you, Adanya. Ziyad tells me that he has great hopes for your future."

A flush rose to her cheeks. "He flatters me, Your Majesty. There is still much I have to learn."

"It is a wise person who can acknowledge that there are things they don't know," the king said.

Ziyad turned to Nehanda, who seemed to have calmed slightly but could not help glaring at Adanya. "What is the lesson today?"

"Creating barriers," she replied. "I've been trying to get her to draw from the energy around her."

"It's been a hard lesson," Adanya admitted. "And my frustration was causing me to be rather disrespectful."

"It takes time." Ziyad lifted a hand and a glowing blue light emanated from it. "Our connection to the people around us is much different than the way other sorcerers are connected to their elements. While we all have a degree of control over our respective magic, dealing with people's energy can be much trickier. Sages can draw strength from the people around them in multiple ways and redirect that strength for specific purposes. Sometimes for healing, sometimes protection." He touched Adanya's hand. The light swooped and whirled around their hands before disappearing. "You have the ability inside of you; you just have to learn to unlock it."

Adanya's eyes were wide with wonder, and she looked down at her hand. "Thank you, sir."

"Nehanda. May I have a word?" Ziyad guided her a short distance away so that Adanya could not hear their conversation, leaving her alone with the king.

"He's a good man, Ziyad," King Keon said with a smile. "When he came to me with the idea to find magical children and train them, I knew he had everyone's best interests at heart. He tells me that you were living in the woods?"

"Yes, Your Majesty. My abilities scared the other children in the orphanage, so they sent me out to fend for myself when I turned eleven."

"Eleven? How old are you now?"

"Sixteen, Your Majesty. It wasn't all bad!" she added, seeing the sadness on his face as well as feeling it. "There are many parts of my abilities that I am far more in tune with now because I was in the woods. I can commune with the animals, and I can survive in the woods for years without help from others. I'll admit that sometimes it is harder for me to use social graces because I spent so much time away from people, but Nehanda has been helping me to learn those as well." She was surprised at herself for sharing so much with this man she'd never met; her introversion often made it hard to speak to people she didn't know. But something about his energy made her feel more comfortable with him than anyone she'd met—even Ziyad and Nehanda.

"You truly are remarkable. I look forward to seeing how your life progresses." He paused, smiling. "Have you seen the capital city?"

"I haven't, Your Majesty. I was brought here when I was found, and I haven't really left since, except to visit the woods."

"I have a proposal," King Keon said as Ziyad and Nehanda returned. Annoyance was rolling off her in waves, though Adanya could sense she was trying to suppress it. "I'd like to take Adanya on a carriage ride through the city, since she hasn't had the chance before."

"I don't know if she could handle it," Nehanda said quickly. "She is still learning to control her Sage abilities; she might be overwhelmed by all of the people."

"I think it would be a perfect opportunity for her," Ziyad said, looking reproachfully at Nehanda. "She'll have to experience it sooner or later, and sometimes training doesn't offer you the same opportunities to learn as being out in the world."

"Wonderful." The king took Adanya's hand again. "We'll leave right away. I'll have her back by sundown."

Ziyad nodded with a smile, and the king guided Adanya out of the Arena.

#

When they returned at sundown, Nehanda was waiting for her in the circle. Adanya was full of energy and excitement, wanting to recount everything she'd seen.

"There are so many people! So many different energies all mixing together! I was overwhelmed at first, but I was able to filter it down and see the differences and similarities between them. Oh, it's so amazing! And then to see how they love King Keon—it's such a warm feeling." She danced around as she spoke, unable to contain her excitement.

The trip had been truly eye opening, from the smells of the marketplace to the colorful clothes on sale, so different from her simple novice robes. She'd felt fear from some people as they realized she was a sorcerer, but most people didn't even notice her. Maybe the world wasn't as anti-magic as Nehanda feared.

As if sensing that last thought, Nehanda interrupted tightly, "We have training to finish."

Adanya stopped dancing and stared at Nehanda. "Training? But the day is over; we always stop at sundown."

"We would have, except your field trip has taken time away. We have a certain amount of hours that we must devote to your training daily, so we have to finish now."

"We can't just start earlier tomorrow? I couldn't possibly focus on training now."

"You'll have to learn." Nehanda walked closer, frustration radiating from her. "I understand that today was a big day for you. But you have to learn to take such experiences with a grain of salt. You won't make it out there in the world unless you heed my lessons and apply them."

"Why just your lessons?" Adanya asked defiantly. "You're not even a Sage! Why isn't Ziyad training me?"

Nehanda's eyes flared again. "Ziyad is the Head of Council. He doesn't have time for training, not when he is the king's closest advisor."

"So he stuck me with an Ember? That doesn't seem fair."

Nehanda controlled herself no more. Flames rolled down her arms, and for a moment, her entire body was surrounded by a halo of white fire. "Little girl," she boomed, "there are many things in this life that aren't fair. Whining and complaining about it will solve nothing."

Adanya cowered away, covering her face from the heat of Nehanda's fire and the rage coming at her in waves. "I'm sorry, I'm sorry!"

She gingerly looked over her fingers, watching the flames disappear as Nehanda gave a short exhale. Her face was troubled, but she composed herself to come over and place a hand on Adanya's shoulder.

"No, I'm sorry," she said. "I look a right fool telling you to control yourself when sometimes I struggle to keep my own feelings under control. But you must understand." She took Adanya by the shoulders and turned her to face her. "I'm only looking out for you the best way I know how."

Adanya dropped her head. "I know that you are. I'm sorry."

Nehanda visibly seemed to struggle to return a lilt to her voice. "Well, now, let's not stand around moping. A few more tries tonight, at least?"

Chapter Nine

U pon returning to the cottage, they found that Waed had been joined by several others dressed in similar worn traveling gear, all sitting around the fireplace drinking after their meal. They rose in awe at the sight of Adanya, immediately realizing who she was after years of seeing her statue. Then they bowed respectfully.

"Please, that's not necessary," Adanya said, still embarrassed by the attention.

Waed made quick introductions, and then the others moved to the dining table to allow their leaders some privacy by the fireplace.

"Did you find anything helpful?" Waed asked.

"We found this." Sefu pulled the journal from his belt and passed it to Adanya. "Nehanda's journal from before she took power."

Adanya ran her fingers over the worn leather, a twinge of excitement mixing with a slight feeling of fear running through her. "Hopefully there is something here that can give us some clues how she was able to acquire all of the other powers."

"Perhaps they can help you to gain the other powers as well?" Sefu said hopefully.

"I don't know if I'd go that far—though, after what we've learned so far, it might be a possibility. I'm sure that it will take time."

Adanya could sense Sefu hesitating, and she turned to face him rather than looking into his mind. "There's something on your mind?" she asked.

"I know this is a big thing to ask of you," Sefu said, "but I still believe you are our only hope of changing the tide of this war against Nehanda. We will support you the best that we can, of course. But will you help us?"

Adanya considered his request. "It will be dangerous. I know she'll be furious that I'm awake and working against her. We're at a considerable disadvantage since I don't know for sure if I can tap into these other powers. Hopefully I'll find more answers in here." She tapped the journal on her lap. Her eyes grew misty as the immense grief threatened to undo her, and she turned to look out of the window. "But everyone I've ever known is dead now because of her. I must make her pay for that. I have to undo all of the wrong that she's created." She had to pause again as she came to grips with what she was about to say. "I will help you. But we need to make plans."

"Agreed," Sefu said, struggling to keep his voice even but failing to hide the excitement on his face.

They moved to the map table. Adanya slipped into the seat at the head of the table, as she once had during council, while Sefu and Waed sat on either side of her.

"Explain to me how things have been working so far," she said. "I'm assuming that you don't have a standing army, and you haven't been attacking full out."

Sefu shook his head. "Our numbers are steady, but no match for her forces. We've tried cutting supply lines, even going undercover to get into the different palaces, but nothing has worked. We've only ended up losing people. Occasionally we'll strike groups of her army when they travel, but that's only to get weapons. If we try to keep everyone together, we're too big a target. So we're spread out; some of our forces are living in towns, supporting farmers and other workers to meet Nehanda's demands for output, while others roam throughout the kingdoms acting as a spy network."

"Nehanda controls entire countries and their armies," Waed added. "Since direct attacks don't work, we do what we can to support the people and give them some measure of hope."

"If the opportunity arose, how quickly would you be able to get word to everyone?" Adanya asked.

"Our network is strong," Sefu said, and she could sense the pride rolling off of him. "A week, at most."

Adanya filed that away for future use. "Have you been able to track where Nehanda is at any given time? Does she move around on a regular schedule?"

"It's been difficult, to be sure," Sefu said. "She travels quickly and without much notice, likes to keep her stewards on their toes. She also travels heavily armed and guarded, and she goes straight to the palaces, so it's impossible to get her while she's traveling."

"And certainly not while she's *in* the palaces," Adanya mused. "She's probably using strong magic to keep herself protected."

"We've been considering a new tactic, but we don't know how successful it would be without some reorganizing," Waed said. "We have spies in all of the cities; if we could pinpoint when she leaves a city, then that city would become our target. She wouldn't be as focused on it because she'd just left, which would give us the chance to infiltrate the city and free it from her control."

"Do you have the numbers for that?"

Sefu shook his head. "Not immediately. It would take time. We'll have to find people from those kingdoms who are familiar enough with the land to get into the palaces. We know open warfare is only going to get us all killed, but if we can remove the stewards, then we'll be able to recruit others to liberate and defend the cities."

"There's no way that Nehanda would leave the cities completely unguarded. We can be sure she'll have something magical to keep them under her control." Adanya paused, thinking. "I need a council."

"What?"

She looked at Sefu. "When the council was alive, we drew on each other's strengths to make ourselves more powerful. There is no way that my magic alone will be enough; we'll have to find the others."

"But how? There haven't been any sightings of sorcerers since before you went to sleep."

"Sorcerers are nearly immortal," Adanya explained. "They can live thousands of years if they so choose. Some sorcerers die in battles or something similar—my predecessor died defending the country against the Ugwe—but some choose to live more regular lives, passing on when they feel ready. There's a chance that some of the council is still alive, or their descendants with magic are, and they're staying hidden because they know Nehanda would try to destroy them. I should be able to sense and find them; we can try to convince them to join us."

"Is it important that they are the descendants of the council?" Sefu asked.

"I believe so. Not only would they have passed on some of their magical essence, even if it did skip a generation or two, but it is likely they would have passed on the knowledge of Nehanda's betrayal. They'd be easier to convince to join us."

"It would certainly give everyone a boost of confidence if we had more than one sorcerer on our side," Waed said. "No offense meant, ma'am."

"None taken. I feel the same way." She considered reaching out to search immediately but decided against it. She still had a lot to process, which would make it impossible to focus. "Would a day be too much of a delay?"

"We've waited for generations," Sefu said with a shrug. "Another day shouldn't make a difference."

"Okay. I need some time alone."

"Of course; I'm sorry that we've thrown so much on you, especially after what you've been through," Sefu said apologetically.

"Will I be safe enough in the woods?"

Sefu and Waed shared a glance. "If you stay close enough that we can hear you if you call for help, it should be," Sefu said.

Adanya felt another twinge of pain. Rashidi had been like that; sometimes he disagreed with things she did, but he understood when it was something she needed and would make sure she was taken care of. She rose, nodded to them all, and left the small house, leaving the path and walking into the tough underbrush.

Her ears perked up when she heard a river running nearby; the river always reminded her of the calm times in her childhood. Following the sound, she found the riverbank and settled herself on the ground with her back to a gnarled old tree, its branches stretching out over the water.

Resting her staff on the ground before her, she closed her eyes and listened to the water rushing past, the birds chirping overhead, the sounds of deer and squirrels moving around nearby. It was so calm and peaceful, reminding her of the days when everything had been simple, orderly, and made sense.

She wished she could relax into that peacefulness, but there was something she still had to do. Her hand shook as she pulled the journal from her pocket and untied the leather around it.

After taking a few deep breaths to steady herself, she began scanning the contents. Many of the entries were mundane, discussing the finding and training of other magical children and her work with the council. But Adanya paused as she saw her name.

This girl, Adanya. There's a magic within her stronger than any I've encountered before, even Ziyad. I suspect that she may be able to manifest more than just Sage abilities; I'm going to do some more exploring in her training and research her background. That would explain the glimpses of other magic I've seen in her. There's no way that she is just randomly this powerful.

Powerful? Nehanda had only ever called her uncontrollable. But Adanya was more troubled by the mention of glimpses of other magic. Nehanda had seen it all along?

Her brow furrowed, she flipped to the next page.

I knew that my instincts were correct. Her mother was a commoner who worked at the palace when King Keon was still a prince, before his marriage. They had a relationship that was commonly known among the palace staff, though no one outside of the palace knew of it. From what I've gathered, he was madly in love with her and wanted to marry her. She cared for him as well, but not nearly as much as he cared for her. When she fell pregnant, she decided that her future—and that of her daughter—would be better served outside of the palace. So she left, but did not tell the prince of her condition and did everything she could to hide herself from him. He searched for her for years until his father told him it was a lost cause, and his hand would be more valuable marrying a princess from another country. He doesn't know that Adanya is his daughter. This explains why her magic is so strong; she has royal ancestry.

Adanya's breath caught, and tears sprang to her eyes. "He ... he was ... my father?" she whispered.

Suddenly, more pieces began to fall into place. The way the king had almost immediately felt familiar to her. His interest in her beyond just as a sorcerer. His constant wishes for her well-being and happiness.

Her mother had never spoken to her about her father before her death; Adanya just assumed he'd been uninterested in them and therefore didn't try to search for him at all.

This new revelation also meant that she was the only remaining heir to the throne of Rydell.

She shook her head. She couldn't even begin to wrap her head around that; better to focus on the other threads of connection that had already begun to form in her mind.

When she was younger, just beginning her training with Nehanda, the older woman would always talk about using magic to protect other magical folk so they wouldn't have to go through the ostracism she had as a child. Then she gradually started talking about it less and less, until Adanya's election, when she stopped talking about it at all. Her focus seemed to have changed from simply protecting magical people to working actively against everyone else.

She flipped through a few more pages of the journal. Now she found entries that discussed gathering power to herself and keeping it from "normal people." Or destroying the "normal "people" before they had the chance to use power against them. There were a few cryptic messages about controlling the King of Harrun months before she suggested the slumber, but no clear explanation of how she managed it.

She stopped skimming when she saw a sentence that expanded on Nehanda's musings on her, reading the passage more fully.

Adanya is becoming even more powerful than I realized she could. Her powers may even be such that she is more than just a Sage. She may be able to control all of the elemental powers and more that hasn't fully been documented, making her a Sage Elemental. There's only ever been one Sage Elemental, ages ago. But if she is, I need to find some way to prevent her from discovering this. My methods of training her have kept her from being able to sense my dealings, but if she were able to control all of her powers, she would be strong enough to stop me. I may need to find something—or someone—that can help me to keep her distracted to where she won't explore her powers on her own.

The journal dropped from Adanya's hands into her lap as tears flooded down her cheeks, the final pieces of the puzzle falling into place.

If Adanya was really as powerful as Nehanda said, then the slumber was just a ruse to get her out of the way. Nehanda must have been able to wake everyone once Adanya was asleep, using their shared connection to control the slumber of everyone else.

She must have ceased to consider Adanya a threat, because the one person who was supposed to connect with her and wake her was dead. She couldn't find Adanya herself through the magic barrier, even through their connection. But now she was awake, and Nehanda was sure to have sensed her energy if she was as powerful as Sefu said.

Now Adanya knew, beyond the shadow of a doubt, that she truly was the only hope the resistance had.

Exhausted and overwhelmed, she allowed herself to surrender to all of the feelings she had been holding back.

Beside her, the river suddenly flowed quicker and louder, drowning out her sobs. She knew this was necessary. She had to express her grief for all that she had lost: her father figure, her lover, her mentor. Even her understanding of her world and her place in it.

A memory stirred in her head, and she allowed herself to be fully absorbed in it as she continued weeping.

Chapter Ten

"Come in," King Keon's voice called.

Adanya took a deep breath, then pushed open the door to the nursery. She was dressed in all black, as was the rest of the kingdom, in honor of the queen's passing.

The king was sitting in an armchair, holding a tiny bundle that cooed occasionally. His face was drawn and tired, his eyes red as he looked down at his son.

"Your Majesty," Adanya said, bowing.

He looked up at her, and her heart instantly broke as his incredible pain washed over her. "Adanya. I'm so glad to see you." His normally booming voice sounded frail and uneven.

"I'm only sorry that I could not come sooner," she replied.

He looked back down. "Meet Kayode."

She gingerly approached, looking down at the beautiful milk-chocolate-colored baby swaddled in his arms. "He's beautiful."

He nodded. "I should feel different than this, shouldn't I? I have a son, after all of this time. But I don't feel any joy."

Adanya hesitated. "I cannot pretend to completely know all that you are feeling, Your Majesty. But what I can tell you is that all of those feelings are real and must be experienced. Even if they don't seem to make sense."

Keon was silent for a moment. Then tears welled up in his eyes. "This was all that she ever wanted, to have a child. And now he'll never know her."

She searched for a response but could find nothing. Instead, she asked, "May I hold him?"

He nodded again, and Adanya leaned her staff against the wall before gingerly taking the bundle from his arms. She smiled gently as the prince stared up at her with wide eyes. "Hello, little one. You may not know it yet, but you are surrounded by so much love. This world can be scary, but you will never have to go through it alone." She looked back up at the king. "If your father has shown me such love and kindness though I'm not his child, just imagine how much love he'll have for you."

He reached out for her hand, and she carefully shifted the little prince so she could take it. "When my mother died, I was at a loss," he said quietly. "I thought it was unmanly and weak for me to cry. But my father shed tears openly for her. He told me that the strongest thing a man could do was to allow their feelings to show."

"I've not had much experience with loss, Your Majesty, but it seems sound advice."

"I know I must be overwhelming you with all of these feelings."

She squeezed his hand. "I am honored you would share them with me."

Tears began to roll down his cheeks; the feeling was so powerful that Adanya began to cry as well. She had not been particularly close to the queen; she had met Queen Eshe after the king took an interest in the young sorceress and Adanya began to spend more time at the palace. She had been worried that Queen Eshe was unhappy with their relationship, but Adanya soon learned she was a very quiet person who enjoyed spending time alone; therefore, Keon's time spent with Adanya was good for her.

Keon spent more time with Eshe while she was pregnant, doing his best to be attentive to her every need, even before the doctors told them what a dangerous pregnancy it was. Adanya attended to her studies, understanding the need to give him space. But now, seeing him in such a fragile state, mourning for both his wife and the mother his child would never know, Adanya couldn't help but feel she should have done more to support him, or to help her.

"I should see to the arrangements," he said eventually, holding his arms out for the baby.

Adanya gently returned the child, planting a kiss on his forehead as she arranged the blanket around his face. "If you need anything, just call."

He smiled sadly again and nodded.

Adanya made her way from the room and to the wing where she and other members of the council lived. She paused, almost turning to go to Ziyad's room, but instead she knocked on Nehanda's door.

"Come."

Adanya entered, heaving a heavy sigh. "I've just left the king. He's devastated."

"Lucky he has you to comfort him," Nehanda said, glancing up from her journal.

The younger woman sat down across the table from her. "Wasn't there something that I could have done? My powers connect me to living spirits; couldn't I have ... I don't know ... given life to her or something?"

Something flickered across Nehanda's face, but it was so fast Adanya couldn't tell what it was. "My dear child. That's not how magic works. You can use magic to influence others, but giving life? Stopping death? That is far beyond your abilities. There are some things we just have to learn to accept."

"I just hate seeing ... feeling ... how much pain that he's in. I wish that there was something I could do." Even as she spoke, she could feel a sharp remembrance of his pain that brought tears to her eyes.

"I understand. But being a support for him is all that you can do right now." Nehanda's voice was flat and unaffected, a sharp contrast to Adanya's wavering voice.

"How does anyone carry all of these emotions and not break?" Adanya whispered, wiping the tears from her cheeks in a vain attempt to get control over herself.

Nehanda rose and put a hand on Adanya's shoulder. "This is why I'm training you the way that I am. If you don't learn to filter out what's around you, you'll be constantly bombarded with the emotions of everyone and everything. It will drive you insane."

"I suppose you're right."

"I know I am. Come, let's get some training in before the funeral. It seems that you'll need help to keep focused."

Reluctantly, Adanya followed Nehanda through the palace, its windows and people draped in black, and out to the Arena.

Nehanda instructed her to filter out everything, focusing only on her. Though by this point, a year after being elected to the council, Adanya could typically use this filter with ease, today was a struggle she hadn't experienced before.

"You're close to the king," Nehanda mused, pacing around her. "This connection makes you especially attuned to his feelings, which are affecting your own. Even though you weren't that close with the queen, you still feel the pain of her loss."

Adanya didn't answer—not that she knew what she was expected to say.

"But our role as sorcerers is to be removed from that. If we're affected by everything that happens to those around us, we'll lose perspective. Nomags will never understand the burden we have to carry."

Something in Adanya's consciousness twitched. Though she'd never heard Nehanda use the term before—*nomags*—she instinctively knew it meant those without magic. There was a bitterness in that word, more than Nehanda normally let escape when talking about the need to protect sorcerers. Adanya almost commented on it, but she decided against it.

Instead, she turned to face Nehanda, her focus forgotten. "But don't sorcerers have to have a connection with non-magical people in order to work with them? Ziyad and the king work so well together *because* of their connection, not *despite* it. How can we be expected to earn their trust, to prove to them we're of more use than threat, if we're always separated?"

Nehanda's eyebrows lowered, and Adanya could sense the disapproval in her. "Ziyad is much older, much more in control of his powers than you. Just because you think you can sense closeness between them doesn't mean that he actually lets his guard down and *trusts* the king."

"If we can't trust the king, then who can we trust?" Adanya realized it was her connection to the king heightening her own emotions, but at this point, she didn't care. "He is part of the reason that we have any of this." She waved her hand at the Arena, at the barracks around it where young sorcerers lived. "Without connection, what are we? Our separation only gives them more reason to be afraid of us. Isn't that what you've been trying to get me to protect against?" Though she sensed heat slowly building around Nehanda as her anger grew, she kept going. "I've never felt grief like this before. I don't even remember my mother's death, I never knew my father, and no one else that I've been close to has died. But this grief..." She pressed a fist to her heart, the feeling intensifying as the tears returned in full force. "It reminds me that pain like this does exist. It reminds me that the people whose emotions and thoughts I can feel are ... people. And that gives me a connection beyond anything I would get from just studying them like books in the library. It makes me want to keep the people that I have a connection to safe so they never have to go through this pain. People like you. I know how much pain you've been through, and I don't want you to have to go through it again."

"Trying to keep people from pain only leads to more suffering," Nehanda said, her voice subdued, though heat still rose from her.

Adanya reached forward and touched her hand, flinching from the heat but not removing it as she gazed into Nehanda's eyes. "Then please, let me feel this. Let me learn from it so I know how to react if ... when ... it happens again."

Nehanda hesitated, her eyes searching Adanya's. There it was again, that strange shift in Nehanda's consciousness. It was almost ... like surprise?

Before Adanya could fully place it, Nehanda nodded. "Make a clear boundary in your head. Allow yourself to feel, but don't let it overtake you. If you must express these feelings, do it alone, where you know that it's only yours and you're not drawing from someone else's grief and sadness."

Adanya smiled, squeezing Nehanda's hand. "Thank you." That was the most physical affection the two women had ever exchanged, but it was enough to show their understanding.

Adanya turned back to the palace, leaving Nehanda standing behind her in silent contemplation.

#

At the funeral a day later, Adanya stood with the other council members, watching as the late queen's casket was lowered into the palace burial grounds. King Keon allowed his tears to openly fall, a nurse standing nearby with the young prince to allow him space to feel his grief.

It was eerily quiet, only the occasional sniffles breaking the silence. Adanya did her best to follow Nehanda's advice, sensing everyone's grief and marveling at the differences she could feel. Some people who knew the queen more personally—ladies-in-waiting, servants, and the like—had a more visceral type of grief, more like the king's. But many of those assembled held a more distant grief; they loved her as their queen, more like a distant figure, and knew her loss was a blow to the king himself.

Above it all, she felt the king's grief, all-encompassing, shaking him to his very core.

King Keon stepped forward, composing himself a moment before he spoke. "Our kingdom has suffered a great loss. Though the queen was a very private person, I know from many conversations that she was loved by all who knew her. She was a quiet pillar of strength to many, myself not least of all. Her loss is a..." He paused to clear the catch in his throat. "It is a blow to all of us. She blessed us with an heir in Prince Kayode, but there will always be a missing piece in our family. For her final gift, we thank her."

Adanya couldn't help herself any longer. She left her place beside Nehanda and went over to the king, taking his hand. Ziyad simultaneously put a hand on his shoulder from where he stood nearby. King Keon broke into tears, his hand shaking as he gripped hers. She found herself crying as well, silent tears streaming down her cheeks as everyone around them maintained a respectful silence. Ziyad caught her eye and nodded approval through his own tears. She could feel pride beneath his grief, pride in her understanding of the connections around her.

She closed her eyes, surrendering to all the emotions swirling around her. "I'll do all that I can to protect you," she whispered to the king.

Chapter Eleven

Adanya didn't know how much time had passed when she opened her eyes again. Her face was wet with tears, and her heart still felt heavy. But now she had a renewed purpose. Nehanda betrayed them, destroyed everything in her own quest for power. Adanya didn't doubt her mentor had been searching for power that would protect her and other magical people; that power, however, went to her head and caused her to go far beyond a reasonable measure.

Adanya was now the only one who could avenge those lost.

Sefu rose as she entered the house. He was the only one there; the others had gone back out to continue their work now that daylight had returned.

"I think I have a plan," she said, sitting before the fire once more. "I know what powers the other sorcerers had, but it will take me some time to discover if I am able to access that magic. If I can, then I will be better attuned to their energy and be able to find them or their descendants."

Sefu nodded. "It seems a reasonable plan. We can support you by distracting Nehanda while you and I search for the others."

"I couldn't ask you to be with me while I'm doing this. It's dangerous, especially since I have no one to train me and I'll have to figure things out on my own."

"There's not going to be any dissuading me," he said, a smirk on his face. "You're taking an enormous risk helping us, and I'm not going to let anything happen to you."

Despite her thoughts of objecting, she could not help but feel comforted by his words. "Very well." She tapped her chin. "There were seven sorcerers on the council; besides Nehanda and myself, there was an Aqua, an Ember, a Flora, a Fauna, and a Clime. In order to connect to their powers, I'll need to manifest them myself."

"Do you have any idea how you're going to do that?"

She shrugged. "The best I can come up with is finding environments that have the elements I need to control." She stood and began to pace, twisting her rings absentmindedly. "Before and after I was appointed to the council, I spent time with all the members, learning more about them and their powers. Hopefully being around the elements will bring back memories of how they used their magic." *Even though those memories happened only a few years ago, in my mind.*

Sefu brought her out of the sobering thought by asking, "You didn't get to observe other sorcerers while you were training?"

She shook her head. "Sorcerers would train with others that had their kind of magic. Since I was the only Sage in training, I didn't engage with the others much. There was something to be said about learning from the council members as I did, though. I got to know them not only as fellow sorcerers but as friends. They taught me a lot more about life and being around others whose skills may differ from mine."

"The kind of thing you learn when training to be a leader," Sefu said wisely.

She stopped pacing, the pang of sadness at her recent discoveries strong. She struggled to compose herself before answering, "I suppose so." Turning to him, she tilted her head, sensing a similar sadness radiating from Sefu. "How old were you when you lost your parents?"

He looked as if he were trying to keep up a brave face, but he wilted slightly under her gaze. "Fifteen."

She sat beside him as he continued speaking, his eyes trained on the fire. "They were leading a raid on a town in a southern kingdom. There wasn't any reason for things to go badly, so none of us were worried. I stayed behind because I'd fallen ill and my mother insisted I rest. I'll never forgive myself for that." He paused, Adanya feeling the heat of anger mixing with his grief. "Somehow word had gotten to Nehanda's men. My parents and everyone with them were slaughtered. Then I became the leader of the resistance. Waed carried most of it while he trained me, gradually releasing more responsibility to me as I got older and more experienced."

He fell silent.

Adanya bit her lip, realizing she had been so caught up in her own feelings that she'd forgotten to pay attention to the feelings of the others around her, or what was at stake for them. A lesson she thought she'd learned.

Hesitantly, she put a hand on his arm, squeezing comfortingly. "While it may be strange for the both of us, it would seem we were meant to stand together against Nehanda."

He nodded wordlessly, and they sat together for a while in silence.

Finally, he seemed to shake off his thoughts and stood, extending his hand to help her up. "Well, then. You need to start manifesting some powers. Where do you think we should start?"

Though his mannerisms still made her think of Rashidi, she was less haunted by Sefu's resemblance than before; she resolved to keep their shared connection in the present in the forefront of her mind as she took his offered hand to stand.

"Aqua, I think. We're close enough to some water that I can try to connect to those powers there."

Together, they returned to the stream. "Naeemah was an Aqua," Adanya mused. "She could control not only bodies of water but the very moisture in the air. If I can attune my senses to just water, I might be able to make it work."

She tried to think back to the time she spent with Naeemah before she had been named Head of Council, searching her memory for how Naeemah used her powers.

Chapter Twelve

Adanya hurried to the council chambers, where she found Ziyad sitting alone at the head of the table. He smiled as she dipped her head respectfully. "I'm sorry to keep you waiting, sir. You wanted to see me?"

"Come sit with me a moment, child."

She did as he asked, hesitantly sitting in the chair to his right.

"How has your training been?"

"It's been getting better. I've gained a lot more control over my powers."

"I'm glad to hear it." He studied her for a moment with a tilted head, and she tried not to squirm under his examination. "I think that it is time you start going on outings with other members of the council. It will give you a chance to get to see other types of magic at work ... as well as getting to know the council members themselves. Who knows? Maybe you'll end up working among them one day."

"Me? On the council?"

"Why not? Any trained sorcerer can be elected to the council, if the remaining members vote for them. I'm sure you have plenty that you can contribute."

Adanya felt her face warm, so she ducked her head to hide her face with her braids. "I don't have any desire to be in leadership, sir."

He reached over and gently took her hand. "Sometimes that's not for us to decide, child."

Adanya wanted to protest further, to tell him that she would do anything *not* to be on the council despite what others kept saying, but she could feel his belief in her and couldn't bring herself to say anything aloud.

Have some faith in yourself, Adanya. She looked up when she heard Ziyad's voice in her head. *I know that it may take some time, but you have what you need to make a great impact.* He squeezed her hand once, then released it and sat back. "Naeemah is going out to deal with a bridge in Danseg Forest; I'd like you to accompany her. She'll meet you in the palace courtyard."

"Yes, sir." She rose and dipped her head respectfully again, leaving to walk through the palace, heading for the courtyard. Her mind spun. Ziyad thought she was worthy of being on the council? But why? She hadn't done anything special to be noticed by him—or anyone, for that matter. Nehanda always said she could be on the council one day, but wasn't that just how a mentor would encourage their charge?

She was left with swirling emotions as she entered the courtyard. When she saw Naeemah approaching, she pushed them aside. She watched Naeemah in awe; she seemed to glide across the courtyard, her blue gown making her seem like she was floating. Though they were only two years apart in age, Naeemah held a grace and maturity that Adanya wished she could emulate. Named to the council only a year ago, she was already considered one of the senior members due to her wisdom and control over her powers. They had already spent some time together, and Adanya considered her to be one of her few friends.

"Adanya, there you are!" she called, waving.

Adanya came down the steps to join her. "Hi, sorry. I was just thinking."

Naeemah smiled. "You're so in your head sometimes. We've got to break you of that."

"A side effect of having so much time spent alone."

She tossed her long, silky-smooth locks over one shoulder and squeezed Adanya's hand. "Well, that makes sense. But if you're going to be on the council someday, you'll have to learn how to be more vocal."

"You're only the second person to tell me that today. I'm not entirely sure that I want to be on the council," Adanya admitted as they began walking from the palace courtyard out onto the road. "It just seems so lofty... I'm sure that I could do more good just being myself."

"It's a lot of responsibility, to be sure," Naeemah agreed. "Every sorcerer on the council has a different power, and we use them to support each other and make ourselves stronger. We're charged with the well-being of the entire kingdom, and that can be overwhelming."

Adanya drew a little closer to Naeemah as they moved through the bustle of the main square, both so she could speak without shouting to be heard and because the cacophony was still a bit overwhelming to her. "Nehanda and Ziyad seem to think that I can do it one day."

"If they see potential in you, then I don't doubt it. I noticed the king seems to have taken an interest in you as well." Naeemah seemed quite at home with the people around her, even waving and nodding regally in response to greetings from passersby.

Adanya blushed. "I don't know why. But I do feel very comfortable with him; he's teaching me a lot about the world."

"King Keon is a kind man, and I'm sure he'll make a great father one day. But your connection with him could be what pushes you to be on the council. If you think about it, Ziyad is one of the king's closest friends, which helps them to work so well together in the interest of the kingdom."

Leaving the town, they followed a smaller road that led into the forest, the sounds of rushing water growing steadily louder. "I just wonder what use I would be if there is already a Sage on the council," Adanya said.

"Sages are the most powerful," Naeemah explained, "and some of the most rare. It's generally a good idea to have as many around you as possible."

They stopped as they reached the stream. It had risen far above its wooden dam and was flooding the road.

Naeemah surveyed the scene as she determined her next move. "This river has always been so insistent upon crossing this road," she murmured, more to herself than to Adanya. "Perhaps we should make it a new path."

Adanya watched in awe as Naeemah's blue-rimmed brown eyes studied the water, her dress floating around her in the gentle breeze, making her look like a mystical water nymph. The water rushing over the road suddenly floated up like the head and body of a snake, contained in an invisible field created by Naeemah. It continued rushing forward but was caught in her field. After a few minutes of the water pressure building, she tilted her head downwards ever so slightly.

The water moved like a snake, pounding its way into the earth on the side of the road and shaking everything around it. Naeemah continued focusing until the water emerged from the earth some distance away from the road. Now, the stream's course dipped deep under the ground, leaving the road high and dry.

Naeemah raised an eyebrow. In response, a small handful of water left the stream and drifted over to her, where it turned to steam that wreathed her hair and smoothed down anything that had come out of place.

"Have you always been able to do that?" Adanya whispered.

Naeemah laughed, her eyes twinkling. "Goodness, no. I spent most of my training soaking wet!" She took Adanya's arm, and they began walking back to the palace together. "What helped me was to think about how nature can be manipulated in natural ways. If you think about it, it's not just sorcerers who manipulate nature. Farmers, fishermen, sailors, they all work with nature to create things that are needed. Working with water is the same way. You'll get the strongest effect when you work with nature, not against it."

"I don't know how that will help me use my powers." She felt a rush of gratitude as Naeemah guided them around the main part of the city, sticking to the quieter side streets.

"That's because you're thinking too hard. You grew up mostly in the woods, right? How did you survive?"

Adanya answered easily. "I sensed the animals and let them know that I wasn't a threat, and I helped to protect them when I could. Once they trusted me, they would lead me to safe places to stay, clean water, and food."

"Exactly. Even though you don't have the ability to use their senses, you were able to follow them to places they would naturally go. The same is true for all sorcerers."

"I hadn't thought of it that way."

"Even for you, as a Sage, you may be able to influence people around you, but only if there is something deep in their mind that wanted to do or say things anyway. That's why it's dangerous to influence minds, because you may be unlocking something that they didn't even know they wanted. People have intrusive thoughts all the time, but they learn to push them down and ignore the ones that could be harmful to themselves or others. Push them to act on them, and there can be very bad outcomes."

Adanya was silent for a moment, taking in what Naeemah was saying. "That makes so much sense. When I was in the orphanage, I would influence other children to take food or toys that I wanted. I've found that most children, especially if they haven't been taught yet, have those kinds of urges."

"Very true. Thank goodness you know better now, hm?"

Adanya grinned at her friend as they reentered the court-yard. "Yes. Thank you for telling me all of this; it helps to put things into perspective." *In a way that Nehanda doesn't.*

Naeemah laughed, and Adanya blushed as she realized she had shared her last thought out loud. "To be honest, I don't think anyone, including Nehanda, ever expected her to be teach-ing anyone. She's not used to having to share her knowledge in this way; she's always kept mostly to herself. Be patient with her. She's trying her best, and I know that she sees the potential in you."

"I'll try."

Naeemah squeezed her hand with a smile, then waved and walked back inside the palace, leaving Adanya to head back to her rooms and ponder her friend's words.

Chapter Thirteen

Adanya refocused with a start, glancing around to see Sefu standing patiently by. "I'm sorry," she apologized. "I didn't mean to keep you waiting like that."

"Do whatever you need to," he replied with a smile.

Nodding gratefully, she turned back to the water and tried to envision herself using Aqua powers as Naeemah had. She caught sight of a fallen tree branch a bit downstream. It was blocking most of the stream's flow, slowing the rush of the water as it searched for a way through. In time, the water would push the branch away or wear it down ... but maybe she could speed up the process.

"What would naturally happen," she muttered to herself.

She took a deep breath, focusing her energy onto the stream. She focused on the water itself, trying to become one with it—the temperature, the feel of it on her skin, the power waiting to be unleashed.

"You're doing it!" Sefu exclaimed.

She realized the flow of water was obeying her thoughts, moving back and forth. Sefu watched in wonder as the water floated in midair, surrounded by an invisible field that stopped the flow.

"Okay, let's try this," she said aloud.

She looked over at the tree branch. The water followed her direction, pushing the branch with such force that it splintered and shattered instantly under the pressure, the pieces carried swiftly away by the current. The stream resumed flowing as usual, moving quicker since the obstruction was gone.

Adanya blew out a breath, looking at the water in awe. "So it's really true," she said, talking more to herself than to Sefu. "I really *can* use other powers. And she hid that from me."

She clenched her hand into a fist, willing herself to push down the anger she felt. It wouldn't solve anything; better to focus on the task at hand.

"What happens now?" Sefu asked.

"I imagine that I should be able to focus my energy toward—" Her eyes suddenly widened and her jaw went slack as a host of blurry but distinguishable images assaulted her: a young woman using water to fix her hair and making water float through the air, steaming wrinkles from a dress. She stood by a small cottage, comfortably surrounded by a clearing in the woods on one side and the river on the other.

As suddenly as the images appeared they were gone, leaving Adanya disoriented and staggering. Sefu was at her side instantly, catching her around the waist and putting his other arm around her shoulders. "I've got you," he said.

She nodded gratefully to him, then straightened. "I saw her. It must be my Sage magic interacting with Aqua magic. But I had a vision. Whoever she is, she's living near the river that runs through some woods. I don't recognize the area."

She could feel Sefu's surprise, but instead of questioning the magic, he asked, "Is it a wide or narrow river?"

"Very wide. Very still, too." She focused, trying to clear the blurriness from what she'd seen. "It looks like a place where she wouldn't have to leave for anything."

"The river is much wider the farther west you go," he mused. "And it does run through some areas of woods that haven't been cleared for roads."

"Then that's where we should go. Lead the way?"

She suddenly realized their proximity, and her face heated with discomfort. Sefu seemed to both notice and understand. He quickly ensured she could stand firmly on her own before stepping away to give her some space. Then he turned to lead them back through the woods. They started in the direction of the cottage, then veered onto another path that exited the woods. He kept his hand on his sword as they followed the path, which kept close to the tree cover but didn't enter it.

Adanya gripped her staff tighter, very aware that this was not the world she had fallen asleep in and that she needed to be cautious. She was also amazed at how clearly she'd seen the young woman; her powers had never allowed her to see others clearly before, only sense their energy and vaguely connect with them. She wondered if Nehanda knew that was possible, if she'd purposefully hidden it from her like everything else. Belatedly she also realized that if she had that power, it was highly likely that Nehanda had it as well.

She could feel the pull of the young woman get stronger as they continued walking for nearly an hour. Neither spoke, both keeping their eyes open for any sign they were being watched or followed. Adanya would occasionally reach out to the birds chirping merrily in the trees or the odd squirrel she saw cross their path to sense if anything was making them uneasy, but all seemed calm.

Finally, Sefu led her back into the trees, and they began picking their way through the underbrush. "It should be somewhere around here. The river runs through; can you hear it?"

Adanya nodded. She could feel the presence of the young woman, almost as if she were directly in front of her. "Let me lead."

Sefu paused to allow her to pass, then followed closely behind. She followed the pull of the young woman, using her staff to push bushes and branches out of her path.

Suddenly, the trees ended and they found themselves standing in the very clearing she had seen in her mind's eye. The cottage was by the water, and sitting by the water's edge was the young woman.

Adanya had to catch her breath; though not a spitting image like Sefu, the young woman clearly carried Naeemah's features.

She turned in alarm as they approached, her hand on a small knife.

Sefu held up his hands, preparing to give an explanation for their presence, but her blue-rimmed eyes grew wide as she caught sight of Adanya. She scrambled to her feet, bowing reverently.

"My Lady Adanya," she said in an awe-filled voice. "I can't believe it's actually you."

"Just Adanya, please," she said, heat rising to her face as she felt the young woman's excitement. "That title does me no good here."

"I knew that you were coming," she replied. "About an hour ago, I could just ... feel you."

"It was only an hour ago that I learned to use my Aqua powers." Adanya nodded in agreement. "But you don't seem surprised to see me alive?"

"My family always believed that you would be awakened one day. My great-great-grandmother, Naeemah, made sure we all knew and remembered it. I just never thought it would be in my lifetime."

"Did she..." Adanya paused to clear the catch in her throat, the realization that her friend was gone suddenly hitting her with full force. "Did she tell you what happened?"

"Yes. She said Nehanda had betrayed everyone, and the council had to go into hiding in order to survive. She tried to aid Rashidi as long as she could, but there was only so much that she could do while protecting herself. She knew that you would need support when you awakened." She bowed again. "I am honored to serve you in whatever way that you need, my lady."

"What is your name?"

"Abiba, my lady."

"Then rise, Abiba. There's no need for such formality. I am honored that you would join us." She turned and gestured to Sefu. "This is Sefu, the descendent of Rashidi and the leader of the resistance against Nehanda."

They nodded at each other.

"Are you here alone?"

"Yes; I lost my parents many years ago, and I am their only child."

"We are alike in that," Sefu said solemnly.

Abiba smiled at him, then turned back to Adanya. "What would you have me do?"

"Our plan has us gathering sorcerers and trying to take one city away from Nehanda's control at a time," Adanya replied. "I haven't decided exactly what magical influence we'll have, but we will need as much strength as we can get."

"Let me gather my things, and I'll come with you." Abiba turned and hurried into the cottage, returning ten minutes later with a bag slung over one shoulder.

Adanya blinked away a rogue tear that threatened to fall over the loss of her friend, then turned to Sefu. "Lead the way back."

The trio walked back into the woods, Adanya again lost in her thoughts. If this was the process to awakening her powers, it would be a good way to find the rest of the council members—or their descendants. She would have to be careful that her emotions did not take control of her, as she was struggling through just meeting Abiba. She had to come to terms with the fact that there may be more of her friends who decided to let go and let their children and children's children carry on the hope of freedom from Nehanda; but the grief would have to wait.

Along with the anger.

Sefu and Abiba conversed quietly as they walked, sensing Adanya's need to be in her thoughts.

So, who should I try to find next?

Adio.

Weather was a natural extension of water; besides, she had an inkling she had been inadvertently influencing the weather anyway, now that she looked back on things.

Suddenly, she stopped short, eyebrows lowering as she felt the energy of other people in the woods. "Someone's coming," she said, gripping her staff tighter.

Sefu immediately drew his sword and Abiba drew her knife as all three turned their backs to each other to scan their surroundings.

Adanya closed her eyes for a moment, focusing on the new energy to differentiate it from her companions. "At least ten men," she said, seeing the flashes of armed men in traveling clothes pushing their way through the underbrush of the woods toward them. "Armed, but not armored."

"Do you think that they're looking for us?" Sefu asked.

"I can't quite tell."

"Nehanda may have used her magic to prevent Sages from entering her soldiers' thoughts," Abiba offered.

"Which means she definitely knows that I'm awake." Adanya frowned.

"If they see you, they'll know something is up," Sefu said. "Do we fight, or do we hide? If we fight, we'll have to destroy all of them."

"Won't missing soldiers be suspicious?" Abiba asked.

"We hide," Adanya said decisively. "Quickly."

He sheathed his sword, and they moved into the underbrush, each finding their own place to hide. Sefu quickly shimmied up a tree; Abiba crawled underneath a fallen tree trunk; Adanya ducked under some bushes, laying on top of her staff to keep the white wood from showing.

A few minutes later, the soldiers came tramping through the woods with no pretense of silence or stealth.

"This is odd for her, though," one soldier said to his neighbor. "We're always on patrol, but through the woods like this?"

"She seems to be a lot more worried about attacks over the past couple of days," his neighbor agreed. "I wonder what could have changed to make her so uneasy?"

"All I know is that I'm sick of these woods." He swatted at a mosquito as they passed Adanya's hiding spot. "Take me back to the city."

"I wouldn't mind that myself."

Their voices faded as they left the underbrush and continued down the path. The trio waited another ten minutes to be safe, then scrambled out from their hiding places.

"We've got to be more careful, now that I'm certain she knows I'm awake," Adanya said.

"Agreed," Sefu said. "Let's move quickly."

They did so, arriving back at the cottage in less than an hour. Waed was there alone, sketching out positions on maps and reading reports. His eyes widened as Sefu introduced their new member, and he bowed respectfully.

"Were you in contact with any of the other families?" Adanya asked Abiba as they settled around the table.

She shook her head. "No. The story passed down was that they agreed to stay away from each other until you awakened. Everyone gathering together would certainly draw Nehanda's attention."

"That is true. I think my next step will be to find Adio or one of his descendants. It may be easier for me to access those powers. How are things going on your end, Waed?"

"Not much change. We're still working on a bit of a holding pattern."

"We'll have to be extremely careful traveling from now on," Adanya said. "Anyone around me could be in danger, and the more council members we find, the more she'll be able to sense us." She turned to look at Abiba. "It would probably be wise if you stayed here while Sefu and I continue searching..."

Abiba shook her head. "If she's able to sense you, you need to be protected. There's no way I'm letting you go out there without me."

She opened her mouth to protest, but she closed it as she realized the young woman wasn't going to take no for an answer. How very like Naeemah. "Alright. Let's take some time to rest. It's been a long couple of days."

Sefu led her to his room again, reminding her to ask for anything she might need before closing the door behind him.

Once alone, she removed the cloak that hid her robes, hanging it behind the door. Then she removed her outer layer of robes, leaving her in her comfortable pants and a loose-fitting shirt.

Sitting on the side table was a pitcher of water and a shallow bowl, undoubtedly for washing face or hands. Rather than walk over to it, she extended her powers toward it. The water floated over to her. A thought turned it to steam that she moved to wreathe around her, brightening her skin and bringing moisture to her scalp and hair.

She was amazed at how easily these powers came to her now that she knew how to use them; hopefully the other powers would work just as well.

Heaving a heavy sigh, she lay down atop the blanket and was quickly fast asleep.

Chapter Fourteen

Adanya sat with Rashidi on a blanket spread out in the field just outside the capital city, the rest of her guard surrounding them at a respectful distance.

She looked up from the apple she was cutting when she felt Rashidi's attention on her, seeing him smiling at her. "What?" she asked.

"Nothing. I just like looking at you, that's all."

She felt the heat rising to her cheeks, and she turned back to her apple. "That's so odd."

"Why would it be odd for me to look at this beautiful woman of mine?"

Now she giggled. "You're so ridiculous." She handed him a piece of the apple, and he purposefully grazed her fingers with his own as she did. She flushed even more, feeling the familiar electricity in his touch.

He chuckled at her reaction as he licked the apple juice from his fingers, looking seductively at her.

"We are in public, sir," she said, trying to sound unbothered but failing miserably.

"The guards won't say anything if I order them not to." Nevertheless, he relented.

"I swear, sometimes I think that you enjoy getting a rise out of me."

She didn't even have to read his mind, easily reading the look on his face: *you make something rise on me.*

She cleared her throat loudly. "So! Are you ready to meet the king tonight? He told me he's been looking forward to it."

Rashidi mercifully went along with her abrupt change of subject. "I think so. What have you told him about me?"

"Good things," she said with a wink. "He knows how I feel about you."

"Oh? And how do you feel about me?"

She looked up to meet his gaze, unabashedly letting him feel all of the love and devotion running through her. "I feel like you're the best thing to ever happen to me. Like you're the support that I never knew I needed. Like everything in my life has gotten better since you've been in it."

His smile widened, and took her hand, raising it to his lips for a kiss. "I love you too. Hopefully I'm up to his standards."

"I don't know why you wouldn't be."

He raised an eyebrow. "Then why are you nervous?"

Adanya laughed, amazed that he could read her so well without magic. "I mean … the king is the closest thing that I have to a father. I know deep down that he'll love you, but the anxious part of me worries he'll find something that he doesn't like."

"You weren't this worried when Nehanda found out about us."

Now she shifted uncomfortably. "She's … different. She has different views on relationships than the king does."

"I noticed."

"What do you mean?"

She felt his hesitation as he tried to phrase his thought, and she purposefully kept herself from reading his mind.

"Everything that you've ever told me about Nehanda makes it feel like she'd rather be alone, not having to deal with anyone. Especially non-magical people. Honestly, I'm surprised her reaction was as calm as it was, considering her feelings."

Adanya considered that for a moment. True, when she was younger, Nehanda spoke of relationships between men and women as nothing more than a means of procreation—though she was careful to remind Adanya that she shouldn't be concerned with such things without explaining the particulars. As a result, she hadn't paid any attention to the few men she'd been around during her training. Being so introverted from her time in the woods didn't help matters.

Nehanda had told her that most sorcerers chose to remain single, knowing the struggles being magical could have on a spouse, as well as the difficulty finding someone 'worthy' (this was Nehanda's way of saying magical). It wasn't until she began spending time with the council that she discovered how many sorcerers actually desired to raise families; Kamaria, Gabir, and Jabari were all married, Gabir's wife having just given birth to their third child.

Still, when Nehanda found out about Adanya's relationship with Rashidi (catching them kissing in a stairwell), she reacted in a surprisingly civil manner, only reminding her to be careful that she didn't get pregnant.

"Maybe she just realized that I'm too old for her to restrict me from being in a relationship," Adanya said finally.

Rashidi raised an eyebrow.

"Don't look at me like that!"

"I didn't say a word."

She scowled. "What are you thinking? You know I can just look if you won't tell me."

"Nehanda has never struck me as a person to easily change their mind on something this big."

"People can change!" she protested.

He held up both hands in surrender. "Of course they can, love." Without giving her a chance to babble on, he rose and began packing up the picnic supplies. "But we should be getting back. You have a council meeting soon, I believe."

She considered pursuing further but decided to let it go. "Sometimes I think you know my schedule better than I do."

"You're a creature of habit. Makes it easier to keep an eye on you. I am still your guard, after all."

They laughed together as they finished packing, then mounted their horses and rode the ten minutes back to the courtyard.

Once there, they left the rest of the guard as Rashidi escorted her up the stairs and through the doors.

"You don't have to walk me to the council room," she giggled, though she did not let go of his hand.

"I know I don't. I just wanted to give you this." He pulled her around a corner, pressing her back against the wall as he kissed her passionately.

Adanya was enraptured. Being enveloped in Rashidi's love was one of the few times she was truly able to ignore all the other calls to her psyche, just existing between her and him. She could solely focus on the surprising softness of his lips, the feel of his hands on her face and her waist, the undeniable energy between them and the strength of his desires to protect her and ... *have* her.

He left her breathless and flushed as he pulled away, gently rearranging her braids. "I'll see you tonight for dinner?"

"Dinner? Dinner."

"It will be fine. Don't worry about it." He kissed her hand, a mischievous twinkle in his eye, and walked back through the door.

Adanya stayed put for a moment, trying to gather herself before walking up to lead the council meeting. It wouldn't do for her to present herself as she was, grinning foolishly with her heart racing.

She hadn't intended on falling in love with Rashidi. But from their first interaction dealing with the Ugwe, there had been a spark between them. Rashidi had taken to finding ways to "accidentally" see her in the hallways of the palace, walking and talking with her until he finally asked her permission to pursue her. She had initially refused, unsure of the wisdom of it. But she relented. They had been in bliss ever since; he'd taught her so much about relationships and been so patient with her.

Even their first time together in bed was a learning experience. But alone with him, feeling his desire for her and hers for him, Adanya couldn't help but let him lead her.

This was the only secret she'd never told Nehanda.

She sometimes felt guilty about it, the secret and the disobedience of her warning, but the love that had grown between her and Rashidi quickly made that go away. The intimacy she kept for herself; the love, however, was obvious to anyone who knew her.

Like Adio.

"I see that smile," he said, rounding a corner and grinning at her. "How's Rashidi?"

"He's fine," she answered, feeling the heat returning to her cheeks.

"I'd think so, with that look on your face."

Adanya playfully shoved him. "I wish you'd leave me alone."

"What, and miss out on this prime opportunity to tease you about finding true love? Never."

"I don't know about all that..."

He gave her a look, teal-rimmed eyes dancing with amusement. "If Rashidi isn't your true love, then I'm a bear. I've never seen anyone make you so happy. And I'm happy for you."

"You don't think that ... it's happening too fast?"

"Why would I think that? Love doesn't have a set timetable."

"I suppose not," she replied distantly.

He stopped walking and turned her to face him. "Hey. You are quite literally the sweetest, most selfless person I've ever met in my life. If there is anyone who deserves to be happy, it's you.

Don't overthink it." He kissed her cheek, then continued walking.

Adanya smiled, happy for the reassurance that she hadn't known she needed.

#

As dusk fell, Adanya stood nervously at the top of the courtyard stairs waiting for Rashidi. Her face brightened when she saw him climbing the stairs sans his normal working clothes, instead wearing a comfortably fitting pair of white linen pants and a shirt.

"Hello, beautiful," he said, kissing her sweetly. "Are you ready?"

"I'm so nervous," she replied, squeezing his hand.

"I don't think that you need to be. The king loves you, and I'm sure he'll be able to see how much I love you."

"I know that you're right, but I'm still nervous."

"I know you are." He kissed the side of her head as he guided her back inside. "Just letting you know that you don't have to be."

She smiled up at him, again feeling the world fade away so it was just the two of them.

They walked through the palace until they reached the smaller dining room where the king regularly ate when not holding balls or state dinners. King Keon smiled broadly as they approached the table, opening his arms to hug Adanya as he always did when not in council. "There she is!"

Adanya could not help but laugh as she hugged him back. "Hello, Your Majesty."

"Everything go alright in the council meeting?"

"Yes, nothing new to report."

"Good, good." He turned to see Rashidi waiting patiently, smiling at their exchange. "And this must be the young man I've heard so much about." He extended his hand.

Rashidi first bowed, then shook the offered hand. "A pleasure to formally meet you, Your Majesty."

"I know that I've seen you around, but certainly not since you began guarding Adanya." He gestured for them all to sit. "I'll admit I've been curious to meet you for myself, as much as Adanya talks about you."

"Oh? And what has she been saying?"

"Strictly complimentary things, I assure you," he replied as the servants brought dinner to the table. "I was beginning to think you were someone that she made up, because I haven't heard a single negative word about you."

"That's an exaggeration," Adanya cut in quickly, feeling the heat rising to her cheeks again.

"I wouldn't say that." King Keon winked at her. "It's perfectly fine to be infatuated." He turned to look at Rashidi on his left, opposite Adanya. "Truth be told, it makes me incredibly happy to see her so happy and loved."

"She makes me incredibly happy, Your Majesty. I can only hope that she's happy too."

"Believe me, she is. She speaks more of you than she even does about the council."

Adanya couldn't help but smile at the good natured teasing. The love she felt from the two men in the room with her, different yet similar, gave her a feeling of euphoria that she'd never experienced before.

As the dinner progressed, Adanya began to feel an unusual sense of nervousness coming from ... Rashidi? She was puzzled. That man was the epitome of calm. Even in stressful situations, she never sensed anything but confidence from him. Nerves didn't make sense.

"Your Majesty," Rashidi began as the servants cleared the table of dinner, "I'm glad that I have finally been able to sit and talk with you. I know Adanya considers you like a father to her, and I wanted to do this in front of her family."

Adanya gaped, bewildered as he left his seat and came to stand next to her. "Do what?"

Her heart nearly stopped as he got down on one knee and took her hand. "Adanya, I love you. You've become the light of my life in the time that I've known you, and there isn't anything I wouldn't do for you. I realized I would never forgive myself if

I didn't make you my wife. So, Adanya..." He reached into his pocket and pulled out a golden band set with an amethyst in the center. "Will you marry me?"

Her eyes welled with tears, and she found herself laughing and crying at the same time. Her body flooded with a rush of emotions, and she found herself unable to speak.

"You might want to answer him, my dear," King Keon said, smiling broadly. "Being on one knee is none too comfortable."

She finally was able to nod and whisper, "Yes."

Rashidi's nerves vanished, replaced by such a feeling of exaltation that Adanya was almost overwhelmed. He grinned widely, slipping the ring onto her finger and scooping her up from her chair to kiss her and hug her tightly. "I love you, Adanya."

"I love you, Rashidi."

They jumped as the king's arms enveloped them both, his laugh booming throughout the room. "I couldn't think of a better match for her, Rashidi."

Buried between the two people she loved most in the world, Adanya could do nothing but smile. This was what love was supposed to feel like. This wasn't pretend or hidden; she knew exactly how they felt about her, and they didn't care who knew.

She'd never been more happy.

Chapter Fifteen

After a quick breakfast the next morning, the trio headed back out into the woods, this time skirting them instead of going into the depths.

"Adio was a Clime, right?" Abiba asked.

"Yes," Adanya replied. "He was also one of my closest friends. I learned a lot about life among non-magical folk from him."

"When did you start being around non-magical people?" When Adanya glanced at her in surprise, Abiba explained, "I was always told stories of the Arena and the training of young sorcerers. I know that you didn't really go out into the city without supervision until you'd been deemed capable of handling yourself."

Adanya couldn't help but smile. Trust that Naeemah would make sure her descendants knew how things used to be. "I had an outing with the king once when I was still in training, but I didn't start going into the city regularly until I was around seventeen. It was still quite difficult for me; I had spent a lot of my time isolated, so being around people was challenging, especially since I could sense them. Adio was one of the first to really take me under his wing. He's five years older than I am, which you wouldn't think would make much of a difference, but he had so much more life experience than me."

"I imagine his support was helpful."

Adanya looked at her again as she felt a wave of sadness emanating from the young woman. "How long have you been living on your own?" she asked gently.

Abiba sighed. "Nearly five years now. We've always lived an isolated life. Once Nehanda took over, Naeemah married and they moved to that clearing. She and her descendants would only go into town occasionally, and generally it was only those of us who did not have magic. That's how they would meet others, get married, have children. Many of the non-magical family members moved into cities, which made it easier to bring supplies back. And if any of them showed magic, they were brought to live and train in the cabin. Surprisingly, there had been someone magical in every generation until my father."

Adanya nodded. "Naeemah could trace her lineage back to the first king; it's not surprising that her magic was strong enough to pass through generations."

"He decided to stay and keep the cabin safe, just in case his heir had magic. After I turned thirteen and showed signs, he and my mother worked together to protect me from Nehanda's spies and teach me to use my magic from books and journals that Naeemah had passed down. Everything seemed to be fine. But one day my mother fell ill. My father took her to town to see a doctor..." The younger woman paused as her energy changed to pure hatred. "Somehow it got out that they were Naeemah's descendants. They were executed, publicly, to make an example for any other council descendants that might be hiding. I only found out because they hadn't returned, and after two weeks I went looking for them."

Now Adanya could feel Sefu's hatred joining Abiba's, though he remained quiet as he stoically continued to watch their surroundings.

"I made sure that the local magistrate who'd ordered their execution would never hurt anyone again. Then I came back to the cabin to wait and watch for you."

Adanya didn't know how to respond. She hadn't thought about the young woman being a killer, but this was war. There were likely to be many more casualties before all was said and done. A ghost remembrance of the pain from losing towns lodged in her chest, and she realized Abiba had only done what needed to be done.

Shaking her head to bring herself back to the present, she asked, "Have either of you heard of any other sorcerer families? I'm sure more must have been born since my time."

They both shook their heads. "We've searched as best we could, but we've not been able to find any," Sefu answered. "Even though we wouldn't be able to train them as they needed, we knew Nehanda would see them as a threat. So either they haven't been born..."

"Or Nehanda has been finding them first," Adanya finished. "She likely has learned how to sense them." She scowled as she thought of all the young sorcerers in training at the palace, hoping Nehanda had not tried experimenting on them in order to gain her new powers.

"Were there any rumors of how she managed to have all the elemental powers?" she asked after a long pause.

"Most said that she'd had them all along and was just hiding them," Sefu said. "Others think she used some ancient magic to steal it from others. Is it possible she wrote about it in her journal?"

Adanya had forgotten about the book. "Possible, though it's unlikely that she would have written about it plainly. We'll have to look when we get back." A memory pulled at the back of her mind, something to do with Ziyad's research, but she couldn't quite place it.

"In the meantime, where are we going?" Sefu looked warily about. "I don't like being out in the open like this. Especially since we know that they're looking for us."

She paused, bringing her thoughts back to the task at hand. "I need a clear view of the sky. I think that I've been subconsciously controlling the weather all of my life. The effects may not have been as strong because I didn't know I was controlling anything, but my attention to it now should help me to focus that energy. I just need a clear space where I can see the sky." Adanya pointed. "There. That hill is a little higher, but we shouldn't be visible from farther away."

Sefu looked anything but pleased, but he followed Adanya and Abiba up the hill.

They stood off to the side as she planted herself at the top, focusing on the thin clouds that were drifting overhead. Now what was it that Adio had said?

Chapter Sixteen

"So, how did it go?"

Adanya scowled at Adio, who was leaning against her doorframe and grinning at her. "I don't know why you are in my business."

"Because I'm your best friend and I care about you," he answered. "Now spill."

The scowl melted away and she grinned widely, lifting her hand to allow him to see the engagement ring. "Pretty well, I think."

His grin matched hers, and he crossed the room to take her hand and examine the ring. "My, my, he did well! It suits you. And it's about time."

"What do you mean, 'about time'?" she asked, snatching her hand back in mock annoyance.

He laughed. "I know how happy and loved that man makes you feel. All of us know, really. We just wondered how long he was going to wait before marrying you."

Her mouth dropped open. "You all have been talking about this?"

"It's your own fault, really. You were so secretive, we had to make up our own assumptions." He helped her put on her outer robes. "All good ones, I assure you."

"How long have you all been talking?"

"Since you started walking differently."

Her mouth dropped open, and she slapped at his shoulder. "Seriously?"

He dodged away from her, laughing. "I'm kidding! Thanks for confirming, though."

"I hate you!"

They walked through the halls together. "You know you love me. You wouldn't keep agreeing to trips with me if you didn't."

"This is an important visit," she protested. "Seeing how you use your magic gives me insight into what the people need."

"Of course." His tone made it clear that he didn't believe her, but he left it alone. "So when is the wedding?"

"We just got engaged last night; we haven't had a chance to plan all of that."

"So are you going to officially introduce him to everyone? Now that you're engaged?"

"I haven't decided."

"Adanya. You can't just walk around here with an engagement ring and not let everyone in on the news."

"Who says I can't?"

Adio poked her. "I can understand keeping your love life and relationship private, but it's not like we don't know. Besides, we want to be able to celebrate you finally finding your true love!"

Despite her reservations, she smiled at the happiness and goodwill radiating from her friend. "I suppose it couldn't hurt. Since you all have been talking about it anyway."

He clapped his hands together. "Perfect. I'll organize a party."

"A party?!"

He grabbed her hand and squeezed, pulling her along. "I'm kidding. Just wanted to see that look of mortification on your face."

"You're absolutely terrible."

"I'll just discreetly ask the council members to the council room, and you can tell everyone. Bring him too, he'll help take the focus off of just you."

Adanya's face darkened momentarily as she thought of the one person who would not likely be happy to learn of her engagement—though recently it didn't seem like she much cared what Adanya did at all.

I can make sure that Nehanda isn't there.

She realized she'd let her guard down enough to share her thoughts with Adio without even trying. *I'm sorry...*

He chuckled. *You don't need to apologize. I understand.*

She smiled gratefully as they exited the palace.

Outside, Rashidi and her detail were waiting for them on horses. He dipped his head respectfully as he saw her. "My lady."

"Captain," she replied, grinning just a little too wide as she mounted her horse.

He winked at her, then turned his horse to lead the way, skirting the main city in favor of a road that led to the southeast.

"I already feel like a third wheel," Adio muttered as he followed on his horse.

"So, these farmers that we're about to see," Adanya said, anxious to change the subject. "What was their request?"

She suspected Adio saw right through her, but he answered anyway. "The land that they are trying to harvest from has turned into swampland over time due to the changing weather patterns. I'm going to dry it out for them so that they can use it."

"And you just … change the weather?"

He laughed. "It's a bit more complicated than that. I forget you haven't really seen my powers at their full strength. If it was just stopping or starting a rainstorm, or clearing fog, or even changing the temperature, it wouldn't take much more than a thought." As if to prove his point, they all instantly felt the heat from the early morning sun dissipate, leaving them in a comfortable temperature. "Changing climate, though? That takes a little more doing. I have to manipulate the air pressure in the area in a way that makes it more stable."

"It is hard?"

"I wouldn't say hard. A bit more complicated, maybe. Requires more focus to direct my magic."

"I hadn't thought of it that way. I know there are times when I have to focus more on controlling my magic. I don't know why I thought it would be different for other kinds."

"It is different, in a way. I've found that I have to pay attention so it doesn't accidentally slip out. Like my mood making it rain or something."

"That actually happens?"

"More times than I'll admit. It can be so easy to just dump a rainstorm on people that you're mad at." He winked at her as she giggled. "As often as you slip up and share your thoughts with me, I'm sure you understand."

"It's only because you're my best friend!"

"I didn't say it was a bad thing. It's good to know what you're thinking sometimes, especially since you tend to get lost in your thoughts and leave the rest of us in the dark."

Adanya felt the mirth from Rashidi, and she glanced over to see him smirking without taking his eyes from the road. *All right, that's enough.*

I didn't say a word, love.

Your face is enough.

His grin widened and he audibly chuckled.

"See!" Adio exclaimed. "He agrees with me! And if anyone would know, it's him."

"I'd like you both to stop ganging up on me," Adanya said, pouting despite her efforts not to.

"It's loving bullying," Adio said. "We're only doing it because we love you."

"I'm sure that we have other things to talk about," she said in annoyance, though she couldn't keep a smile from her face.

Adio laughed but obliged her and changed the subject.

#

An hour later, they arrived at a large stretch of land in the lower kingdom. There were signs of attempts at farming—shovels, carts, and other things—but clearly they all had failed. There were puddles of stagnant water, clouds of midges, and dense fog floating above them. Clumps of grass and ducktails were vaguely visible. The temperature was humid and sticky, making them all uncomfortable.

Adio cracked his knuckles, dismounting from his horse and walking a few steps toward the edge of the swamp. "I'll have to be really careful. I wouldn't want to have to come back and fix this every year."

Adanya watched him closely, fascinated. Focus radiated from him as he faced the swamp, and the familiar buzz in her psyche told her of his magic working. A stiff wind blew around them, scattering the midges and fog and leaving the swampy ground clear to view.

She sensed his focus shift slightly, and the clouds suddenly disappeared, allowing the sun to come out bright and hot. The water on the ground evaporated in clouds of steam, obscuring their view momentarily. Once the ground was reduced to a muddy mess, the clouds returned and the temperature reached a comfortable place.

One more shift in focus, and there was a noticeable change in the overall atmosphere around them. Adanya could sense the animals nearby reacting, beginning to move to climates more conducive to their survival.

Adio cracked his neck. "That should do it."

"What did you do?"

"Changed the air pressure. The way it was before, the pressure in this area made it very humid and rainy, which created the swamp. Now it should be a more regular pressure system so the rain comes more systematically, which should be better for growing crops."

"You've done this before?" she asked as he swung back into the saddle.

"Plenty of times. Climate is one of the most frequent things that affects planting and growing seasons, so I help out when I can. It drains me a bit more than simple things, and I need to rest from using magic for a few hours, but I don't mind it."

Adanya turned her horse to lead the way to the nearby town so they could deliver the news to the farmers. "I had no idea."

He smiled at her. "You haven't really been around other magic for that long. It makes sense that there are things you're still learning."

"I'm lucky you all keep teaching me."

Two women and a man were waiting for them at the town entrance.

"Lady Adanya," one of the women said as they all bowed.

She nodded her head politely. "Sorcerer Adio has adjusted the area so that it should be better suited for farming. If you have any further concerns, please don't hesitate to let us know."

"We are grateful to you both," the woman said. "We were worried there would be many people unable to work because of the land."

Adanya was already smiling, feeling the warmth of their gratitude radiating through her. "Of course, we're always willing to help."

"If you would like to stay, we could prepare a meal for you."

"That's not necessary; you needn't use your resources on us."

She felt mirth coming from Adio and shared her thoughts with him. *I don't need your commentary.*

It just amuses me that you're so introverted you've found diplomatic ways to keep from interacting with strangers any longer than necessary.

Oh, hush.

They all bowed again. "Well, thank you again!"

Adio chuckled as their group turned and rode back toward the palace.

"Why are you laughing at me?" she demanded.

"For as much as you care about the people, you sure don't like spending a lot of time with them."

"Now that's not true. I just ... I get awkward trying to make small talk."

"I know. I've seen how well you've adapted to talking to people since you became Head of Council. A big difference from that shy little thing appointed to the council a few years ago. I'd like to think I had something to do with that."

"Really, now?"

"Of course. Nehanda teaches you magic, and I teach you social skills. You can say thank you at any time."

She scowled at him. "Oh, I suppose."

"Helped you get a man, didn't I?"

Rashidi snorted before he could help himself, and Adanya whipped her head around to glower at him as he tried to contain his laughter. *I do not feel supported.*

He's hilarious. I always forget until outings like this. He's a good friend.

She sighed, turning back to Adio. *He is, but he can also be annoying.* Aloud, she said, "I didn't know you had such stock in me getting a man."

"Of course I did. You need someone you can be intimate with without worrying about all of that propriety Nehanda drilled into you. Someone you can be vulnerable with and trust."

Adanya was surprised. "That was ... very sincere of you."

He shrugged. "I can be serious, sometimes."

She reached over and took his hand, squeezing it. "Thank you, Adio."

He squeezed back. "Don't mention it."

She glanced back at Rashidi again, who winked at her with a smile. Then she rolled her eyes dramatically as Adio added, "But since I have you both here, who said 'I love you' first?"

Chapter Seventeen

A smile tugged at the edge of her lips as she thought of her friend. "He said he manipulated air pressure," she muttered to herself.

She remembered his energy and focus shifts as he worked his magic. After a few moments, she could *feel* the magic changing within her, even more strongly than when she had tapped into her Aqua magic. She had been experiencing Sage magic for so long she barely realized how it felt. Aqua magic felt like water rushing through her. But Clime? This felt like a cool wind blowing through her while simultaneously bringing the sizzle of lighting that made her hair stand on end.

Sefu and Abiba looked around them in awe as a dense fog settled around them seemingly out of nowhere. Within moments, it was so thick they could not even see each other.

Despite the many emotions still swirling within her, Adanya laughed aloud. "You taught me well, my friend."

As before, a vision flashed before her eyes, freezing her in place as her Sage and Clime magic connected. This time she saw Adio himself, outside a treehouse surrounded by fog. He sat with his legs dangling over the edge of the balcony, looking exactly the same as the last day she had seen him. She was startled when he turned his head and seemed to look right at her, surprise in his eyes. "Adanya?"

"Adio? Can you hear me?"

"Like you're standing right next to me."

"Where are you?"

"Nyota Woods. Come here and I'll find you."

Adanya staggered as the vision passed, Sefu only just managing to catch her as he found her in the fog.

"You've had another vision?" he asked.

Adanya's heart was pounding with excitement. She could feel the pull of Adio's energy as she had once been able to do. "I know where Adio is," she said with a bright smile.

"Tell us where," Abiba said as she found them in the fog.

Adanya turned to Sefu. "Nyota Woods, northwest of the palace. Can you lead us there from here?"

He nodded. "I have to insist we travel under cover this time."

"Of course."

He turned and led the way, the two women trailing closely as they moved into the tree cover.

"Adio was your closest friend, right?" Abiba asked.

Adanya was surprised until she remembered that Naeemah had shared stories before she died. "He is. Many of the sorcerers on the council took me under their wing when I was elected, but Adio and I always had something special. He was like the big brother I wish that I had … like Naeemah was the sister." She hesitated, turning to look at the younger woman as she tried to control the sadness rising in her. "Did … did Naeemah say why she decided to pass on instead of staying?"

Abiba nodded. "She and the other sorcerers wanted to prevent Nehanda from using their magic to become more powerful, which is why they all went into hiding. But Naeemah couldn't bear the thought of not using her magic to help people, so she would go out to the different towns in disguise and help when she could. That's how she ended up getting married. She hoped that, if anything happened to her, her family would be around to help you when you awoke. But somehow word got around of her travels, and she was captured by Nehanda's soldiers." She paused, as if the memory was her own. "She knew Nehanda would try and take her magic, so she summoned a flood and drowned herself and the soldiers."

Tears sprang to Adanya's eyes, and she vainly tried to blink them away. The thought of sweet, kind Naeemah sacrificing herself for others was exactly like her, yet imagining her last moments created a new kind of pain inside Adanya's chest.

"I'm sorry," Abiba said quietly. "It can't be easy to hear this."

Adanya cleared her throat. "My days have been full of things that aren't easy to hear," she replied. "I'm sure that won't end any time soon."

Abiba squeezed her hand comfortingly. "I can't even imagine."

Ready to change the subject—and ease her swirling emotions—she asked, "What did she say about Adio?"

"Something about him always knowing how to have fun."

Adanya could not help but smile, remembering his ability to always make her laugh. "That is very true. He loved telling jokes and often tried to get me to loosen up."

"We need to be more quiet going forward," Sefu warned over his shoulder. "The closer we get to the capital, the more dangerous it gets. We've avoided many spies here."

The women heeded his warning, but Adanya's thoughts were filled with memories of her best friend—and her excitement to see him again.

\#

As they traveled, she began to feel rather than see that she'd walked these paths before. Everything still looked different, but the scent of wild honeysuckle made her feel like she was back in her own time, when things still made sense and her world hadn't been turned upside down.

Adanya's heart pounded as they drew nearer to a grove of trees swathed in fog. They were so near, she could feel Adio beside her. A moment later, the fog parted and the man himself approached. His cheeks were just as rosy as the day she'd last seen him, and his usual bright smile seemed ten times bigger as he opened his arms to her.

"Come here, little girl."

Adanya forgot all pretense of dignity and ran into his arms, tears streaming down her face as she took comfort in his familiar embrace.

"I knew that I'd see you again some day," he laughed, squeezing her tightly. "Someone had to be around when you woke up. I know how hard it is for you to make new friends."

"You've no idea how happy I am to see you."

"Oh, I might have a bit of an idea." He wiped a tear from his own eye as he pulled away from her. "I'm guessing these two are part of the welcoming party?"

Adanya turned back to her companions, trying to regain her calm. "These are the descendants of Rashidi and Naeemah, Sefu and Abiba."

They bowed to him.

Adio was suddenly solemn, something Adanya had rarely seen. "Nothing like seeing the future in front of you," he said quietly. He took Adanya's hand and squeezed it, and they were silent for a moment. Then he cleared his throat. "Well, I'm sure there's lots of work to be done and lots of things to catch me up on. Come on up to the treehouse, and we'll talk." He turned, and the fog cleared enough for them to see a rope ladder leading up onto a wooden platform nestled in the massive fork of the tree before them.

He led the way, climbing up effortlessly. Adanya and Abiba followed, Adanya carefully maneuvering her staff to climb, and Sefu followed once he was sure they were not in danger of being attacked once their backs were turned.

They climbed onto the platform, looking about them in awe as Adio helped them up. Though the fog continued for miles around, the quaint treehouse was surrounded by clear blue sky.

The house looked like any other on land: single storied, a few windows, a front door, and a sloping roof.

"You built this all by yourself?" Adanya asked in wonder as he led them to the door. "I didn't know you had that skill."

"I didn't, at first," he replied. "I was living in an underground cavern for a while while I decided what to do. But you know me, I need the fresh air and the sky to survive. So I disguised myself and apprenticed with a woodsman for a time to learn, then came back and built everything. It's held up for a few generations, so I'd like to think that I did a decent job."

He opened the door and ushered them inside.

It was a simple one-room house. The left wall held the kitchen, with a few cupboards, hooks for drying meat and vegetables, and basins for washing food and dishes. The right wall was the bedroom, with a comfortable bed and dresser with a mirror. The back wall was the dining room, with a single small chair and table.

"I didn't quite plan for visitors," he chuckled. "You're welcome to sit wherever you like."

"Do you spend all of your time up here?" Adanya asked.

"I venture out now and then. Some of the other kingdoms still have decent trade, so I'll go down to replenish my stocks. Didn't want to draw too much attention to myself in case Nehanda decided to start looking for me, though, so I foraged for what I needed, mostly. I get fresh water for washing from the rain whenever I need it, and there's a stream nearby for bathing. Not a terrible existence, really."

"It still had to be difficult for you. I know how much you love being around people."

He shrugged, though Adanya could sense a little sadness. "Necessary sacrifice. Once I knew of Nehanda's betrayal, I knew it was important that someone from our time was alive and well to help you with whatever came next. But how were you able to sense me so strongly?"

"It would appear Nehanda hid the fact that I'm a Sage Elemental," Adanya said, unable to keep a trace of bitterness from her voice. "Sefu found me at Rashidi's grave, and he helped me get to the castle and discovered her journal that held some ... discoveries. Then I was able to find Abiba, Naeemah's great-great-granddaughter."

"You definitely favor her," Adio smiled at the young woman. "But Sefu ... I could swear that I was looking at Rashidi when I look at you."

"My grandparents used to tell me that," Sefu said with a nod from where he stood beside Abiba in the chair. "I am honored that I can assist both of you."

Adio looked back at Adanya, sitting beside him on the bed. "But I get the feeling you have more to tell me?"

She sighed heavily, deciding that now was as good a time as any to tell the others. "King Keon was my father."

Everyone's eyes widened, and Adio asked, "How do you know?"

"Nehanda discovered it after she found me. That's why my magic abilities are so strong, and why she tried to keep the truth of them from me. I don't know if she has also been able to harness those powers, or if she's using other found magical children and controlling them."

"From what I've seen, she has been using the powers for herself. But there's something strange about them. I don't think she has them naturally; the way she uses them is strange. I don't know how she's been able to do it, though."

"I'm sure that she found some dark way to do it."

"We'll have to find out. In the meantime, where do things stand now?"

Sefu took up the story, explaining the resistance and their current plan to liberate the cities. As he spoke, Adanya could sense the hope that always rested beneath the surface when he was around her starting to climb after the revelation she was the heir to the throne. Though becoming queen was absolutely the last thing that she wanted, she only hoped they lived long enough for there to be a throne to inherit.

Adio stroked his chin. "It's a good plan. I think that with the three of us magical folk combined, we should be able to get started on the liberating as soon as we know our target." He glanced out of the window, noting the sun's position. "If we travel at dusk, I won't have to use my powers to hide us. It would be wise to keep Nehanda blind to our doings as long as possible."

Then he took Adanya by the hand and led her back to the door. "If you two would excuse us, I'd like to catch up with my friend alone."

Leaving them inside, the pair sat on the edge of the platform side by side, looking out over the fog as their feet dangled over the edge. They were silent for a while, drinking in each other's company. Adio tilted his head, and the fog thickened around them.

Understanding immediately, Adanya smiled. The fog dissipated almost instantly.

"Doesn't look like you'll need any training," he chuckled. Then he turned to look at her. "How are you doing?"

"It's an adjustment, but I'm alright." She didn't turn to look at him.

He raised an eyebrow. "You know good and well what I meant. I see how strongly that boy resembles Rashidi. That has to hurt, knowing he should be your great-great-grandson as well as Rashidi's."

Adanya's face tightened as she struggled to hold back the tears that suddenly sprang to her eyes. "It makes sense that he would have moved on. There was no way for him to find me, no reason he should have waited to create a family."

"But...?"

"But ... there's a part of me that is so angry with him. We'd planned on living life together, loving one another until we died.

But I was gone, and he married someone else. Had children with someone else. Loved someone else. All of that, he was supposed to have with me. I know that it's irrational, but I almost wonder if he ever loved me at all if he could so easily move on."

Adio was silent for a moment as he considered his answer. "Do you remember when my younger sister lost her husband in an Ugwe attack?"

Adanya could remember the pain his sister had experienced, and how similar it felt to her own. "Yes. She was devastated."

"But a few years later, she remarried."

"I remember. I couldn't understand how someone could just ... start over after having lost the love of their life."

"She always loved her first husband; never forgot him, never stopped holding a place for him in her heart. But life goes on, no matter how much we want to live in the past and hold on to the one we lost. My sister found new happiness because she was willing to move forward." He took her hand. "I know your situation is much different, but the same idea rings true. For all intents and purposes, you were dead, lost to Rashidi forever. It only made sense that he married and started a family of his own. For my part, I'd like to think he knew, somehow, that his descendant would be able to help you when you awoke. Like Naeemah did, in a sense. Doesn't make it better, I know. But something to think about."

She didn't look at him, but she squeezed his hand as she allowed a tear to escape her eyes. "I'm glad that you decided to stay for me," she said quietly.

"Wouldn't have done anything else, little girl."

They returned inside after sitting in silence awhile. Adio served them all a simple meal of rolled oats and honey with fresh rainwater. Then, as dusk fell, they climbed down to earth and began making their way back to the cabin.

Adanya stayed close to Adio as they walked. Despite finding herself in this strange new world, it was comforting to have someone from her time that was familiar and close, the big brother she'd wished to have when she was younger.

Chapter Eighteen

Adanya lay in the fork of a great tree, one leg dangling listlessly while she stared up into the leafy canopy, disassociating. It had been another difficult day of training—that happened more often than not—and she just wanted to escape from all that was being demanded of her for a little while. She didn't notice the sky darkening as huge gray storm clouds drifted in from the west, promising a heavy rain. She was only roused when a fat raindrop splashed onto her forehead, startling her so badly she fell from the tree with a yell of surprise.

She scowled as she pulled herself to her feet, dusting off her robes and shaking stray leaves from her braids as raindrops fell around her.

"As if this day couldn't get any worse," she muttered.

Just as suddenly as the rain had started, however, it stopped. She looked around in surprise, finding a light-skinned man grinning at her.

"I hate when that happens," he said, his light sandy-brown eyes twinkling. "Already having a bad day, and then it decides to rain."

She was puzzled. She could sense magic flowing through him, different from her own. "Did … did you stop it?"

"Seemed the polite thing to do." He made an elegant bow, causing Adanya to giggle. "Adio, at your service. Resident Clime."

Her eyes widened. "You're on the Council of Sorcerers!"

He laughed. "Doesn't actually make me that special." He came closer. "You, on the other hand … I've been hearing a lot of good things about you."

"Me?"

"It's been a long time since we've had another Sage training here. Before my time, I'm sure. Sages are pretty rare, and myself and the rest of the council have been watching you with interest. From what I hear, you're pretty powerful."

She blushed, ducking her head so her braids covered her face. "I wouldn't say all that. Besides, from how my training is going, I don't get the impression that I'm doing so well."

"Nehanda's always been a hard-ass."

Adanya's eyes widened, having rarely heard such language uttered around her—and certainly not about an authority figure in her life.

Adio grinned. "Ah, so that's what it takes to get your head back up where it belongs? Noted. But Nehanda's like that with everyone. She can think you're the most gifted sorcerer to ever live, but she won't let you know it. Doesn't know how to give people their flowers. But she's shared with the council how impressive you are. There's a good chance you'll end up on it with me, one day."

"But there's already a Sage on the council, and he's the Head."

"No rule that says there can't be two. Ziyad always says having someone with the same abilities around can help you to sharpen your craft. I'm sure he wouldn't mind at all, especially since you are so rare." He came over and leaned his back against the tree trunk. "Don't let Nehanda get to you. Just keep at it, and I'm sure you'll make it far. Hey, stop that!" he added as she ducked her head again. "Here, I'll teach you a lesson that Nehanda probably hasn't even thought of."

He lifted her head so she was looking at him. "You were given a lot of power when you were born. I can tell that you're the shy, quiet type, but we don't really get that luxury as sorcerers. You've got to learn to navigate this world with confidence, even if what you want to do most is hide away. I'm not saying you need to just change your personality, but you do have to learn how to get through the things that make you uncomfortable. There's a whole world out there that will pull for your attention; it's up to you to figure out what will help you stay grounded and focused. Having other sorcerers around you helps, believe me. They can understand what you're going through. But the first thing that you have to do is learn to have some confidence in yourself. Keep that head up."

Adanya smiled at the motivational speech and the good will radiating from him. "You're right, Nehanda never went over that with me."

They shared a laugh.

"Have you seen the council chambers yet?" he asked.

"No. Nehanda said that I'm not allowed unless I've been summoned."

"Summoned? Sometimes I wonder how she was chosen to be an instructor," Adio said with a shake of his head. "Come on, I'll show you."

He took her hand before she could protest. They went through the main gate of the palace and inside, up the stairs to the sorcerers' wing. Adanya grew more and more nervous as they approached the door to the council chambers, feeling as if she were doing something terribly wrong.

Adio squeezed her hand. "You won't get in trouble; I brought you." Without waiting for her to answer, he pushed open the door and led her inside.

Her eyes widened in awe as she looked around the room.

Though it was not heavily decorated—in truth, it was rather plain—Adanya was struck with a feeling of awe and reverence as she looked around. Around the walls were shelves full of books, scrolls, and maps. A few side tables for serving food and drink were underneath the windows. But what took up most of the space in the room was a long oak table surrounded by high-backed chairs. At the far end, away from the door, sat an elaborate chair with worn red cushions differentiating it from the others. That must be where Ziyad sat, she thought.

Adio watched her with a smile, and then walked over to one of the bookcases. "These shelves hold many things. A complete history of our kings, from the first one until Keon. The writings of former Heads of Council. Crop production, animal husbandry, land ownership ... any and every thing of importance is recorded here."

"But why here?" she asked. "Surely there are recorders, a place for these histories elsewhere in the palace."

"Everything that has happened in our kingdom, magic has had some hand in it, whether directly or indirectly," he explained. "We keep these records here to monitor magical involvement and to determine if we are doing too much. Any of the royal recorders are welcome to examine these documents, except for when we are in council."

"I didn't realize how much magical involvement there was," she said.

"That means we're doing our job." He walked over to a seat in the middle of the table and sat down. "Just think, one day you'll be a more formal part of it. I know, you don't believe me," he interrupted as she opened her mouth to protest. "I need you to have a little more confidence in yourself, little girl."

"I wish that you wouldn't call me that," she said, miffed. "I may not be a full sorcerer, but I'm anything but a child."

The mischievous twinkle returned to his eye. "I don't know. Seems like you might need that little push."

"I don't know what you're talking about."

"He does have a tendency to tease." A new voice said.

They both looked toward the door to see Ziyad had entered, so quietly that neither of them noticed. Adio rose and bowed his head respectfully, while Adanya dropped her head again. He smiled at them and walked over to his seat, resting his staff on the back of the chair before sitting.

"What are we discussing?" he asked.

"I'm trying to convince the young one of her potential," Adio replied, sitting back down.

"I shouldn't think that she'd need convincing." He shifted to look at her. "Even without the full use of your powers, I can tell you will be a part of greatness, one day."

"I'm a orphan from the woods, sir," Adanya replied, her head still bowed. "I don't think that anyone should expect so much from me."

"They won't if you don't expect it of yourself."

She looked up, confused. "Sir?"

He beckoned her over. "Come here, child. Adio, can you give me the map?"

They both did as they were asked, Adio spreading the map out on the table before Ziyad while Adanya came to stand on the other side of him.

Ziyad tapped a portion of the map near the western border. "Do you know what this is?"

She peered at it. "I'm afraid that I don't, sir. I haven't had much chance to study maps."

"It isn't anywhere, really. A small town with less than fifty people living there. But they have proven themselves invaluable to the kingdom. You see, this town is surrounded by some of the richest, most fertile soil in the world. Most of the food that we use in the capital and at the palace comes from this town. And it was acquired completely by accident. The people who have now lived there for generations kept mostly to themselves; it almost became part of the territory of the western kingdom, but they did not realize the importance of the town, so it fell to us. Nothing much was expected of the land until the leader of the town presented himself to the king and proved how important their town was to the kingdom. He knew what the land was worth, and he wanted to make sure that his people were given what they deserved for it. If he hadn't, we never might have known."

He looked up at Adanya. "I'm sure that you're wondering why I'm telling you this story."

"I imagine it's to remind me to be confident in myself and hold myself at my true worth?"

"Precisely." He patted her hand good-naturedly. "If I may be so bold, I think Adio would be a wonderful person to learn that from. He almost wasn't a part of the council, but his confidence in his abilities and what he could bring to the council won out."

"Of course they did!" Adio said indignantly. "My experience is what set me apart from other Climes."

Ziyad chuckled. "You see?" *I think it's time that you start experiencing the world with other sorcerers.*

She blinked as she heard his voice in her head. *But Nehanda is the one training me.*

There's a reason that people are educated by more than one person. Everyone brings their own experiences and views on how they use their magic. It can help us to understand our own better. You're more powerful than I think any of us realize, and I want you to get as much experience as you can. Adio is a good place to start.

Before she could answer, Adio made an excited noise.

"I've got an idea." He tapped the map. "You said that you haven't studied maps much. I'm guessing you haven't been around the country, either?"

She shook her head. "I've only visited the capital city with Their Majesties a few times."

"Well, I think we need to change that. With your permission, Ziyad, I'd like to take her on a tour. It would be good for her to get out into the country and learn more about the kingdom."

Ziyad smiled and nodded. "I do think it's a good idea. I'll inform Nehanda where you are. Go and grab a few things."

Adanya could not help but smile, and she lifted her head. Her outings with the king and queen had been exciting; how much more would traveling the country be?

Chapter Nineteen

After they returned to the hideaway and made introductions, Waed shared news.

"Nehanda just left the Western Kingdom, Ferandar," he said, pointing to the map around which they all stood. "We've been building up our forces near the capital since we got the news, but we need a solid plan as to how we'll take the palace."

"The moment that we use magic, Nehanda's going to know what's up," Adio warned.

"I don't think we have any other options," Adanya said. "Without us, they're outnumbered."

"They don't use magic to defend themselves," Sefu said. "They certainly wouldn't know what hit them."

She shook her head. "The longer that we can keep Nehanda from finding out that we're gathering sorcerers, the better."

"What if you blocked her?" Adio asked Adanya. "You can keep people from sensing others, can't you?"

"I've never done it on a scale like this," she replied. "One or two people, sure, but a whole army?"

"It wouldn't have to be a whole army. Just me."

She tilted her head. "What are you thinking?"

"Ferandar's capital city sits on a high plateau, remember? If a hard enough storm hits—one that would make it impossible for the guards to be outside, for example—then our people can get in and take over the palace. If you were able to hide me long enough, I could make it look like a naturally occurring storm and she wouldn't know I had anything to do with it."

"It's risky. Her Sage magic has probably made her aware that I've woken up, so she's got to be on high alert. Though I don't think she's been able to pinpoint where I am."

"But if we don't help, then the resistance won't be able to make any progress," Abiba pointed out.

They fell silent, looking to Adanya for her decision. Her eyebrows were lowered as she thought, her eyes studying the map.

There was considerable risk with this plan. Sefu's fighters may not have the numbers to overtake the palace. Nehanda could find them before they got close, or she could arrive in the middle of their assault. There was even a chance that Nehanda did leave some kind of magic defense behind. Adanya was uneasy about revealing the reunification of the council before they were at their full strength. And yet this was not an opportunity they could waste. The three sorcerers together—especially Adanya, as she uncovered her other skills—were likely the push the resistance needed to start liberating the other kingdoms. In this case, it seemed waiting wasn't an option.

"Alright," she said finally, "we'll do it. But we need to have everything planned to the letter. Waed, I need troop numbers and locations. Adio, have you ever been inside that palace?"

He shook his head. "But I know where the palace is and can change the weather over us before sending it there. It would be less obvious if the storm rolls in from elsewhere. I'd have to get started a few hours before the attack was to take place."

"One of our men managed to get in and out a few months ago," Sefu said, rummaging around the papers on the table until he found a letter and a hand-drawn map. "He was able to give us an idea of where things are in there—the throne room, bedrooms, and so on. This can be the guide for when we get inside."

"Will the outer wall be difficult to navigate?" she asked.

"There are water troughs and a postern gate on the back of the palace wall. They haven't been attended to, likely because no one can ever get close enough to them. Besides, there are so many guards in the courtyard and on the walls that approaching hasn't really been an option."

"I don't like the idea of leaving that to chance," Adanya frowned. "We need to know there is a surefire way for the resistance can get inside."

"Wait, I do remember that there was something peculiar about the palace architecture..." Adio screwed up his face as he thought.

Adanya could not help but briefly smile at the familiar sight; it always made him look like a child.

"Tunnels!" he suddenly exclaimed. "Because the palace was built on a plateau, the builders ensured the royal family would be able to escape through a hidden exit if the palace was assaulted from the front. So they built a tunnel system that would lead them safely out."

"Wait," Abiba said, "if there are tunnels, we might not need to send the fighters in at all!"

"Why not?" Sefu asked.

"If we can find the other end of the tunnels, then we can flood them out!"

"But they'll be sloped away from the palace," Waed said. "There's no way we'd be able to get the water to actually go into the palace."

"Wait a minute; she has a point," Adio said. "She is an Aqua, after all. If my storm can send enough water into the surrounding area, then she can make the water go up the tunnels and into the palace. With enough force, she could even take the foundations down and take the whole palace down, too."

"But then that's two of you whose powers I'd have to conceal." Adanya frowned again. "And we have no idea where the entrances to the tunnels are. That would take up valuable time we just don't have."

"It's not like trying to open the gate doors or grates would be any faster," Adio said. "The flooding would be a safer option, as well; the resistance fighters wouldn't have to enter the palace until most of the soldiers inside were dead or trying to escape the water."

"We already have to send messengers to tell our units there to prepare for the assault," Waed said. "We could send word ahead of us that they need to find the tunnel openings. Then, by the time that we arrive, they likely will have found them."

"We're leaving a lot up to chance," Adanya said.

"Can't control everything, little ... Adanya." Adio caught himself before using her nickname, clearly wanting to give her respect.

She hesitated, then nodded. "Alright. Waed, send word to the units that they need to find the tunnel openings, then be prepared to assault the palace when we arrive."

"Tell them to look for groves that are within a few miles of the palace," Adio added. "It would be a likely place to hide them."

Waed bowed. "At once."

"The messenger will leave within the hour," Sefu said as Waed went to the living quarters to find someone to serve as a messenger. "We should rest for a couple of hours. We can leave when the night is darkest; if we travel light, we should arrive in two days. I'll see to gathering provisions. There are a few empty rooms in the back where you can rest." He also bowed and went to make preparations.

"I could use a good nap," Abiba said. She smiled at them both, then disappeared into the back hallway.

"When's the last time that you slept?" Adio asked.

Adanya shrugged, sitting down in front of the fireplace and resting her staff beside her. "I'm not entirely sure."

"I need you to do better than that, little girl." He came over and put a hand on her shoulder. "You still have to take care of yourself."

"There isn't time for all that," she replied, staring into the flames instead of looking at him. "I have to wrap my brain around how to keep you two hidden, think about our future plans for finding the rest of the council or their descendants, consider how best to go after Nehanda, prepare for the trip..."

"Adanya," he interrupted softly. "I know you. You preoccupy yourself when you're worried to avoid thinking about things. What's wrong?"

She was silent for a moment. "What isn't?" she whispered. "I feel so under-equipped for all of this. The closest that I ever got to planning and being involved in battle was against the Ugwe. The stakes are so much higher now. I'm ... scared. All of these people's lives will be in my hands, and the last time that happened, they were all slaughtered. What if I fail?"

"Hey, now." He crouched down in front of her so he could look up into her face. "You didn't fail. You were deceived, same as all of us. You can't blame yourself for what happened to the people. And I have faith in you. Look at what you've done in only a few days since waking up! You've started discovering your own powers, you've found Abiba and me, and now we're about to start liberating the world from Nehanda's rule. That's more than some people could boast for a lifetime."

She sighed heavily but didn't answer.

"What else is bothering you?"

There were tears brimming in her eyes, and she struggled to control the sadness welling up inside of her. "Whenever I close my eyes, I have so many memories from before all of this happened. Most of them are with Rashidi. It feels so good to have him near me again. But when I wake up, it's like I'm losing him all over again. And ... it hurts. So much."

Adio immediately took her in his arms as her voice broke, letting her cry into his chest as he stroked her hair. "You have every right to feel that way. My poor little girl. You're carrying the weight of the world on your shoulders. But I want you to remember something." He gently wiped the tears from her cheeks, lifting her head up to look at him as he had done when they'd first met. "You don't have to carry all of this alone. Those two in the back have proven they'll do all they can to support you, and you already know that I'm here for you. I can't take all of the pain away, but I can certainly take things off your mind to make things easier. But the first thing that I need you to do is sleep. Just for a few hours."

Adanya wanted to argue, but she knew that he was right. "Alright," she said finally. "Thank you, Adio."

He kissed her forehead before shooing her gently toward the back hallway. "Go on now, you hard-headed thing."

Once again in her underrobes, she got under the thin blanket and fell asleep almost instantly.

Chapter Twenty

Adanya scowled as she studied the maps and papers spread out on the table of the council room, heedless of the glorious summer day just outside of the windows. She was still dressed in the black of mourning, even though it had been nearly a month since the death of Ziyad and her election to Head of Council. The Ugwe had finally been driven from the kingdom, leaving Adanya to settle into the day-to-day operations of running the council. But now more than ever, as she sat in the chair that was once Ziyad's, she felt wholly unprepared for the position.

Just as she let out a frustrated groan, Rashidi appeared in the doorway, rapping his knuckles on the open door to announce his presence.

"Everything alright in here, my lady?"

She looked up, surprised to see him inside of the palace. Belatedly she realized he had been in her thoughts, and she might have accidentally telepathically called for him in her frustration.

"I'm sorry," she stuttered. "When I'm not focusing on my magic, sometimes there are latent effects on the people I know."

"No need to apologize, my lady," he answered, flashing her a warm smile that somehow made her calmer. "I was actually coming to find you anyway."

"Coming to find me?"

"I wanted to get your feedback on your protection detail. I know that we weren't able to prevent your injury"—he gestured to her shoulder, which still throbbed occasionally when she moved it—"but hopefully we've done well otherwise."

Adanya could sense something behind his request, but she couldn't suss it out. "My shoulder gets better as time goes on; you and the guard kept much worse from happening to me. I know that the king is grateful for your hard work and dedication. He was..." She paused, remembering the feelings of regret from the king over Ziyad's death. "He was worried about me."

"He has every right to be, my lady. Ugwe are no easy thing to overcome. But you faced them without much fear, so I think that you'll be alright."

She smiled and gestured for him to join her at the table. "I do wish to learn more about you, since it seems that we'll be spending more time together." She surprised herself with this request; talking to people she didn't know was still a struggle for her, but she was finding it easy to talk to him.

"What do you want to know, my lady?"

"How long have you been a captain?"

"About four years now, I believe. It tends to start running together after a while."

"Have you always been on guard detail?"

"Occasionally, but it wasn't too frequent. I was mostly in charge of patrolling the trade routes, dealing with roaming bands of thieves, things of that nature."

"That sounds dangerous."

"It could be. It taught me a lot, though. I will admit, I've found this assignment to be the most fulfilling." There was that sense of something she couldn't put her finger on again.

She couldn't help but snort. "Watching me bumble around and try to look important? Why would that be fulfilling?"

He chuckled. "You shouldn't be so hard on yourself, my lady. You're doing an amazing job for someone so young, and everyone can tell you're throwing yourself into the role."

"I ... thank you, Captain." She didn't know why she didn't truly believe his words, especially considering the earnestness behind them.

He smiled, then looked over the maps and things she had scattered across the table. "What are you working on? Perhaps I can offer some assistance."

She sighed again, her frustration returning. "I'm trying to understand all of these reports. Part of my job as Head of Council, now that the Ugwe have been dealt with, is to oversee things like the finding and training of new sorcerers and delegating tasks to the other council members. I also have daily councils with the king, though that part is easy."

"The king is a very easy man to get along with, from what I've seen." Rashidi nodded in agreement. "But I'm assuming that these other tasks are a bit overwhelming for you?"

"I've never been in charge of anything before, Captain. I never wanted to be. I didn't get any kind of training on how to be a leader, and now it's all been thrown on me. It's like someone threw me in the ocean and told me to swim."

"Well, I wouldn't quite say that."

She gave him a look. "What do you mean?"

He smiled. "I mean that you weren't thrown in without help. The king clearly supports you, and your fellow council members all want you to succeed. They wouldn't have elected you if they didn't think that you could do this."

"Or they elected me because I'm the only Sage."

"I've seen how the others treat you. They truly value you and want you to succeed. No one expects you to do this completely on your own."

"But I'm the Head of Council, I'm supposed to know what I'm doing on my own!"

Rashidi paused, looking as if he were trying to decide how to phrase his next thought. "May I ask you something?"

"Of course."

"Please don't take this disrespectfully, I don't mean it that way, but why is it so hard for you to ask for help?"

"I beg your pardon?" She frowned. "What does that even mean?"

"It means that you have plenty of people around you who are ready and willing to support you. But I get the sense that you never ask. I'm wondering why that is?"

For a moment, she was affronted. How dare he ask her something like that, so personal and ... and actually a good question. But she could sense the characteristic good will that always seemed to radiate from him and knew he was genuinely trying to be helpful.

She was silent as she tried to find an answer. "I spent most of my childhood alone in the woods. I had to make do on my own. There wasn't anyone to ask for help. I just ... I'm used to having to figure things out on my own. And I don't want people thinking that I can't do this job now that I have it."

He nodded at her explanation. "I understand that you want to do your best. But my lady, sometimes part of doing your best is knowing when to ask for help. When I was first promoted to captain, I learned that the only way to fully complete the missions I was given was to ask questions. No one thinks the worse of you for it; in fact, you gain their respect because they know that you know when you need their support instead of trying to do it on your own and messing things up."

"I suppose you're right," she said slowly, absorbing his words.

He looked over the mess of papers on the table again, then turned back to her with a twinkle in his eye. "You know, I have a lot of practice with organizing papers and things."

She stared at him, sensing there was something behind his words but trying to avoid just jumping into his mind.

When she didn't answer, he said, "I'd be happy to help, if you ask me."

"Oh. I..." Despite her mind's immediate agreement, she found herself struggling to form the words.

"My lady." Now he spoke in a firm but gentle tone that made something low in her belly start fluttering. "Ask me for help."

She shouldn't have asked, she should have been upset or annoyed that he had told her to do something, but she wasn't. Instead, she was ... intrigued.

"Can you help me to get all of these reports and maps organized?"

He smiled. "Of course, my lady." He began shuffling through the papers. "If I may be so bold," he added as he continued, "I was hoping I would be able to spend more time with you, outside of leading your protection detail."

She blinked, confused. "Spend time with me? Doing what?"

He shrugged. "Whatever you'd like. Sitting and talking, taking a meal, walking through the gardens."

"Whatever for?"

He paused, looking up at her with a bemused smile. "No one has ever asked you something like this, I gather?"

She shook her head.

"Well. A man normally asks a woman to spend time with him to get to know her better because he is interested in pursuing her," he explained patiently.

"Pursuing? You mean like ... starting a romantic relationship?" She tried to ignore the jump of excitement from her heart as she spoke the words.

"You say it like it is so taboo," he chuckled.

"I ... it's not been something that I've worried much about."

"I can tell. If you're uncomfortable with the idea, you can say no. I won't be offended."

"I'm not, I just … I'm not sure how to react to the idea."

"You could say yes. If we spend some time together and you're still uncomfortable, that would be the end of it."

She could sense his hopefulness, and also the underlying fear she would say no. As she thought about it, however, she realized she'd already decided in her heart that she did want to spend more time with this man and the captivating energy she sensed in him. She just hadn't said it aloud. "I would like that."

The widest smile she'd ever seen on his face appeared, and she could almost physically feel his excitement. "I look forward to it, my lady. Now, shall I explain how I've organized these?"

Chapter Twenty-One

Adanya looked up as she finished dressing in Sefu's room, sensing Adio approaching. He pushed the door open with a smirk.

"I'd be lying if I said I didn't miss you in my head," he said. He looked at the barely disturbed bed. "Get any sleep?"

"A little. I wouldn't exactly call it restful, though."

"Well, no one promised that. You ready to go?"

"As ready as I can be, I suppose. Though I still can't fathom how I'm going to manage hiding the both of you at the same time."

"You won't need to, remember? I'm about to conjure up a storm to send ahead of us. It will reach the palace before us, then I'll just be there for backup and you can focus on hiding Abiba."

She blew out a sigh. "Yes, of course. I knew that."

He came over and squeezed her hand. "I know you're nervous. But you've got us around; everything doesn't fall on you."

She swallowed the lump that caught in her throat, remembering Rashidi telling her the same thing. "I know."

He squeezed her hand again, then reached over to pick up her staff and hand it to her. "Well then, Head of Council. Shall we?"

Abiba and Sefu were waiting for them outside, already mounted on their horses. Waed was holding the reins of two other horses.

"I'll stay behind to continue monitoring communication," he explained as he helped Adanya onto her horse.

She nodded, then looked over at Adio. "Well, my friend, time for some stormy weather."

He grinned again. "How many days' journey to Ferandar?"

"Two, if we ride hard," Sefu replied.

Adio nodded, then settled his unfocused eyes ahead as he used his magic. Adanya focused all of her power on shielding Adio's magic from anyone who might be searching for it. Her own magic flowed through her, connecting with his and making them both stronger. As he worked, gray storm clouds rolled in from the west, obscuring the stars and moon and plunging them into almost complete darkness. All that anyone could see of each other were dark silhouettes until Adio sent the clouds scudding away into the distance.

"Should get there before we do," he said, climbing on his horse. "I've left enough cloud cover to help us travel without drawing attention. Assuming you know the way, Sefu?"

"I've traveled this road many times," Sefu replied with a nod. "Let's go."

They all kicked their horses into a gallop, following Sefu as they began their journey down the road.

The night was brisk, the wind speeding past them as they traveled and making them grateful for the cloaks in which they wrapped themselves.

It will take much more effort to shield Abiba. Adanya shared her thoughts with Adio rather than shouting across to each other as they rode. *Her task is a lot longer than yours.*

I wouldn't say a lot more, he replied.

I almost feel like we're putting too high expectations on her. She's lived by that river all of her life,; she's never needed to use her powers with such force before. What if she can't handle it?

Then you'll help her, he replied simply. *But I don't think that will be the case. She's seen and heard about generations of her family being destroyed by Nehanda. That's got to drive her almost as much as Nehanda's betrayal drives you.*

This is a big step, Adio. What if we're moving too soon?

We've got to seize the opportunities where we can. I know that you've never been involved in a war, Adanya, but this is how things go. We strategize, we make plans, and when we see an opening, we take it.

My second-guessing everything certainly isn't making me seem like a very confident leader.

It makes you a competent leader. You're trying to find every possible thing that could go wrong and plan for it; while doing that in your day-to-day life is a little obsessive, in situations like this it can be the difference between winning a battle and losing it.

Adanya hesitated before sharing her next thought. *If Nehanda shows up ... I'm not ready.*

I didn't expect you to be. There's a lot of unpacking you still have to do about her, and you haven't exactly had the time to do it. You've also learned a lot about yourself that you didn't know, and are still learning. The fact that you're still making plans and pressing ahead is amazing. Don't get so into your head that you start doubting yourself.

Sometimes I think that you know me too well. She glanced over to see him shrug.

What are friends for?

She went back into her own mind, considering next moves and possible scenarios as they rode.

Occasionally, she used to listen to Rashidi explain battle plans from old campaigns—different tactics, soldier placements, and why certain plans worked or didn't depending on the terrain, numbers, and a host of other factors. She never quite understood all that he was talking about, having no experience in battle, but she loved just listening to him talk and watching his face light up as he shared his area of expertise. She remembered smiling at him as he talked, nodding occasionally to show she was following his explanation.

She realized some of his words must have sank in, even though she hadn't realized it at the time. Troop numbers and placement weren't really her focus, but she did have an idea how they all worked, enough that she would be able to follow along when discussing such things with Sefu.

In the silvery glow of the moonlight, she could see Sefu leaned slightly over the neck of his horse as he rode, leading the group down the road. She couldn't imagine living a life like he had, constantly on alert and learning to fight and lead from a young age. A pang of guilt went through her as she realized he and Abiba were both victims of her lack of awareness. If she had paid more attention to the signs, asked more questions, been able to step out of her comfort zone ... maybe none of this would have happened.

But, she realized, what ifs won't get you anywhere.

Just as Sefu had been thrown into leadership without much choice in the matter, so had she when she was elected to the council. If he could take control of his situation, why couldn't she?

A roar shattered the calm of the night. Everyone pulled their horses up short, looking for the source. Adanya knew instinctively what it was, and she paled as she gasped, "Ugwe!"

Sefu and Adio drew their swords, directing their horses to face the direction they guessed the Ugwe was coming from. The earth shook as the creature thundered toward them, and Adanya and Abiba struggled to control their panicked horses.

Adanya's mind was racing, trying to think of how she could best help. She was frightened about getting into its mind in her state, especially since there were other people's lives to consider. Her eyes searched her surroundings until she caught the telltale glimmer of a small creek running through the woods.

Abiba! We can drown it!

What?

Concentrate the water around its nose and mouth, in a bubble.

Using our magic? But Nehanda...

I'll shield us. She didn't know how or why, but Adanya had sudden confidence that she could.

Abiba's eyes were wide with fear, but she nodded her understanding.

Keep it as near the woods' edge as possible! Adanya told Sefu and Adio.

They both gave short nods without question, and she sensed their immediate trust in her.

She wasn't sure if she trusted herself at the moment, but there wasn't time to second-guess.

The Ugwe burst from the trees, knocking over old trunks and branches and scrabbling with its massive claws to change its direction to face them. If they looked fearsome by daylight, they were absolutely nightmarish at night, with the scattered moonlight illuminating every wicked muscle on its lithe form as beady eyes glinted in the semi-darkness.

The men charged, riding around the beast to get its attention. Adanya found herself radiating calm to the others before she fully realized she was doing it, instead focusing on the water and sharing Abiba's magic while simultaneously shielding their magic to keep from being discovered. She was keenly aware that, while Sefu was a seasoned warrior, Adio only knew enough to defend himself in an emergency; indeed, she'd never even seen him wield a sword, which made the current situation even more worrisome.

Between Abiba and Adanya's efforts, a bubble of water formed, drawing from the creek to feed it. They both worked to control the water, Adanya holding the bubble and Abiba pulling in the water. They hadn't even discussed it, but Adanya could feel the Aqua magic flowing through both of them and connecting them in a way she had never experienced before. They could hear the men shouting and the horse's hooves dancing around the Ugwe, trying to dodge its flogging tail.

"Adanya!" Adio's cry came. "Much longer?"

She exchanged glances with Abiba, who nodded. The bubble was large enough to encompass the whole head of the creature.

Keep an eye on its tail!

The two women jointly turned their attention to the snarling creature behind them, who was still focused on Adio and Sefu. As one, they moved the bubble quickly, dodging and moving to follow its head until they managed to get the bubble around it.

It roared in confusion, though the sound was muffled through the water, and thrashed back and forth. Adanya and Abiba's faces were strained as they focused on moving the water with its head. Out of the corner of her eye, she saw Sefu slash wildly at the tail when it got too near to them.

Slowly, ever so slowly, the monster's movements became sluggish. It dropped down to its haunches, swiping at the water bubble to try and dislodge it. But Adanya and Abiba's joined energy kept it firm, and the Ugwe finally collapsed, its chest stopped heaving, and its tail ceased its twitching. The women released the water, letting it splash onto the ground below the monster. All was silent save for the resuming sound of insects and birds.

They all sat frozen on their horses, trying to recover.

Sefu found his voice first. "We should keep moving."

Everyone nodded their agreement, and they carefully maneuvered their horses around the corpse before kicking back into a gallop.

Adanya's hands shook where they clutched the reins, trying to understand how she'd been able to use her magic that way. It was almost ... instinct. It was as if joining her magic with Abiba's had brought out something in her that she didn't even know existed. And it was stronger. She hadn't used Sage magic with Ziyad, save for the occasional telepathic conversation, so there hadn't been a chance to see how their magic would have amplified each other.

Though she did remember reading something of it in Nehanda's journal after she awakened.

Wonderful. Something else to figure out.

She glanced over at Adio, sensing his worry before seeing it on his face. *I'm alright. You?*

Managed not to wet myself and my sword arm feels like I've done 100 one-armed push-ups. But I'm still alive, so great! She could tell that he was attempting levity for her sake, but decided not to comment.

Hey. You were amazing, I hope you know that.

I don't know where any of that came from.

He shrugged. *I'm sure there's some part of your subconscious that always knew what you were capable of. You're just finally getting to experience it.*

I think I need to have another look in that journal, see if there's anything else I've missed.

And I don't think you have to be worried about Abiba handling things once we get there. She's shown she's up to the task.

Agreed.

For now, chill out. You've used a lot of magic and your body isn't used to that.

She nodded, focusing on the road ahead. There was a lot to think about.

Chapter Twenty-Two

The mood in the council room was dour, everyone dressed in black and struggling to reconcile with the death of Ziyad. His chair sat empty, a further reminder of his loss. Nehanda, as the second-highest ranking member after Ziyad due to the length of time she'd been on the council, took control of the proceedings.

"As we all know, it is tradition that a new Head of Council be appointed as soon as possible after the death of the previous Head. Since we are all present, we must now cast our votes. Please, take a few moments to consider, then we will elect our new leader."

Adanya's mind was anything but focused, the loss of Ziyad seeming stronger to her because he was the only other Sage that she had known. Understanding the gravity of the situation, however, she forced herself to look around the room to consider who would be a good replacement.

None of her companions had expressed a desire to be in leadership, save Nehanda. Adio had made it clear he enjoyed the freedom that not being in charge gave him. Kamaria, Gabir, and Jabari all had families to care for; the demands of being Head of Council would take them away from their roles as parents and spouses. That left only Naeemah and Nehanda. How different the two women were! Naeemah, calm and graceful, with seemingly endless patience and care for those around her. And Nehanda, with her fiery temper and need to have things just so.

Part of her wanted to support her mentor, knowing her desire to keep things in order would be beneficial to the effective running of the council and protection of the kingdom. But then she worried that Nehanda's inflexibility could prove dangerous in a role that required taking many factors into account to make decisions. Her only choice, then, was Naeemah ... but speaking the name aloud, or even writing it, would instantly raise Nehanda's anger against her and possibly change their relationship forever.

As she contemplated, she suddenly became aware of a puzzling energy in the room. Despite everyone's sorrow, it felt strongly positive, radiating toward her. Surely this was only because everyone knew how important Ziyad had been to her ... right?

"We're all thinking it, might as well say it," Gabir said. "I nominate Adanya."

Adanya looked at him in bewilderment, her surprise growing as she looked around and saw the others nodding in agreement.

"But, me?" she stammered. "Certainly someone else, someone with more experience on the council..."

"Experience isn't the only thing to recommend someone to leadership," Jabari said wisely. "And a desire to be in leadership doesn't always make one a good leader."

Nehanda finally found her voice. "But Adanya is so young! She's only been on the council for two years. She still has much to learn before she would be ready for a position with such responsibility."

"But despite that," Naeemah said, revealing a letter from her pocket, "it was Ziyad's wish."

Nehanda's mouth dropped open as Naeemah unfolded the letter and read it aloud.

"'It is my wish that Adanya succeed me as Head of Council when I am gone. While the tradition of voting should still be upheld, know that my full support is behind her. Written in the sight of and given to Naeemah by Ziyad.'" The raven-haired beauty folded the letter back up reverently. "I think he knew that his time was coming," she said quietly. "He gave this to me a month ago. I couldn't fathom why."

"I suppose that settles it, then," Kamaria said. "If there was anyone whose judgement of a person we could trust, it was Ziyad. He must have seen something special in you, Adanya."

Adanya was speechless, overwhelmed with not wanting the role, Ziyad's support of her, and the smoldering anger radiating from Nehanda. Before she could react, Gabir rose solemnly. "All in favor of Adanya becoming the new Head of Council, please raise your hand."

Every hand at the table immediately went up ... except for Nehanda's. "She's too young," she repeated. "Surely someone with more experience, someone trained by Ziyad would be more suitable."

"The decision is made," Kamaria said firmly. She picked up the velvet bag which lay upon the table and withdrew the ring of office that used to rest upon Ziyad's right hand—a simple golden band with a small black stone set in its center—and came over to slide it upon Adanya's finger. "I have faith that you'll make us all proud," she said supportively, placing a hand on Adanya's shoulder before stepping back to allow all to see.

Nehanda stormed out of the room without another word, a rare outward sign of anger from her.

Adio smiled apologetically. "She'll come around. It's no secret that she's wanted to be Head of Council almost as long as she's been on the council."

Adanya was still speechless.

Naeemah came over, hugging her friend. "I know this is a lot. Go to your room and get some rest. We'll take care of the transition preparations and inform the king."

Wordlessly, Adanya left the room. She started walking automatically to her room, but she stopped when she'd almost reached it. With a quick look around to make sure no one was watching, she turned and ran down the hall, out the side door, and into the forest.

Once there, she pressed a shaking hand to her heart, trying to slow her breathing and keep from hyperventilating. What had just happened? Surrounded by the trees and the open air, the gravity of her new appointment seemed so far away, like something from another world. But the ring on her finger reminded her that it was oh so real.

Why had Ziyad placed such faith in her? She'd barely graduated from her training regimen with Nehanda, just starting to learn from the other council members; she'd done nothing notable that would have esteemed her above the others. True, Ziyad had kept a close eye on her since the beginning of her training, and had spent more time with her, but that couldn't have been enough to recommend her, could it?

And Nehanda's reaction... Though she herself knew of Nehanda's desire to be the Head of Council, she never could have imagined her opposition to Adanya's election would be so strong. She would always be indebted to Nehanda for her training, but today made her question if the woman had ever truly cared about her.

She slumped down against the trunk of a thick tree, attempting to organize her thoughts and think clearly. But her conflicting feelings made it hard to do so. She felt scared, angry, betrayed, and, overall, alone.

What would happen if she just ran away? Returned to her simple life in the woods, alone, without having to take any more responsibilities or be accountable for the safety of the kingdom.

But that would mean leaving the king, the man who had become like a father to her, who clearly cared for her and wanted her to do well. Naeemah, who'd taken her under her wing and helped to build her confidence. Adio, who seemed determined to support and uplift her. Even Gabir, Jabari, and Kamaria, who had not spent much time with her but clearly saw her value, even if she didn't. Could she leave them all?

So engrossed was she in her thoughts that she did not hear or feel Adio until he sat down beside her on the exposed root of the tree.

"Thinking about running away, little girl?" he said gently.

"How did you know?" she asked without looking at him.

"Hey, now; I'd be a terrible friend if I didn't know you by now. Talk to me. What's going through that head?"

Unable to control herself, she released all of her emotions and thoughts into his mind at once. He physically leaned back for a moment, blinking rapidly. Then he reached down and took her hand. "Well. If I was feeling all of that, I'd want to run away too. What have you decided to do?"

"I don't know," she admitted. "I wish that there was time for me to ... to think, to get my head around all of this."

"Sometimes that's not a choice that we have. Those of us who were born sorcerers have a responsibility to use our powers for the good of others, whether we want to or not. Some can't handle the pressure; they seek to use their power for their own good, and that is what destroys them. But the rest of us? Our lives have to be dedicated to others, in whatever capacity that is. Almost like royalty in a way."

She was quiet as she contemplated his words.

"So I'm not going to stop you. If you feel like you're not up to it, you can go into the woods and I'm sure that no one will find you. But I can promise you this: if you go back, then I'll always be by your side. And I know the rest of the council will be there to support you as well. Even Nehanda, once she comes around."

"*If* she comes around."

"*When*. She doesn't quite know how to show it, but she loves you."

Something about the day's proceedings made her doubt that, but she kept this to herself. Her eyes moved back to deeper in the woods, knowing that if she chose to stay, she wouldn't get the chance to run again.

Finally, she sighed a heavy sigh and stood resolutely. "Well, then. It looks like we've got work to do."

Adio smiled, enveloping her in a tight hug. "No matter what happens, little girl, I'll do my best to be there for you."

Chapter Twenty-Three

After a two nights' hard ride, well hidden by Adio's fog whenever they stopped to rest during the day, they resumed their journey at dusk. Adanya marveled at how much the landscape had changed; since all of the inhabitants of the kingdom had perished, regular upkeep had vanished and nature had been allowed to reclaim the land.

Now they were slowing their horses as they approached Ferandar's capital, Lumumba. The plateau that held the palace had been visible for miles, their western approach shielding the rest of the city from view—though they could see distant plumes of smoke from chimneys and forges showing its location. Their side of the palace was surrounded by an open plain, with trees coming in thick on either side. The walls were high and thick, with flags bearing a strange standard flapping in the wind. As they directed their horses deeper into the tree cover, they could also see soldiers pacing atop the walls. It was well placed for defending.

A whistle, like that of a bird, directed them farther into the woods, where their forces were waiting for them. Sefu dismounted first and went to speak to one of his captains as the other three dismounted, looking about them in awe.

Beneath the trees were nearly a thousand men and women dressed in traveling clothes of gray and brown and armed with bows, swords, and spears. All were spattered with mud from Adio's storm. They clearly were not unused to battle, all grim-faced and moving purposefully to carry out their orders.

But many stopped and stared at the sight of Adanya, recognizing her from her statue and the tales that had been told of her. Her face reddened, and she ducked her head a little so her braids swung to hide her face.

Adio nudged her. "None of that, now. They've been waiting for you."

With an effort, she raised her head and tried to look more confident than she felt.

Sefu returned. "We've found the entrance to the tunnels, though it looks like they haven't been very well maintained."

"Let's see."

He led them to a small hill, situated besides a fast-flowing stream that snaked its way through the forest, swelling past its banks from Adio's storm. The tunnel had been dug into the side of the hill, the entrance hidden by a screen of vine and leaves that disguised it from the casual observer. Inside, the walls had been shored up by wooden braces; here and there they had fallen, leaving the tunnel partially blocked.

Abiba and Sefu went a bit into the tunnel, discussing and examining.

"What do you think, Abiba?" Adanya asked as they emerged back out into the forest.

"I can make it work. These cave-ins look fairly recent, probably because they've been unused this far out. The ones on a higher incline wouldn't be under the kind of pressure that caused these cave-ins."

"Is the rest of the tunnel going to be strong enough to withstand the water?" Adio asked.

"It should be. The water will be rising slowly, not rushing through like the stream."

Adanya took charge. "Sefu, what does the approach look like from the other side of the palace?"

"There's nearly a mile of open plain between the palace gates and the rest of the city. These woods extend to either side of that plain, but not close to the road. Anyone trying to approach would be easily spotted."

"Is the gate guarded?"

"Heavily. Guards both inside and out, and on the ramparts. It can only open from the inside."

"It will keep the water in, if nothing else," Abiba pointed out.

"We need to draw any survivors out to this plain," Adanya said decisively. "Keep them away from the city. Once the water has risen enough to drown as many as possible, we need to push the survivors back here."

Sefu nodded. "I'll have a company sent around front to nudge them along, and the rest I'll spread through these woods."

"Abiba, how much time do you think you'll need to get the water into the palace?"

Abiba had been moving between the tunnel entrance and the edge of the wood, gauging the distance and incline. "At least six hours to get it there, a few more to get it to cover at least the ground floor."

"I want the water to get at them while most of the palace is asleep, so they'll be caught more off guard. We'll need to start soon. We'll also need to send in a company to capture the steward."

"I'll see it done," Sefu said.

"We strike when Abiba has finished."

Sefu moved off to give orders.

Adio turned to the two women. "A bit of advice: trust yourself. You know the plan. You know what you're trying to accomplish. Trust yourself and you'll be successful. I've seen what you two can do when you work together." He put a hand on Adanya's shoulder and squeezed supportively.

She took a deep breath. Then she looked at Abiba, and they nodded to each other. "Let's get started."

Adanya settled herself on a flat-topped rock a short distance from the stream, sitting cross-legged with her staff on her knees and taking a moment to clear her mind. Then she focused all of her energy on Abiba, the world around her fading as she mentally weaved an invisible hedge of protection over the younger woman, much more focused now that she wasn't also fighting a monster at the same time.

Upon seeing Adanya's nod, Abiba turned to the stream. She focused on the water, and it seemed like an invisible hand was moving the water from the stream bed into the tunnel entrance.

The water was brown, carrying along broken sticks, rocks, and dirt from the runoff. But it moved steadily under Abiba's guidance, flowing into the entrance as easily as if it were still running its natural course.

Adanya was vaguely aware of her surroundings, though she had little concept of time. Adio sat nearby, polishing a sword he'd gotten from one of the soldiers. Sefu came and went as he gave orders and checked on their progress. It was almost as if she were in a dream, the things in her periphery taking on a hazy dissonance. She also felt Abiba's magic working and was able to join her own Aqua magic with it while still maintaining the protection. The light around them slowly grew dimmer as the day progressed, the two sorcerers still hard at work—though to the outside viewer, it seemed like nothing was happening at all.

Ironic that one of the skills Nehanda had worked on with her the hardest was helping Adanya to fight against her.

Chapter Twenty-Four

Adanya let out a frustrated sigh as she entered her room and slammed the door behind her, throwing her staff down bad-temperedly. Rashidi looked up from the chair by the fireplace where he was sharpening his sword.

"That doesn't sound good," he remarked. "Is everything okay?"

"No. No, it is not okay."

He put aside his sword and came over to her. "What's wrong?"

"You're going to say 'I told you so.'"

He chuckled and put his arms around her waist, kissing her forehead. "No, I won't. Just tell me."

She looked down at Ziyad's ring on her finger. "It's been nearly a year since I was made Head of Council. But Nehanda is still treating me like a stupid child in need of training. I'm not saying I know all there is to know about magic and controlling it and being in a leadership position, but she could give me some credit! It's so hard for me to trust her blindly, like I did when I was younger, after how she reacted to my election."

"Did something specifically happen today that made it worse?"

"She questioned my judgement in front of the council! And not in a way that would be constructive. She clearly thinks I don't know what I'm doing."

"Did anyone else say anything?"

"Jabari told her to be respectful, and Kamaria reminded her that I'm Head of Council. But you know that Kamaria and Nehanda have never seen eye to eye, and I had to end the meeting to give the two of them time to calm down before they burned every scrap of paper in the room. Adio suggested that I come and talk to you."

"I knew I liked him."

She didn't laugh, instead pushing past him to plop into her chair by the fireplace. "Things have been so strained between us since I was voted in. I've spent more time with Nehanda since I left the forest than with anyone else; I thought that I knew her, that I could trust her with anything. I thought she was my biggest supporter, but now? I'm starting to have my doubts."

He followed her over, sitting in the other chair and waiting patiently, knowing she needed the space to pour out her thoughts before getting any kind of response from him.

"She always wanted to be Head of Council. It was like she was training herself for it. She always used to talk about using her position to help other sorcerers, to protect them from being mistreated and misunderstood. But lately she talks more and more about the people around sorcerers, and how we have to be careful of non-magical people. It's like losing this position changed her whole mindset. Sometimes I feel like she actively resents me."

She fell silent again, a few moments passing before she continued voicing her thoughts. "I suppose I can see how this was a blow to her. It's all that she ever wanted, and I got it without wanting it. It makes sense that she'd be a little jealous. And it makes sense that she'd be more wary of non-magical people because of the way she was treated. I guess it just comes out and she doesn't know how to share her feelings without coming across harshly; the Ember in her."

Feeling the slight change in Rashidi's energy, she looked over to see him trying to suppress a frown. "What?"

"Do you want my opinion, my advice, or nothing?" he asked.

She sighed. He'd gotten into the habit of asking her this when she came to vent; while she didn't particularly want to hear the truth, she knew that he only shared from a place of love and support. "Opinion," she said quietly.

He reached over and squeezed her hand. "I never saw your relationship with her before you were elected Head, but if it has changed as much as you say, then maybe you should start distancing yourself from her. She's perfectly valid in having her own feelings; it's understandable that she would be disappointed. But if she really cared about you, she'd learn to put that to the side and do her best to support you."

"I … maybe."

"I know she's the closest thing that you have to a mother, so it's hard. But my love, there are so many more people around you now who want nothing but to love and support you. You don't have to solely depend on her."

She sighed heavily, squeezing his hand back. "She's the one who taught me to truly harness my powers. The one who found me in the woods. I wouldn't be where I am today without her."

"Sometimes people are only meant to be in our lives for a season, and then we have to let them go. It's hard, but sometimes it's necessary for growth. I'm not saying that you need to cut her off completely; it's impossible, really, since you're both on the council. But you could start to limit the time you spend alone with her. It makes sense; you have many more duties to perform now, so it wouldn't seem like you're just pulling away out of the blue."

"I suppose."

Hearing the reluctance in her voice, he gently pulled on her hand to guide her over to him, sitting her down in his lap and wrapping his arms around her. "It's just my opinion. You don't have to take any of my suggestions."

"I know. But I think that some part of me knows that you're right."

"Well, whatever you decide, you know I'm here to support you."

She sighed again. "I know."

He tilted his head back for a kiss, and she obliged, gently running her hand over his scarred head.

She tensed slightly as she felt Nehanda's presence, her spirit betraying her intention to find Adanya.

"No." She focused her energy on hiding her and Rashidi's presence from Nehanda, her eyes looking off into space.

Rashidi raised a puzzled eyebrow, but waited to see what she was doing. After a few moments, Nehanda's energy faded away, and Adanya's eyes regained focus.

"I missed something?" he asked.

She leaned in for another kiss. "Nothing. Just making sure that we were undisturbed for a while."

Chapter Twenty-Five

“The lights have all gone out,” a soldier reported to Sefu.

“Maybe an hour more,” Abiba said without stopping in her work.

“Move the invasion force into position,” Adanya said, pulling slightly away from her focus on her magic. “You’ll need to be ready to move as soon as the water has taken out the floor level.”

Sefu moved to follow her orders.

“Where do you want me?” Adio asked.

"With us. You have actual sword skills to help protect us; we'll have to reserve our magic for extreme circumstances, so we'll need to stay safe and hidden."

"Understood."

Adanya could feel her heart starting to beat faster. While she wasn't leading the troops into battle, she was, effectively, taking charge. She'd never seen herself in such a position, however she knew this was what was required of her. Rather than give in to her worries, she returned her focus to her task.

An hour later, they heard sharp whistles being passed along throughout the trees. "Let's go!" Sefu ordered, leading his soldiers to the fringe.

Abiba relaxed her magic, allowing the water to return to its regular flow. Adio directed a few fighters to keep the water from flowing backwards by throwing large stones and branches across the entrance of the tunnel.

Adanya waited a few minutes to be safe before releasing her protective shield. Then she rose and joined Adio and Abiba as they all moved toward the edge of the tree cover.

On the plateau, lights began to shine from the upper floors of the palace. It was clear something was happening, though from their distance all they could hear was the chirping of crickets and the rustle of wings from birds in the trees.

Several breathless minutes passed. Adio reached over and stilled Adanya's hand where her fingers were anxiously tapping her staff. "Patience," he said softly.

"I hate not knowing what's going on," she muttered.

"Didn't you tell me once that you could see things in other places?" he asked.

She turned to look at him in surprise. "How did you remember that?"

"Just because I've been awake for many more years than you doesn't mean I forgot the things you've told me," he said, tapping his temple with a chuckle. "And as strong as your Sage magic is getting, you could probably still keep yourself shielded from Nehanda."

Now she closed her mouth before she could utter the argument he'd preempted. "Well."

Before she could talk herself out of it, she closed her eyes, took a deep breath, and sent her mind to the palace gates. Almost instantly she could see the road before the open gates, now flooded and choked with mud. Sefu was leading a skillful charge, waiting for the water to recede before moving closer, defending against any soldiers who managed to put up a resistance. The scene was chaotic, somewhat murky in her mind's eye, but it was clear enough that their plan was working. At the same time, she could feel her protection energy still surrounding her.

She fluttered her eyes open, about to share what she'd seen; however, a messenger from Sefu was there, breathlessly giving the same report. Strange; she hadn't even sensed his approach.

"The palace has been breached. The gates are open and they're battling on the road. There's water coming out; it looks like their losses were heavy."

"Makes sense," Adio nodded. "They concentrate soldiers on the ground floor because that's where an invading force would enter first. There will be a lot fewer soldiers on the upper floors."

Abiba squinted and pointed. "Is there something waving over there?"

Adanya followed her finger. They could see a small pinpoint of light waving from the top of the wall. Her eyes widened. "It's a signal. They must have reinforcements hidden somewhere..."

A shout came from behind them as someone spotted a responding pinpoint of light waved back from the trees across the field.

Adanya turned to the messenger. "Tell Sefu to send as many men as he can spare to us here. The enemy has another force, and they're attacking from the field."

The messenger took off at a run. Adanya turned back to the edge of the field, seeing dark shapes emerging from the trees in the lengthening darkness.

"How did we miss them?" Abiba asked aloud.

"It's clever, actually," Adio mused. "Someone knew the palace could be attacked from the front, cutting them off from escape. We'd all expect the back to be unguarded because of its excellent position; what better place to hide a separate defense force? They were likely hidden deeper in the woods where we wouldn't have noticed each other's movements."

"The problem is, do we have enough forces to counter them?" Adanya asked. "We're at a disadvantage in this darkness."

"I can move the clouds," Adio offered. "I know that it was helping to cover our movements, but that might be a moot point now."

Adanya chewed her lip as she contemplated. "There's a chance Nehanda may already be aware of the attack here. But on the other hand, she may not know, and using magic again risks her attention being drawn to us. My protection can hide us, but used too often, she'll be able to sense that magic is being used." She paused only a moment more before nodding. "Do it. I'll shield you."

Without hesitation they both went to work, she weaving her protection shield before Adio began working his magic, sending the overhead clouds away into the distance.

Almost instantly the night was nearly as bright as day, a full moon and stars bathing the land in silvery light. The enemy soldiers came charging out of the woods, knowing their advantage of darkness was gone and hoping instead to overwhelm them with numbers.

Sefu appeared at Adanya's side. "Our archers in the trees will attack from the sides, and I'll lead a charge down the field."

"What about the palace?" Adanya asked.

"The soldiers who are still alive have nearly been destroyed, and I already have a contingent entering the palace to get the steward. More of them were wiped out by the water before we even got there; pity we couldn't reach them before someone was able to send up the alarm. There's a force in reserve in case either contingent needs support."

"Alright, go. We'll stay here. If we need to use magic as a last resort, we will."

"Keep out of sight." He charged off, gesturing for his men to follow him as he ran.

The trio of sorcerers found a large rock to hide behind that afforded them a view of the battle. Adanya had to suppress a shudder as she watched Sefu go; the matter-of-fact, take-charge manner in which he spoke during tense situations reminded her of Rashidi, now more than ever.

Adio noticed, gently squeezing her arm for support.

They watched as the two forces clashed, swords clanging, arrows whistling through the air. There were casualties on both sides, but it was clear the enemy had not expected them to be so well organized and prepared.

Sefu was a blur of motion, jabbing here, dodging there, throwing a knife or cutting arrows from the air. Now and then he gave an order that did not reach their ears from that distance, and his troops followed, moving as a unit in one direction or another. They were keeping the enemy from retreating into the woods, Adanya realized, pushing them toward the plateau on which the palace was sat to put their backs to the wall.

"He's amazing," Abiba breathed, her eyes fixed on the action.

"The fact that everyone is so in sync without having trained as a unified army is impressive," Adio added.

Adanya could not help but feel a bit of pride for the young man. Rashidi certainly would have been proud of him. And if the people rallied behind him as much as the resistance fighters did, then their chances of success were starting to look a little higher.

"Ma'am!" A soldier appeared behind them. "The palace is taken. We have the steward in custody, and any enemy forces have been either captured or destroyed."

"Make sure the palace is secured, then go into town to make sure there aren't enemy soldiers there," she ordered. "See if there is any aid that we can offer the people."

"Understood." The soldier disappeared back into the forest.

"Look at you, being a commander," Adio said, pride in his voice.

"Just doing what makes sense," she said with a blush.

"That's what a commander does."

They turned their attention back to the battle, watching as Sefu continued to battle madly right in the heat of it. His forces moved with skill that the enemy soldiers could not match, and it was clear the enemy forces were dwindling.

Soon—though Adanya, having never been in a battle, could not fully track the passing of time—Sefu waved his sword aloft to signal victory.

Adanya felt her heart leap but warned herself not to get too excited.

"We won?" Abiba asked. "We did it?"

"It seems so," Adanya replied. "I'll admit I expected far more complications."

"This was just the first step," Adio said. "Whether she knows that magic is involved or not, Nehanda is going to put her guard up to keep from losing any more kingdoms."

"Do you think she'll try to retake this one?"

"It's possible, though I think from a tactical standpoint it would make more sense for her to strengthen the defenses around the other kingdoms than to come back for this one. Besides, I've got a feeling the people in town will have a stake in making sure she can't come back."

Sefu rejoined them, splattered with blood and dirt and a few small wounds. "The town has been searched and cleared. Once the water recedes in the palace, we can clear it out and refortify it for our own defenses."

"Where's the steward?"

"We're holding him in the forest."

"We should question him. He might be able to give us some insight into Nehanda's movements and what she might—agh!" She had risen as she spoke, and she cried out as an arrow thudded into her shoulder, knocking her from her feet.

Sefu quickly fired off a return arrow, felling the offending archer as Abiba and Adio went to Adanya's aid.

She gritted her teeth in pain, though more from being knocked over than the actual arrow wound. "The water, Abiba! Take it back so our forces can get inside."

"But..."

"Now!" she ordered.

Reluctantly, Abiba turned her attention back to the water, not bothering to push the logs and debris out of the way.

Sefu took charge, directing his fighters to eliminate the few enemy soldiers who had slipped into the trees. Adio tended to Adanya's shoulder, testing the arrow to see its depth.

"Have to push it through," he said apologetically. "If I try to pull it backwards, it will cause more damage."

"Do it." She winced as he broke the feathered end off, then gripped his arm as he pushed the arrowhead forward so that it pierced her back. Then he pushed it the rest of the way through in one fluid motion. She only grunted, her energy focused on shielding Abiba for as long as possible. Blood seeped from the wound, staining her gray robes.

Adio ripped a swath of cloth from his shirt, wrapping it tightly around her shoulder. She grunted again, her face filled with pain as she tried to keep her focus.

"We need to cauterize it," Adio muttered, looking around for something to start a fire with.

"Done!" Abiba gasped as she slumped down, exhausted. With the water moving, it was enough to let gravity carry it down.

"Let's go," Adanya said, trying to stand while simultaneously sending a message to Sefu.

"You can't ride like this!" Adio protested. "You'll lose too much blood!"

"And if we stay here, we risk drawing out Nehanda. I'm too weak to fend her off now. They'll bring the steward to us."

Reluctantly, Adio scooped her into his arms and carried her to his horse, insisting that she not ride alone. Once he saw Abiba mounted, they spurred their horses off.

Adanya watched the landscape speed by, littered with the bodies of friend and foe alike. She struggled to keep her consciousness, drifting into the darkness.

Chapter Twenty-Six

"What part of rest do we not understand?" Adio said in frustration.

"I'm the Head of Council, and there's work to be done! Besides, it's not that bad of a wound." Adanya tried flexing her arm to prove her point but winced.

Adio crossed the council room in two swift strides, pointing an accusatory finger at her where she sat in her chair. "Aha! See? You need to sit down somewhere and recover. It was better, but you keep stretching your skin. It won't heal fully unless you rest."

"There isn't time for that. Besides, Nehanda said..."

"Nehanda will work until she drops dead and pushes everyone around her to do the same. That's not the person you should be listening to right now. I understand that it's not as bad as it could have been, but if you keep pushing like this, it's going to get worse. Infections are nothing to joke about."

"I don't think it's that dramatic. I need to get my head around all of my new responsibilities now that the Ugwe problem has been solved."

"And there will be plenty of time for that. No one—except Nehanda—expects you to know everything all at once. You did an amazing job in solving the Ugwe problem. Rest on those laurels for a bit, hm?"

"I don't know how to do that."

"Well, then I'll just have to force you."

Adanya was about to protest when she felt the approach of Rashidi. She turned to spot him coming through the doorway, smiling before she realized it as her mind flashed back to the gentle kisses he'd given her for the first time only days before.

Adio noticed. "Captain!" he called.

Rashidi approached, bowing his head respectfully. "Yes, sir?"

"You've been wounded many times during your career, I'm sure?" Adio questioned.

"Yes, sir." Rashidi nodded.

Adio glanced back at Adanya while she tried to determine where he was going with this line of questioning. "How important was rest during your recovery from these wounds?" He continued.

"Extremely important, sir. Your body needs all of the energy it gets so that it can heal."

Adio smirked victoriously. "The Head of Council is finding it hard to actually relax while she's in the palace. Could you take her somewhere relaxing? Maybe the spring by Hasfar?"

"It is a wonderful place to relax. I'd be happy to gather a guard company to escort you, ma'am."

Adanya tried to protest again, seeing the look of understanding that passed between the two men.

"We'll leave within the hour, ma'am." Rashidi bowed again and swept out of the room.

"I'll get the kitchens to pack you a lunch," Adio said, following him.

Alone in the council room, Adanya sighed. While still stressed about learning her new duties, she had to admit the prospect of some rest was appealing.

She looked up as Nehanda entered the room, clearly preoccupied as she scribbled in her notebook.

"I need some reports," she said, not even looking at Adanya as she walked over to the bookshelf. "There are some rumors about the Harrun that we need to investigate at today's council meeting..."

Adanya took a deep breath, knowing that directly contradicting Nehanda usually didn't end well—even though now, Adanya was her superior. "We're not meeting today. I'm taking some time to rest."

Nehanda stopped in her search, and Adanya could feel the heat coming from her, both physically and from her energy. She slowly turned to look at her. "Rest? There isn't time for that."

Adanya tried to sound braver than she felt. "There will be plenty of time to get things done when I am better healed."

"You're the Head of Council; you don't get the choice of just not working."

"I'm no good to anyone if I'm distracted by my body not being fully healed. Besides, it wouldn't be good to need a replacement so soon after my ascension."

Nehanda's eyes flared at Adanya's defiance, but she took a deep breath and managed to keep herself calm. "If you think it's best," she replied with a small bow that Adanya knew was mocking.

"I'll see you when I return." Adanya walked out, her heart pounding as she still could feel Nehanda's anger.

She decided to go speak with the king to inform him of her trip and to have their daily conference. She found him in the garden, pruning rosebushes.

"Ah! Have I lost track of the time?" he asked as he saw her.

"No, Your Majesty." She bowed. "I wanted to inform you that I'm ... that I've been *forced* to stop working for the day and rest."

He smiled widely. "I'm glad to hear it. Judging by your reluctance, I'm guessing it was Adio's idea?"

"Yes." She could not help but pout.

He laughed heartily. "I'm glad you have such good people looking out for your best interests. I was sincerely hoping that you would take some time to rest."

"You too?" she asked in surprise.

"I didn't think it was my place to say," he admitted. "But I don't want to see you pushing yourself too hard. I'll admit I was much like you when I was crowned king, working extremely hard to catch up with all of my new duties and not allowing myself time to rest. It was Ziyad who encouraged me to find the balance between working and resting. I'd like to encourage you to do the same."

"I ... I guess that I don't have a choice. I suppose I should get going."

He winked at her, then turned back to his pruning.

#

Rashidi and the guard escorted Adanya to the outskirts of Hasfar, a few hours' ride from the palace. Here there was a natural spring surrounded by a lush forest. Adanya spread out a blanket and the lunch Adio had given her, then sat watching the water as she ate in silence. Using what she'd learned, she shut out the energy around her and quieted her mind.

All the energy, save for one person.

"Captain?" she called.

Rashidi drew closer from where he had been standing guard. "Yes, ma'am?"

She was aware that he liked to maintain a professional manner when they were outside of the palace, so she asked carefully, "Do your duties prevent you from talking to me while we are out?"

"Not at all, ma'am. But I didn't want to intrude; you seemed very focused on something."

She smiled. "Nothing, actually. Focused on nothing."

"That sounds like it might actually be quite relaxing. I imagine that always sensing everyone around you must be exhausting." He had asked her a few questions about what it was like to be a Sage during one of their walks together—not probing, but genuinely trying to understand and learn more about her.

"It can be. But you get used to it, in a way. Learn how to take time to tune everything out and reset. It's much easier now than it used to be."

"I can only imagine. None of my experiences would likely compare."

"Very few things compare to magic," she chuckled. "I imagine that's why sorcerers tend to spend time together; we can understand the burden we carry." She could not stop her eyes traveling to his muscular arms and imagining what it would be like to be wrapped in them.

A slow smile crossed his face, and Adanya's eyes widened as she realized she'd accidentally shared that thought with him.

I've been wondering the same thing, he thought in reply.

She cleared her throat loudly, sipping from her cup as she felt the heat rising to her face.

He chuckled quietly, but mercifully he didn't comment further.

Eager to change the subject, she asked, "How long have you been enlisted, Captain?"

"About seven years now, ma'am."

"Do you enjoy it?"

He nodded. "It's a fulfilling career, ma'am. Difficult at times, but that only adds to the fulfillment."

"Sometimes I wonder what it would have been like to actually choose a career." She sighed. "Being chosen for something doesn't quite hold the same appeal."

"I'm sure that you wouldn't have been chosen if you didn't have the ability to hold the position."

Her eyes flicked up at him in annoyance. "That isn't the first time that I've heard that recently."

"Probably because it's true." He smiled disarmingly.

Adanya felt something low in her stomach flutter at the sight of his smile. She'd seen it before, of course, during their now frequent walks through the palace. But outside, in the warm, late summer light, it seemed to be the perfect adornment to his handsome, rugged face.

His eyes seemed to take in her reaction, and they twinkled ever so slightly as his smile widened. He took a step closer to her. "If I may be so bold?"

She blinked, thinking he was referring to holding her until she noticed he was gesturing at her injured arm. "Oh … of course."

He gently took hold of her arm, rolling up her sleeve to see her injury. It had already begun to heal, but the welts on her skin were still an angry red. "It was well tended to. But your friends are right. It will only get worse if you don't rest and allow it to heal."

Adanya tried again to repress the delightful shiver that ran through her at his touch. "I suppose I can't ignore someone who has experienced it."

He rolled her sleeve back down, grazing her hand with the tips of his fingers. "Oh? Is that what it takes, ma'am?"

"Maybe it is." Again feeling the heat from his gaze, she turned away and glanced at the sun. "We should probably get back soon. I'd like to be back home in time to watch the sunset."

"Of course, ma'am."

Adanya's focus was solely on Rashidi as they rode back, her mind racing. She wanted to spend more time with him, to learn more about him ... and to feel his touch without worrying about others seeing.

When they arrived back at the palace, Rashidi waited for her to dismount before turning his horse toward the stables.

"Captain!" Adanya blurted, unable to help herself. "Would ... would you mind walking me to my room? I believe you and I have more to discuss."

There was that smile again. He dismounted, tossing his reins to one of the soldiers. "It would be my honor, ma'am." He climbed the stairs after her and offered his arm.

They walked in silence as they passed through the more crowded parts of the palace, with servants and nobles going to and fro. These people paid little attention to her beyond a courtesy bow or nod due to her station, and no one seemed to notice or care about Rashidi's presence.

Which was probably for the best, because her heart pounded so hard she was sure her voice would shake if she tried to speak. What was happening? She'd never experienced feelings like this before and was entirely unsure of how to deal with them.

They soon reached a quieter part of the palace and slowed their walk.

"So, ma'am," Rashidi said. "What was it you wanted to ask me?"

"I…" She giggled awkwardly. "Now that I have you alone, I forgot."

He chuckled, the sound rumbling deep in his chest. "It wouldn't have anything to do with thoughts of my arms around you, would it?"

"…Maybe."

He stopped walking, turning to face her and lifting her face to his with a gentle hand. "You do realize that you don't have to dance around it? I'll happily have you in my arms any time." Before she could fully react, he gently pressed a kiss to her lips.

Adanya thought she was going to explode. As had happened the first time he kissed her, everything else in the world seemed to melt away. The only thing she could sense was his lips against hers and his arms as they gathered her into them. What was this? All of these sensations were new and confusing, and yet she knew she wanted to experience more.

She opened her eyes as he pulled away, seeing him smiling at her reaction. "Are you alright?" he asked.

"I, um…" She struggled to form words, finally settling on, "Can we go to my room?"

Amusement danced in his eyes. "If you would like to."

She nodded furiously, and he took her hand to guide her the rest of the way.

Once there, she backed against the closed door and looked at Rashidi as he glanced at his surroundings.

"I don't understand what's happening," she finally said. "I've never felt ... whatever this is before."

He took a step closer to her, then paused. "Would it be easier if you used your magic on me? It might help you to share what you're feeling, instead of trying to find the words to explain it."

Adanya considered. "It might, actually. Though, since I've never experienced this, I'm not sure how it will come across."

"Perhaps I'd better sit down, then." Rashidi took off his sword belt and the rest of his armor, resting it against the door, then walked over to one of the chairs in front of the fireplace.

After a moment, Adanya followed, sitting in the chair beside his. He watched her expectantly. Gathering herself, she carefully shared her feelings with him. As attraction, longing, and curiosity passed between them, his smile returned to his face. She waited breathlessly as he processed everything with his eyes closed before opening them to gaze at her.

"Thank you for sharing that with me," he said gently. "I think I understand." Then he extended a hand to her.

She took it with relief, happy she hadn't overwhelmed him. "I was worried it would be too much," she admitted. "I've never shared those kinds of feelings with anyone before, and I wasn't sure if I could control them."

"I hope you don't feel like you have to control them," he said seriously. "Especially since they're quite normal ... and I feel the same way."

Adanya gasped before she could stop herself. "You do?"

Rashidi laughed, gently rubbing his thumb over her knuckles. "Why else do you think I asked to start seeing you?"

"I ... okay, you have a good point." She was suddenly very distracted by that thumb and the sparks racing through her.

He rose and came to stand in front of her, pulling her up to her feet. "I understand that you don't have any experience here. But I would be honored if you would let me guide you through it and teach you."

Adanya looked up into his warm brown eyes, sensing his honesty but also enraptured by the way those eyes looked in the light of the setting sun as it streamed through the window. "I would like that," she whispered.

He cupped her cheek in one hand, stroking it before leaning down to kiss her again.

Adanya completely forgot the sunset, the fireplace crackling, even the dull throb in her shoulder as he kissed her deeper, wrapping his arms around her to pull her even closer. As their bodies pressed together, she could not help but wonder at how the world seemed to melt away in this moment—and how she hoped it would not be the only time.

Chapter Twenty-Seven

Adanya woke with a scream of pain as a red-hot iron was pressed to her shoulder. Abiba held her down while Adio cauterized her wound with the blade of his sword, heated in the small fire lit in the clearing where they had settled for the night. The night was still bright, so they hid in the shadow of the trees, the horses nosing about in the nearby grass.

Abiba grasped her hand as Adanya fell back onto the makeshift pillow made from her rolled-up cloak, shaking from the pain.

"Got to do the other side," Adio said apologetically, pushing her braids from her face. "You ready?"

She couldn't speak but nodded, tightening her grip on Abiba's hand. Between them, they lifted Adanya so that Adio could get a good look at her shoulder.

"Brace yourself, love." At her second nod, he pressed the hot metal to her wound. Her skin sizzled and burned as it sealed the wound shut, and she groaned to try to keep from screaming. She fell back down, nearly retching at the smell of burnt flesh and delirious from the pain.

Abiba quickly doused a rag with water and dabbed at the sweat beading on Adanya's forehead. "You shouldn't move any more tonight. You need to sit still."

"We ... we need to talk to the steward," Adanya muttered. She reached out with her magic to find Sefu, sensing him despite the pain that pulled her focus. "He's bringing him to us."

"Until he gets here, rest, little girl," Adio said, gently pushing her to lay back. "I can't send you to a spring, but I can still make sure you get some rest."

Despite her pain, she smirked. "You are always going to make sure of that, hm?"

"And don't you forget it. Go to sleep."

Adanya closed her eyes, knowing the pain would prevent her from sleeping but deciding to humor him. After a while, she heard her companions talking quietly beside her.

"I would have felt safer at the cabin," Adio said. "But we've already moved her much more than she should have been."

"She's so amazing," Abiba said admiringly. "She's still able to think straight when she must be in so much pain."

"She always has been, though sometimes she doesn't believe it. She's more powerful than even Nehanda probably realizes, even without her magic. But with it? She'll be unstoppable."

"Is there a way for us to help her? I mean, I couldn't imagine being as powerful as she is and not believing in yourself."

"The words people say are powerful, too," Adio reflected. "Nehanda was the one who trained her, and she was always prone to use words that were more hurtful. It started getting better as Adanya was elevated and began to be surrounded by people who only gave her encouragement. But negative words are hard to overcome."

Adanya had to struggle to keep from showing her surprise at his words. Though she had started to realize something about the way Nehanda used to speak to her was wrong, hearing it stated so directly made everything fall into place. Her difficulty believing in herself was grounded in the words spoken to her during a vulnerable time of her life, when she was learning and growing. It made sense that she was having such a hard time pushing past the self-doubt and asserting herself to be all she could be.

Knowing it was one thing, but how was she supposed to overcome it?

She woke up at the sound of approaching hooves, not re-alizing she'd fallen asleep. The sun peeked above the horizon, bathing the land in golds and oranges, and the fire had died down to embers.

Abiba was already awake on watch; Adio, sleeping beside Adanya, was also just waking.

"Help me sit up," Adanya ordered. "It's Sefu."

They did so, propping her up. Adio fashioned her a sling from her cloak and carefully placed her arm in it.

Sefu rode up with two horses behind him, one carrying a gagged and bound man. The soldier on the other horse dis-mounted and helped Sefu pull the man down from his saddle. None too gently, they seated him before Adanya and her com-panions.

Give me a minute, she thought, projecting her thoughts to her three allies.

She studied the steward, a rather plump man dressed in rich clothes (though they were now covered in a layer of dried mud from the flooding of the palace) with a well-kept beard and a balding head. His eyes were wide with fright, darting from one face to another as he tried to determine who was in charge. Digging deeper, she saw he was not a particularly clever man, and prone to cruelty due to his power. Just the sort of person that Nehanda could keep control over; he had no ambitions beyond being rich and comfortable, and she easily supplied him with that.

Sefu, ask him the questions I tell you.

Sefu took the gag from the man's mouth and stood beside Adanya, one hand resting threateningly on his sword hilt. "What is your name, steward?"

"K-Kofi, my lord," the man stammered.

"How is it that you became the steward?"

"My family has been stewards for two generations. The Great Nehanda appointed us after she conquered the kingdom."

Adanya's and Adio's jaws tightened at both the reminder and the exalted title, but they managed to keep it as their only reaction.

"Did you send any message to Nehanda to tell her that the palace had been attacked?"

He shook his head vigorously. "By the time I realized what was happening, it was too late."

"And there was no one else in your court who would have known how to give the signal?"

"Oh no, she only entrusted it to me. Besides, she doesn't allow stewards to keep a court. She lays out how she wants things run, and we stewards do it. There isn't much decision making to be done."

Keeping things close in hand, Adanya thought and saw the others nod in agreement.

"What do you know about the other kingdoms and stewards?"

"Nothing more than I told you. The Great Nehanda only tells us what we need to know to run our respective countries."

"How often do you see her?"

"Maybe once every three months? She used to come only once a year, but her visits have increased this year."

"Have you noticed anything different about her?"

"Other than her visits? No."

Sefu gestured to the other soldier. "Take him out of earshot."

Adanya's face was pensive. "She must have sensed that I was waking."

"How?" Adio asked. "And if she knew that, why didn't she try to find you?"

"She may have Sage powers now, but that doesn't mean she would be able to break through my protection magic." Her mind was churning, piecing things together as she remembered something she'd seen in Nehanda's journal. "If she knew what a Sage Elemental could do, even if neither of us had become one yet, she'd know I was a danger to her plans. So putting me to sleep kept me out of the way."

"But why did things change? Why did you wake up if Rashidi wasn't there to connect with you and bring you out of it?" Abiba asked.

Her eyes flickered to Sefu as she realized, "Because I had a connection with someone else. You must have gotten close enough to my cabin to connect to my magic, even if you didn't know it."

His eyes grew wide for a split second before he resumed his calm demeanor, though Adanya could sense his amazement. "I had wandered farther into the woods than normal that day."

"And you found me."

They all were silent for a moment, contemplating what they'd just discovered.

Finally, Abiba ventured, "It's only a matter of time before she realizes that she doesn't have control in Ferandar anymore. And she's bound to know you had something to do with it."

Adanya frowned. "I wish I'd thought to mask my resting place to delay her discovery. I'm sure she'll visit sooner or later to see for herself. If she can find it without magic masking it, she'll know for certain I'm awake."

"That couldn't be helped," Adio said. "You didn't know what was going on."

She scowled but turned to Sefu. "What were our losses?"

"Less than fifty. Your strategy worked greatly in keeping the losses minimal. But we need to start planning for our next attack."

"He isn't much help." Adio gestured with his chin at the steward. "She did well to keep them in the dark about each other."

"We also need to find the rest of the council," Adanya pointed out. "Or their descendants. Our magic together was strong and effective, but it's going to take more than just the three of us to defeat her."

"You can't do much of anything until you've gotten some strength back," Adio cautioned. "Using your magic now to awaken your other skills could kill you."

She frowned again, knowing that he was right. "What should we do with the steward?"

"Send him back," Sefu suggested. "The people in town will keep him in check. From what I saw, none of them cared too much for him."

"Good. We'll regroup back at the cabin and start monitoring to determine our next target." She glanced up at Adio. "Can we at least get back there? I understand that I need to rest, but we're too exposed here."

Adio sighed. "Back to the cabin. But you're riding with me, and you're getting right into that bed when we arrive."

"Trust me, I'm not feeling like arguing right now."

Without further delay, everyone mounted and rode toward the cabin.

Chapter Twenty-Eight

A year after her election, Adanya stood scowling at her reflection in the mirror, running her hand over the scars that striped her shoulder. Rashidi came up behind her and kissed her shoulder, brushing her braids from her neck so that he could kiss it, too.

"What are you scowling at, beautiful?"

"This scar is so ugly. Look at it! I'm never showing my shoulders again."

"You don't exactly wear them out now," he chuckled.

She huffed and pulled away, readjusting her shirt to cover her scar. "I hate that I have this."

"Why? You got that scar helping to protect the country. That scar is something to be proud of."

"I'm not exactly a beautiful woman to begin with; I didn't need anything to make it worse."

"Who exactly are you trying to impress? Because you already have me."

She wasn't amused by his attempt at levity, glaring at him as she made her feelings known.

He came over and took her into his arms. "Now you listen to me, Head of Council. You are one of the most beautiful people I've met, inside and out. I don't know who put it into your head that you aren't, but they were dead wrong."

"You're just saying that because you love me," she muttered.

"No. Well, yes, but that's not the only reason. I'm saying that because it's true. You don't think there are men all over the kingdom who wish they could be with you?" He gently caressed her face. "When you're in your element, helping people and doing what makes you happy, your face is as bright as the sun. And I'm the lucky man who gets to call you mine."

Adanya's face softened, and she smiled ruefully. "Keep talking like that and I might start believing you."

"Good." He kissed her. "You need to start being nicer to yourself, anyways; you'll believe it even more if you keep saying it to yourself."

"If you say so."

"I do. And don't think I haven't noticed that you're only focusing on your looks because you're feeling insecure about something else."

Her mouth dropped open, wondering how he knew she was doubting her ability to be an effective Head of Council again.

"I told you, I don't need magic to know and understand my woman." He chuckled in response to her expression. "Now, we should be getting you to your outing." He helped her put on her robes, then smacked her ass playfully as he kissed her again. "I'll meet you out there."

Adanya smiled as she watched him go, enjoying the warmth of his love lingering behind. Talks like these were becoming far more common the longer they were together; Nehanda's seeming contempt for her was more and more obvious, making her insecurities worse. Rashidi, while he would never say anything against her mentor directly, was clearly unhappy at the way she treated Adanya and did what he could to bolster her ego.

Outside, Rashidi awaited her with Jabari. He had been appointed to the council after her, though he was nearly ten years older than her. His appointment came after the death of the previous Fauna, who had tried to use his powers to control the Ugwe.

Jabari was an intimidating man with a powerful frame punctuated by muscular arms, which he always wore bare save for leather cuffs on his wrists where various birds often landed.

His dreads fell to the middle of his back, though they were usually pulled back from his eyes with a length of leather. Today, a fierce-looking hawk was perched on his shoulder.

He bowed on his horse when he saw her. "Lady," he said respectfully, his deep voice seeming to rumble in his chest.

"Jabari," she replied with a nod, mounting her own horse. "Are we ready?"

"I'm following your lead."

Adanya nodded at Rashidi, and they and her escort galloped from the courtyard, taking the road to skirt the town and head to the northwest. She glanced up at the hawk, which flew above their heads as they rode, and marveled at how the wild creature seemed completely at ease with them without having been hobbled.

Jabari noticed her look and grinned at her. "I forgot that you haven't really had the chance to see my powers in action," he called.

"I haven't. Do all creatures behave like that around you?"

"Only the ones I speak to and take the time to build a relationship with," he replied. "Faunas are considered to have a 'lesser' magic, one that requires more intelligence to wield effectively. I can speak to animals in their own language, and when they respond, I can understand. I can also sense animals, even from a great distance."

"I imagine it gives you a chance to use some of their natural abilities."

"Absolutely." He made a screeching noise, and the hawk screeched back before shooting off into the distance. "My friend there can see for miles; he'll let me know if there's anything amiss."

"Are you expecting anything?"

"Always best to expect the unexpected. Especially considering where we're headed."

"Surely the danger is lower now that the Ugwe are gone."

"Lower, yes, but there are still plenty of other animals that can prove dangerous. Which is why we're heading to the forest now. These bear attacks are getting out of hand ... I'm starting to wonder if something is pushing them out of the forest."

"What could possibly do that?"

"Any number of things, really. Bears are more afraid of humans than we are of them; if humans are in their habitat, it might be scaring them into going into the towns instead of staying in the woods."

They rode for an hour more, slowing their pace as they reached the outskirts of a thick wood. The hawk returned, landing on Jabari's outstretched arm and having a whole conversation with him before resuming its perch on his shoulder.

"Nothing seems out of the ordinary, from what my friend sees," Jabari reported. "Still, things may be different in the woods themselves. Keep your eyes open, everyone, and follow my lead."

Everyone dismounted, leaving the horses to nose around in the grass. Jabari led the way into the woods, Adanya slightly behind him and Rashidi directing the company to protect her sides as he took up the rear.

As they moved further in, the breeze that had followed them on their ride ceased, leaving them feeling stifled and warm. A few birds sang overhead, sending the hawk's head turning this way and that from Jabari's shoulder. Insects droned loudly from the underbrush, and the sound of running water reached their ears from a distance as their feet crunched through the leaves.

After a short distance, Jabari held up a hand to halt, then bent down to the soft ground. "Looks like our friend has been here recently." He beckoned for Adanya to come closer, pointing out a bear's paw print. "Do you see how deep it is, here? This fellow was running from something."

"From something?" she echoed. "What could possibly be scaring a bear so badly in its own habitat?"

"A fair question. Especially considering how deep into the forest we are."

"Is it close?"

"Judging by the freshness of these tracks, I'd say so. Keep your eyes open, everyone. We want to avoid killing it, if we can." He resumed leading them through the woods, occasionally pointing out other tell-tale signs: broken twigs, claw marks, the occasional half-eaten bird.

Suddenly, he tensed, sending Rashidi to order the guard closer to Adanya.

"What is it?" she whispered.

Instead of answering, Jabari turned and dove at her, knocking her out of the way of the enormous black bear that came thundering toward them. The hawk cried out and flew upwards, perching in the branches of a tree as it continued screeching. Rashidi barked an order, and the guard came between them and the bear with their spears pointed forward.

Jabari leapt to his feet and pushed past them, holding up his hands non-threateningly. He growled and barked at the bear, trying to communicate with it as it turned back to the group. Adanya watched in awe as Rashidi helped her to her feet, thoroughly checking her over.

The bear seemed to have been running for ages; its jaw was covered in spittle, sides heaving, and black fur plastered to it with sweat. It reared onto its hind paws, swatting at the air with massive claws that threatened to rip them all to shreds. Though it was no Ugwe, Adanya could appreciate the immense power and ferocity the bear had.

Jabari continued his attempts, slowly inching toward it. The bear continued growling, though it rested all four paws on the ground and seemed to be trying to understand. Finally, it tilted its head like an oversized dog and sat down, its eyes still studying Jabari.

Adanya's eyes were wide as he went right up to the beast, gently stroking its head as he continued talking to it.

"It's alright, he won't hurt us," he called over his shoulder. "He knows that we're here to help."

No one else in the party seemed convinced, staying a good distance from the bear.

"Did he tell you what's wrong?" Adanya called back.

"Seems we've got a rogue sorcerer on our hands," he replied. "He's been practicing his fire magic on our friend here, pushing him around the woods. Killed his mate and their little ones."

Adanya frowned. "That would explain a lot. Can he tell us where he last saw this sorcerer?"

Jabari asked, then gave the bear a comforting pat before returning to the group. "By the water, he says. There's a cottage there."

The bear shuffled off in the opposite direction, as if it wanted nothing else to do with magic that day.

"Lead the way," she said resolutely, gripping her staff.

They fell into single file, all the more cautious now that they knew they were dealing with magic. Before long, they came upon a small cottage by a swift-flowing stream. Adanya was about to ask Jabari and Rashidi the best way to proceed when an older man came flying out of the door, flinging fire at them.

Everyone ducked out of the way, the flames dancing through the air before vanishing.

"Get out of here!" he cried. "This wood is mine!"

All fear forgotten in the moment of duty, Adanya stood erect and reached out to the man's mind with her own. He froze in place, hand outstretched as he struggled against her control.

"We don't want to hurt you," she said calmly, deciding her words would have more impact out loud in this situation. "Let us help."

His eyes blazed with fury. "There is no helping me!" he grated angrily. "All I want is to be left alone!"

"I'm afraid that's no longer a possibility. I know you think that you're just protecting yourself from the bear, but you went so far as to kill its family. Now it's venturing out of the woods and hurting the townsfolk." Her eyes swept over his ragged clothes and unkempt hair as she wondered just how long he'd been roughing it alone in the woods.

"It serves them right! They never understood me, they only feared me! Now they have a taste of what it feels like to be afraid."

"Non-magical folk respond to sorcerers differently. The only way we can all live in peace is if we show them the best of us."

"They don't deserve it! All my life, they've treated me like I was a disease and wanted nothing to do with me! Well, I'll show them."

Adanya's face twitched, feeling the force of his hatred pushing against her power. "Please. Let me bring you to the capital. We're working to protect sorcerers, to find ways their powers can be used to help others in a way that is fulfilling to them."

"I want none of your charity! You're just another one of those sorcerers who let them put a leash on you instead of being free. Well, I won't be leashed. I want revenge!" With a sudden effort, he wrenched himself from her control, sending her physically staggering back a pace or two.

Before he could raise his hand to send fire toward her, Jabari screeched. The hawk came out of nowhere, darting around the man's head and pecking at him. He flailed widely, yelling as he tried to focus enough to send his fire. Adanya tried to concentrate again, this time trying to extend the paralysis to put the man to sleep. But the screeching, flapping, and yelling drew her focus too much; beyond that, his immense hatred was still fighting her.

He managed to bat the hawk away long enough to stretch his hand out toward Adanya again.

She gasped in horror as a dagger seemed to suddenly grow from his chest, sending him back a few steps. Blood blossomed through his shirt. He gurgled painfully, shock on his face as he looked down at the dagger, then back up at where Rashidi stood. The fire died away from his eyes, and he collapsed to the ground.

Rashidi gently put his arm around her shoulders, turning her away from the grizzly sight. "There wasn't anything for it. He wasn't going to come with us, not without causing serious injuries."

"Your captain is right," Jabari agreed as the hawk landed back on his shoulder. He stroked its breast feathers. "When we can't catch them early enough, the ways of the world can sour a sorcerer. You did all that you could."

"Somehow I don't feel all that convinced," she said quietly.

Rashidi squeezed her shoulder, then turned to the rest of her guard, giving orders to bury the man and bring word to the townspeople that the threat was gone.

Jabari came over to her. "I know it's unpleasant when you want to help someone but can't. But part of being a leader is realizing that you can't save everyone."

"I just ... I've never seen it happen in front of me like this. I've never felt such hatred, from anyone. Even though I was there to help, he wanted nothing to do with it."

"Emotion is powerful. Sometimes it's good, like with love." He nodded in Rashidi's direction, causing Adanya to blush. "And sometimes it's hatred. That hatred can poison and overwhelm a person until they are unable to listen to reason. We all have that instinct to protect ourselves, my lady. But when emotion gets in the way, that protection tends to come with no regard to what it may do to others."

"You speak wisely, Jabari," she said quietly, though his words brought little comfort.

He patted her shoulder, then moved to take the lead to guide them back out of the woods.

Rashidi saw her distress and took her hand, squeezing it reassuringly. His touch calmed her somewhat, but she could not help but think about another Ember in her life, and how similar the rogue sorcerer's words were to hers.

Chapter Twenty-Nine

After two days of forced rest with periodic updates from Sefu—which revealed that nothing much was happening—Adanya was going stir-crazy. She'd flipped through Nehanda's journal several times without finding anything new or useful; most of it seemed to be written in some code that she couldn't figure out.

"We're using time that we don't have," Adanya said with a sigh.

"But if you're not healed fully..." Adio protested.

"Adio. You know I'm right. I'll be careful, but we've got to find the rest of the sorcerers."

He heaved a sigh, realizing that fighting wouldn't get him anywhere. "Fine."

She looked at her council, sitting around the map table. "I think we need to find Jabari next."

"Why him?" Abiba asked.

"He knew Nehanda longer than anyone on the council, even me. Perhaps he'll be able to give us some insight."

"If he's still alive," Sefu pointed out.

Adanya closed her eyes for a moment, feeling the slightest tug on her magic she recognized as Jabari. "I don't know how to explain it, but I feel that he is."

"So we need to find an animal for you to talk to?" Adio asked.

"I suppose so. Though ... he was always very close to birds. Maybe that's where I need to start."

"Waed," Sefu said, beckoning his friend over. "We'll need to keep on high alert. Any whisper of where Nehanda is, or what her plans may be moving forward, I want to know about immediately. We're going back out."

Waed nodded his understanding. "Be careful."

Adio fussily adjusted Adanya's shoulder sling and bandages, trying not to scowl. "You still stress me out, little girl."

"I think you're doing a bit much."

Abiba picked up Adanya's staff as she reached for it. "I'll carry that."

"I'm not an invalid!" Adanya protested.

"Of course not," Abiba said cheerfully. "And we're going to make sure you don't become one."

Now Adanya scowled. "Fine. Let's go."

They left the cabin and traveled into the woods, following Adanya's lead. They walked for a while until they were fairly deep into the woods. A hawk's cry drew her attention, and she stopped, looking upwards.

"Just talk to it," she murmured.

She concentrated on the hawk, trying to communicate with it rather than simply sensing its energy and intentions as she would have before. She felt something in her magic shift, and she opened her mouth to speak.

"Hello, friend," she said.

The hawk soared into sight, perching on a tree branch a short distance away from the small party. "You're the Sleeping One," it said to her.

"Yes," she replied.

"It's good that you're awake. The land needs you."

"I'll do what I can to save it."

The hawk dipped its head to her, then flew off again.

Adanya turned to her companions to see them all standing slack-jawed, staring at her. She realized she must have been screeching back and forth with the hawk, not speaking plainly as it seemed to her.

"I guess it worked."

Her eyes grew wide as a vision of Jabari pushed into her sight, standing with his back to her at the entrance to a cave and looking out into the sunrise. A lynx stood beside him, tail curling around his legs. He suddenly turned, looking straight at her.

"I'm glad to see you," he said with a smile.

"Where are you?"

He turned and called in his booming voice, "Come!" He held up his arm, and a stunning hawk flew to him, landing on his wrist. "Bring Adanya to me," he commanded. The tawny feathered bird zoomed away.

"My friend will find you and lead the way," he said. "Be careful."

Sefu was ready this time, supporting her as she came out of her vision.

"He's sending a hawk," she said after reorienting herself. "We should wait here."

They all sat down in the shadows of the trees, Adio softly fussing over her shoulder. "I really wish you would have taken more time to let this heal."

She flexed it experimentally, wincing at the dull pain that didn't yet seem ready to go away. "You and I both know we don't have the time. I'll be fine."

He adjusted her sling. "I know, I know. But I worry about you, little girl."

She smiled. "I know."

They glanced over to where Sefu and Abiba were talking to each other, comparing the stories they had been told all their lives.

"It's still a bit jarring," she murmured. "All of the things that we've done, our experiences and accomplishments, are legends to them and everyone else. But to me, it's just a week ago."

"Definitely disconcerting," he agreed. "It wasn't as strong for me, since I spent most of my time alone. But being among other people, especially people who need our magic to win, has put things pretty sharply into contrast."

She hesitated before voicing her next thought. "How long do you think she was planning this?"

"Nehanda? It's hard to tell, exactly. I feel like I began to see changes in her after your election. But I have a feeling that she'd started to change long before then."

Adanya sighed, remembering Nehanda's outburst at the council meeting and her subsequent harsher treatment. "I think you're right. Even before I was elected, I knew that I was starting to see her change. Reading her journal makes it a little clearer. But I was so blinded by the way she used to treat me that I missed signs that were obvious to others. Rashidi saw through her in an instant and was always trying to tell me without openly speaking against her. I didn't appreciate the tact he used so well back then ... I'd give anything to have it back now."

He squeezed her hand comfortingly. "I know."

They fell into silence as they waited, looking upward to see if they could catch a glimpse of the hawk.

After some time, the hawk she'd seen with Jabari soared into sight, circling their heads as it waited for them to get to their feet. Once it saw them up, it began flying low through the trees, slow enough for them to make their way through the underbrush. An hour of travel found them coming to the edge of the woods; across a clearing, they could see a large hill with a cave opening sloping down into it.

The hawk screeched—*she's here,* Adanya understood—and Jabari appeared at the entrance to the cave.

"Well," he said with a smile, "aren't you a sight for sore eyes?"

Adanya smiled back, feeling his happiness radiation toward her. "I could say the same!"

He carefully hugged her, commenting, "What's this? A war wound? Things have certainly changed."

"More like me being careless," she chuckled.

Adio came over and the men shared a back-thumping hug before Adio introduced the rest of the party.

"The resemblance is uncanny," he remarked as he shook Sefu's hand. "Come on in."

He led them inside the cave, tree roots weaving in and out of the smooth, packed earth walls. In some places, the roots were exposed enough to serve as seats. In others, simple handmade furniture made the space quite cozy. A fire pit sat in the center, which he stoked back up as they all settled around it. "I haven't heard a human voice in some time now," he said. "It's just been me and the animals. I figured it was safer that way."

Adio nodded. "Interacting with people brings its share of risk."

"I knew you wouldn't be able to stay completely away, extrovert that you are. Still, I'm glad you stuck around."

"Had to; couldn't leave Adanya completely on her own."

"I felt the same." He turned to Sefu. "I've been talking to the animals; I know about your latest offensive. Well done."

Sefu nodded respectfully.

"I've asked them, especially the birds, to keep an eye out for any signs that Nehanda may be moving. They'll be less noticeable than your spies will."

"How long have you known what's going on?" Abiba asked.

"I've only started poking around in the last week or so. I wasn't sure that Adanya was awake, but something told me it was time to get things moving."

"Jabari," Adanya ventured, "you knew Nehanda long before any of us. Do you think you might have any insight that would help us to understand her present course better?"

He considered for a moment and then sighed. "Maybe. But I don't know that it will be anything more than you've probably figured out on your own."

"Anything would help."

He paused, stroking his chin. "I knew her while we were training under Ziyad. He was the first one to show either of us any care; though my upbringing was nothing like yours or hers, there was still a lot of distrust for non-magical folk who weren't my family. Ziyad helped me push past all of that, and I began to enjoy learning from and spending time with others. But Nehanda? She never quite lost that mistrust. Learned to hide it, I suppose, though you know her temper would slip occasionally. I never did quite understand why Ziyad passed the duty of finding and training young sorcerers on to her. Although ... I did see a change in her once she found you."

"A change?"

"She'd never been a patient woman, but I could see her putting forth the effort to be patient with you."

"What was so different about me?"

"You were like her in a lot of ways," Adio said wisely. "Orphaned, kicked out of the orphanage because of your magic, forced to survive on your own in the woods; she saw your similarities."

"Maybe that's why Ziyad asked her to train me personally. He probably thought that our similar backgrounds would help us to connect." She sighed. "And it did work, for a while."

"She was proud of you, in her own way," Jabari said. "I remember coming to visit her a couple of years before you were appointed to the council. You were all that she could talk about; she'd always taken her training duties seriously, but she was especially proud of you. I think that she could tell early on how powerful you were, even though she wasn't sure of the extent of your powers. She knew you were destined for greatness."

Adanya contemplated his words. "I think you're right. I didn't realize it at the time, but she would push me so hard. And I was the only one who she gave private training. I thought it was because I was the only Sage in training, but it must have been more than that." She looked up at Adio and Jabari. "But what could have made her change so drastically from wanting to protect sorcerers to wanting to control the world?"

"As terrible as it sounds ... I think it was your election," Jabari said gravely. "Everyone knew she wanted to be Head of Council so she could be a bit more aggressive in protecting sorcerers. But Ziyad knew she was just too emotional to make objective decisions on those matters, and she would do more good if she focused on finding and training sorcerers."

"Before you were named to the council, she was always suggesting more proactive measures concerning protecting sorcerers," Adio added. "Ziyad always shot her down; he'd tell her that our place was not to force people to accept sorcerers but to teach them to live in harmony with us. She was never quite on board with that."

"I knew she was disappointed when I was elected instead of her," Adanya said. "The whole way that she treated me changed—slowly at first, but it started becoming more obvious to me, and Rashidi. I never dreamed in a million years that she would have gone so far as to sacrifice everyone in the kingdom."

"It's not really that far-fetched if you knew how truly damaged she'd been by her experiences. I don't think we knew how powerful she was, either," Jabari said.

"And once she knew that you would stand in her way, she had to get rid of you," Adio said. "So she concocted the scheme to put you to sleep."

"But why just put me to sleep? Why not kill me? She had to know that I'd wake up, sooner or later."

"Maybe she knew that she wasn't strong enough to kill you, even if you didn't know the full extent of your powers," Abiba piped up from where she and Sefu had been listening attentively. "From what I understand, she didn't have all of the powers that she does now when you went to sleep. Tricking you like she did would get you out of her way."

"If she thought that the only person who could wake you was dead, she wouldn't have worried about you anymore. She couldn't have known that I would accidentally find you and wake you," Sefu concluded.

"It makes sense." Adanya sighed. "If I could go back and let her be Head of Council to avoid all of this, I would."

"Not too sure we wouldn't have still ended up in similar circumstances." Jabari shrugged.

Everyone was silent for a while.

Finally, Adanya straightened her back resolutely. "Well, I think that we know what needs to be done now. We've got to find Kamaria and Gabir, or their descendants. By that point, I should have accessed all of my powers, and we can think about a more direct attack on Nehanda."

"Agreed," Jabari said as Adio nodded.

They all looked up as the lynx bounded into the cave, coming straight to Jabari and communicating in a series of growls and snarls, which Adanya could understand. *Someone is coming.*

"Could someone have tracked us?" she asked, paling.

"Not sure, but it's not safe for you here." Jabari helped her to her feet as the others rose. "Out into the woods; that way we're not trapped in here. I'll cover the rear."

Adanya stopped short as she realized what he was doing, sensing his determination and courage. "No," she said firmly. "No sacrifices. You're coming with us."

"The important thing is that you're safe," he replied just as firmly. "Now go!"

She hesitated, her voice dropping to a whisper. "I can't lose anyone else."

He squeezed her good arm as he guided her out of the cave. "Don't you worry about it. Now hide, and shield the others."

Reluctantly, Adanya went with the others into the underbrush while Jabari stood at the entrance to the cave. She extended her powers to shield their presence from whomever was coming, and they waited.

A sudden gust of wind kicked up, and the dirt in front of the cave began to swirl and dance. A small dust devil swirled up, growing steadily larger until it was the size of a man. Then it disappeared almost as quickly as it had come and a tall, stately figure was left standing with their back to Adanya and the others.

Adanya had to struggle to keep her composure as she recognized the figure, even from behind. There was no mistaking that bone-straight posture, that close-cropped black hair, and the black robes that flowed to the ground. She shuddered as she heard the voice, the same as it had been the last time she'd heard it.

"Well, Jabari, you were a difficult one to find," Nehanda said.

"That was the idea," he replied calmly, leaning against the cave wall. "Couldn't make it easy for you."

"Why did you decide to linger? Surely you knew I'd find you sooner or later."

"Turns out, it was later. How did you find me?"

She tossed something onto the ground from beneath her robes; though Adanya couldn't see what it was, she felt Jabari's distress and realized it had to be his hawk. "You've got to be more careful dealing with wild animals. They can be a little careless."

Jabari stooped to pick up the broken bundle of feathers, his normally stoic face heavy with emotion. "Why, Nehanda? Why are you so hell-bent on destroying everything around you?"

"Oh, don't act like you don't know," she scoffed. "With the world under my control and sorcerers protected, we don't have to live to appease the people anymore!"

"Protected? Then why didn't you protect the sorcerers who were being trained when the kingdom was slain? I could see you wanting to get rid of the council, but those were innocent children who had nothing to do with it!"

"Don't you see? They'd already been indoctrinated by the council. I needed people around me that were like-minded, and everyone had been corrupted. So I started over, finding my own sorcerers to make my own council. But it wasn't enough. I had to take matters into my own hands."

Jabari shook his head sadly. "It seems that the Nehanda I loved is gone."

Despite her focus on keeping them hidden, Adanya couldn't help but be surprised at his words. Nehanda also seemed to be affected, her back stiffening. She fell silent for a heartbeat. The moment passed, however, and Adanya sensed intense hatred.

"Love is weakness. It can make you blind to the threats around you. Why else do you think I encouraged Adanya to get on with that guard?"

"I guess it backfired, because Rashidi always saw right through you."

"She was distracted enough not to know what I was doing behind the scenes. But now, old friend, it's time for you to help me."

The wind returned, suddenly and forcefully, as Nehanda turned to fully face Jabari.

"You're not getting any help from me," he said, raising his voice to be heard above the wind.

"I wasn't asking."

The wind blew harder, whipping leaves from the trees and creating a small whirlwind. It slammed Jabari against the cave wall, unable to resist. The four hidden in the woods could only watch in horror as his skin began to glow, his face contorted with pain. Adanya realized what was happening, and it took everything within her to keep her focus as Jabari's magic was sucked from his body, floating through the air in a glowing green ribbon. It surrounded Nehanda, settling onto her. Jabari's body quivered as the last of his magic was drained, the glow leaving his eyes last. Then Nehanda dropped her hand. The wind stopped immediately. Jabari seemed frozen as Nehanda walked over to him, leaned forward, and blew gently. Immediately, his whole body crumbled into dust, scattering onto the ground as if he'd never been.

Nehanda exhaled loudly, then turned around. Adanya shook with rage and grief, fighting against the pain Jabari had shared with her in his last moments and the urge to leap out and challenge her. The sight of Nehanda's face, now stamped with an open cruelty, almost made her see stars.

Nehanda stared in their direction for a moment, almost as if she could see them. They all held their breath. Then she turned away. The whirlwind reappeared, and she stepped in and vanished.

Adio rose quietly. "Sefu, Abiba, give us some time. We'll join you when she's ready. I'll keep an eye on her."

They could see her distress and didn't argue. Rising, they retreated farther into the woods.

Adanya couldn't move. She couldn't think, tears streaming down her face as a jumble of emotions fought for control inside of her. Adio gingerly came closer, putting out a hand to touch her shoulder. "Adanya..."

When his hand touched her, he was thrown back by a surge of power bursting from Adanya as her head whipped around to him. All of her emotions exploded at him, shooting through his head like a thousand shouting voices, incoherent in their madness. She herself was silent, staring at him as he grabbed his head, writhing on the ground. In that moment, she didn't even know who he was—much less herself.

"Adanya!" Adio grated through the pain. "Come back! It's me!"

Something about his voice cut through the turmoil in her mind, and she blinked, immediately silencing the voices and releasing Adio. She watched him in horror as he staggered to his feet.

Though his concern was immediately for her, she scrambled backwards, wincing at the pain in her shoulder as she tried to avoid his touch.

"No, stay away from me!" She sobbed. "Don't you see? Everyone close to me gets hurt! Jabari is dead because of me, and I just watched! I have no idea what I just did to you; I could have killed you!"

"There's a lot to process, little girl. I understand."

"I'm the reason that all of this happened! If she hadn't been jealous of me, if she had been elected Head of Council, none of this would have happened! We'd be back in our own time, everyone would be alive, things would be different!"

"We can't know that. Besides, not everything that happened was bad. Being Head of Council allowed you to meet Rashidi."

"And he's gone too!" she screamed. "Married to another woman with the family I should have had with him!"

Adio had been slowly approaching her, and now he was close enough to wrap her in his arms without hesitation, as if what had just happened were a distant memory. She struggled against him for the briefest of moments before sobbing brokenly into his shoulder, words lost as emotions continued to flood through her. He stroked her hair gently, shushing her. "It's going to be alright, little girl. Give it some time."

It took nearly ten minutes for her crying to subside. She fell into an almost catatonic silence, her face blank as Adio dried her face with his sleeve and pulled her to her feet.

"Come on. Let's get back to the cabin where it's safe, then you can have some time to think."

She didn't respond, allowing him to take her hand and guide her back through the woods where the others were waiting.

Chapter Thirty

Adanya sat under the awning at the edge of the Arena, watching with interest as Kamaria and Jabari worked with their trainees. Over a year after her ascension, she'd more firmly settled into her role of Head of Council and had more time to spend on other projects, such as finding and training young sorcerers. Nehanda was still in charge of the efforts—Adanya felt it wasn't right to take the role from her, especially after not being elected—but Adanya tried to make it a point to be visible, as Ziyad had before her.

As she watched, she could not help but compare what she was seeing to her own experiences with Nehanda. Both Kamaria and Jabari were far kinder to their students, pushing for growth yet offering encouragement and kindness as they worked. Rashidi's voice was in the back of her mind, reminding her of the space that she had been putting between her and Nehanda.

Though it troubled her somewhat, she also realized the separation had been good for her. She no longer felt like she was being treated like a child, and the support from the rest of the council had helped her come into her own as their leader. Still, her interactions with Nehanda were terse at best, and Nehanda was starting to actively avoid her.

"What have I told you about showing your emotions on your face?"

Adanya smirked as she heard Adio's voice behind her. He sat beside her, watching the training. "Keeping your emotions out of other people's heads is one thing, but you're still giving away the game looking all gloomy."

"I was just thinking," she sighed.

They ducked as a tongue of flame shot past them, struggling not to laugh at the horror on the young trainee's face.

"I'm so sorry, Lady Adanya!" she said. "I don't know what happened!"

"It's fine," Adanya said comfortingly. "No harm done. I know that learning your powers can be difficult."

"Besides, singed edges are fashionable these days, so I'm told," Kamaria said, chuckling as she patted the trainee's shoulder. "You could have just told the Head of Council that she needs to upgrade her wardrobe."

The council members all laughed as Kamaria led the young woman away, gently giving instructions as she went.

"Is that jealousy I see?" Adio asked, seeing the look cross Adanya's face.

"My training was nothing like that. Sure, she taught me a lot, and there were times she showed a little vulnerability, but it was never so open."

He nodded. "I think that her upbringing makes it difficult for her to really warm up to anyone or to make connections. Even if she does think you're exceptional."

"I doubt she thinks that anymore," she snorted.

"Hm. I have noticed the frostiness."

"I'd be worried about you if you didn't."

"She'll come around. You know how much she wanted to be Head."

"Hm." Adanya very much doubted that, but she kept her thoughts to herself. She rose, adjusting her robes. "I'm off to the council room. Some of the trainees are studying history, and I promised them I'd stop by."

He chuckled. "This is the most people that room has ever seen go through it."

"Nice to have some life in there."

She left the Arena, choosing to walk though a side gate and up a tree-covered path outside the palace walls rather than walking through the hallways. It was a lovely spring day, with the trees blossoming and birds chirping merrily overhead. A slight breeze stirred the leaves, toying with her braids and robes.

She paused to take a deep breath of the fragrant air. A smile crossed her face as she sensed Rashidi's presence a few seconds before she heard his voice.

"Mm. You should stand in the breeze more often. I can honestly say it's one of my favorite views."

"Did you sense me outside of the palace walls without you?" she said with a smirk, turning to look at him.

"I just know your fondness for the outdoors and had a feeling that you'd come through this way." He wrapped his arms around her and kissed her tenderly. "How's my beautiful lady today?"

"A little distracted," she admitted.

They laced their fingers together and continued walking side by side. "What's got you distracted?" he asked.

"Reflecting on the past. Thinking about how different my training was from what the young people have now."

"Hm." He hummed, encouraging her to continue.

"Sometimes I wonder if my training had been different, how things would have gone. How my relationship with Nehanda would be now."

"There's no guarantee that it would have made any difference. A person's history truly shapes who they are and how they treat other people in turn."

Adanya thought about her own history. "That's true."

"I don't doubt that she cared about you, at some point, in her own way. But she clearly cares more about herself now. And I need you to do the same. Don't let her have such an affect on you."

"Kind of difficult when we still work together."

"You know what I meant."

"I know."

"And you know that you haven't felt as much pressure or stress since you've been pulling away from her. Everyone who cares about you can see it." They stopped in front of the gate to the garden, and he gently pressed a kiss to her forehead. "Sometimes you just need to do what's best for you." He stroked her cheek, then returned the way that they had come.

Adanya watched until he disappeared around a bend in the path, smiling wistfully. He was right—he generally was—about her separation. And how much better she felt. Still, she sometimes wondered if pulling away from Nehanda would have consequences no one could foresee.

After a moment, she turned and pushed open the gate to the garden.

As was customary for that hour, King Keon was in the garden. Today he was not alone; the little prince toddled alongside his father, watching in wonder as he watered and pruned, all the while narrating what he was doing.

Adanya bowed as he came into view, smiling. "Am I interrupting a lesson?" she asked.

"Not at all. I was just finishing up for the day." He dusted off his hands and picked up the boy. "His mother loved the garden; I want this to be a place he associates with her memory."

"I think that's beautiful, Your Majesty."

"How are things going with you?" he asked as they walked inside together. "I hear that the training has been going well."

"It certainly has. We've found more young sorcerers in the past three months than we have for years. I'll admit I'm enjoying seeing all of the young faces. And we've shifted our focus from just training them to use their magic to really educating them on history, science, and other things they'll need to be successful in life. Not everyone will end up on the council, but they can still bring some good to their communities."

The king smiled proudly, and Adanya could not help but smile at the fatherly warmth radiating from him. "I'm glad to hear it. I knew you'd grow into your own once you had some time. Where are you heading now?"

"The council chambers to check in with some of the trainees studying history there"

"Well, don't let me keep you." He leaned over and kissed her cheek, as he always did; Adanya was delightedly surprised when Kayode sloppily kissed her chin before his father pulled back.

She kissed the little boy's head before bowing and heading to the council chambers.

There she found three trainees, all in their teens, poring over old tomes that had been spread across the table. They rose respectfully as she entered.

"Please, don't let me stop you." She walked over to her chair and sat down, resting her staff against the bookshelf behind her. "Finding anything interesting?"

"It looks like Ziyad was annotating a lot of records," one of the two girls said. "We've been tracking his handwriting in the records."

"Really?" Adanya said in surprise. "What kind of records?"

"They're from much earlier in our history, closer to when the kingdom was first founded," the young man said. He found a specific book on the table and laid it open in front of her, pointing out Ziyad's familiar precise handwriting in the margins. "This was the first note that we found. This section details the powers of the different sorcerers that had been discovered."

Adanya examined the note. *Six powers mentioned here; however, it seems like another power was redacted from these records.*

"Another power?" she echoed aloud.

The young man pointed at the section in question. "But he's right; it looks like someone had started to write something else but erased it and wrote over it with the next section."

"So we decided to do some digging," the other girl said, "looking through other early records to see if we could find more of his notes. And we did! So many!"

Adanya listened with furrowed brows as the trainees continued to explain what they'd found: hints and riddles scattered throughout different historical accounts, as well as reports taken from people throughout the kingdom.

"So, if I fully understand what you and Ziyad found … there's another power?"

"Yes, ma'am; a sorcerer who possessed all of the powers, as well as increased mental powers, called a Sage Elemental. But this is someone who would only be born very rarely."

"That would be something, wouldn't it? But it seems like he didn't find any definitive proof. It may just be a legend."

"It could be, ma'am, but if it's true, that means there could be someone out there right now who has all the powers and doesn't know what to do with them."

Adanya was silent, contemplating the discovery. If Ziyad had been researching, there was no doubt he believed there was some merit to the rumors. However, there wasn't a good way to search for such a sorcerer, if they truly existed. She looked up at the young recruits, who were watching her with excited anticipation.

"Was there anything else you found?"

"Yes," the young man piped up. "There are also several mentions of a sorcerer being able to take the powers from others to bolster their own strength."

"That one doesn't seem quite as likely, though," one of the girls said.

"Did Ziyad have notes on those as well?"

"A few, but there weren't as many records on that to begin with."

Adanya paused, trying to process all of this new information. "We don't quite know how much he was able to find," she said carefully. "But if you're up for it, I'd love for you to keep looking."

Their faces lit up, and they thanked her in overlapping sentences.

She smiled at them. "I'll expect a report when you think that you've found anything more." Rising, she left them to their task. Her face was pensive as she left, her thoughts puzzled. Why had Ziyad been searching for this? What could it all mean?

Chapter Thirty-One

Hours after returning to the cabin, Adanya still sat in a catatonic state, completely dissociated from everything around her. Unlike her usual dissociation, she could hear everything being discussed around her, almost as if being filtered through water before reaching her ears. Sefu and Waed spoke in low tones over the map table, while Abiba and Adio sat at the dinner table, watching her.

"We need to do something," Abiba said, her forehead creased with worry. "Now that we really know how powerful Nehanda is, we've got to move faster. Have you ever seen anything like it?"

Adio shook his head. "I'd heard rumors that a sorcerer could take another's powers, but it was just that, rumors. Superstitions from the time when non-magical folk didn't know much about us or how to deal with us. There was never any real proof to show for it."

"That's got to be how she had enough power to take over all of the kingdoms on her own."

"Not completely on her own. And not just by magic. The King of Harrun didn't much care for magic; she would have had to charm him some other way. I'm sure the promise of spoils was enough to entice him. Then, when she didn't have need of him to control his forces, she got rid of him. Now she rules with fear, much as he did."

Abiba lowered her voice. "If she's really that powerful ... how are we supposed to defeat her?"

Adio nodded toward Adanya's motionless figure. "Adanya's the only one who can. Perhaps her powers are stronger now because they come naturally, not stolen."

"If she ever comes out of it."

"You have to understand about her, she's always had such a heart for others. If she thinks her actions caused harm, especially to those she cares about, it takes a toll on her. I've never seen it hit her this hard, but she'll come out of it. We can start thinking ahead about our next steps, though."

"Who's left on the council to find?"

"Kamaria and Gabir. Ember and Flora. Though, considering that they had children of their own, they might not have decided to stay."

"There were two Embers on the council?" Abiba asked in surprise.

"Generally there were two of at least one type of magic on the council. The Head of Council tended to have the same powers as someone else on the council, like Adanya and Ziyad. It happened through the years that we'd occasionally have two who weren't Head together, like Nehanda and Kamaria. Though, now that I think about it, the Embers never did quite get along."

Sefu joined them, spooning himself a bowl of soup from the pot that sat at the center of the table. "Good news and bad. We know where Nehanda is now. She was spotted at the Southern Kingdom's palace a few hours ago."

"That must have been where she went after she left the caves," Adio mused.

"What's the bad news?" Abiba asked.

"The guard on the other kingdoms has been tripled. We don't have the numbers to take any of them."

"Without numbers, we'll have to rely on magic," Abiba said with a frown. "Even with all of the council reassembled, will we be able to defeat her?"

"Adanya will," Adio said confidently. "She'll find a way."

As if summoned, the fog over her consciousness broke. Adanya suddenly took a deep breath and sighed loudly, her body slumping slightly. The others came over to her, concerned looks on their faces, as she tried to catch her bearings amid the intense feelings of worry radiating off them.

"Probably not the best question right now, but how are you feeling?" Adio asked gently.

She considered as she came out of the haze of her dissociation. "Not as despairing as before," she answered, her voice husky after hours of disuse. She reached out for Adio with her good hand, and he took it and squeezed. "Thank you for taking charge, my friend. Who knows what I might have done if you weren't there."

"You know I'm always here for you."

Abiba brought her a cup of water, which she sipped gratefully.

"Adio, what I did to you when I was angry ... have you ever seen anything like it before?"

He shook his head. "You projected voices into my head once before, when you were feeling conflicted. Nowhere near as strong as what happened today. But it falls in line with your Sage abilities. It's like you'd somehow taken the spirits of everyone we've lost and used their energy against me. I could actually hear voices screaming in my head."

She took another deep breath as she continued to regain control of her mind—it had never taken this long to reorient after dissociating, something that worried her slightly. "I think that's what I did. I couldn't explain to you how I did it, but I could feel their energy as I once could when they were all alive. Do you remember when the towns were falling, before I went to sleep? I could feel when the people's lives were ripped away from them. Maybe I took all of them in, somehow."

"That would explain a lot."

"Regardless, we've got a lot of work to do."

"We need to figure out our next move," Sefu agreed.

"There's a strong possibility that any sorcerers born since Nehanda's rule are either working with her or she's taken their powers," Adio warned.

"We need to find Jabari's descendants," she said distantly. She looked up at the council. "And ... I think it's time I call them to me."

"Using your powers to call them?" Sefu said, confused. "But won't Nehanda be able to find you if you use your powers like that?"

She was feeling stronger now that her mind felt back in place, buoyed by her decision. "We have to weigh our options. She already knows I'm awake. If she hadn't sensed it herself, she will know from what she drew from Jabari. We're running out of time. And I'm sure Jabari may have inadvertently shown her where his family is in his last moments. They're in danger now." She shook her head. "There just isn't time to find them and Gabir's descendants and Kamaria. I'm certain Nehanda is going to be making moves sooner rather than later."

Adio tilted his head. "How do you know that Gabir isn't with us?"

Adanya winced as the echo of Jabari's screaming voice in her head returned. "Jabari told me."

They all fell silent.

"Sefu, can your men find a place where I can call the sorcerers to? Somewhere that won't reveal our headquarters here if anything goes wrong."

"I'll put them right on it," he said, rising.

"Abiba, how are your fighting skills with weapons?"

"I could stand a bit more practice."

"I agree. It's always good to have a backup. Magic clearly doesn't care about arrows." She managed a wry smile as she gestured to her shoulder.

"I can train with her," Waed volunteered.

"Thank you."

As they went off together, Adanya sighed again as a familiar throb moved through her. "I'm sure my shoulder needs redressing, my friend."

"I'm glad I'm not going to have to fight with you about it," Adio said with a smile. He left, returning with fresh bandages and salves a few moments later.

"Adio..." she said as he worked, staring into the fire. "Can you ever forgive me?"

"Forgive you for what?"

"What happened in the forest. I could have seriously hurt you without even knowing it."

"But you didn't, and that's what matters. And now that you know you have those powers, you can use them."

"I don't know if I want to," she said, her voice dropping to a whisper.

He looked up from his work, turning her face so that she would look at him. "You're going to have to do a lot of things that you don't want to before this is all said and done, little girl. The best thing to do is to remember the end goal. I'm confident that you're not going to make any decisions without a lot of thought; that's really all you can do."

She managed a smile, though she was only a little comforted by his words. She turned back to the fire, losing herself in thought as she watched the flames lick hungrily at the wood.

She was exhausted, the onslaught of emotions affecting not just her mind but her heart and body. She had to take advantage of the time that she had to rest ... but that didn't mean her mind would stop.

She was very afraid, but she managed to hide it from Adio. Not afraid of Nehanda, even though there was plenty of reason to be after seeing what she was capable of. No. She was afraid of herself. Afraid of all of these powers she was manifesting, afraid she could accidentally hurt those she cared about.

But she was also angry. The anger that she felt toward Nehanda for taking everything from her had been smoldering silently beneath the surface, and she could feel it trying to break free. She knew it served no purpose, that it could make her reckless—something she couldn't afford, not now.

Still...

Nehanda would deserve every bit of retribution coming to her.

Chapter Thirty-Two

"We're running out of space to put them," Nehanda reported to the council curtly. "While it's true that we have been finding more sorcerers than ever before, we lack the space and resources to support and train them."

"Perhaps it is time we begin extending ourselves," Adanya mused, ignoring the sharp rebuke that she felt rather than heard from Nehanda.

"What do you mean?" Adio asked.

She looked around at the rest of the council members. "For as long as any of us can remember, the training of new sorcerers has been done by current members of the council, correct?"

They all nodded.

"Considering there are only six of us, perhaps it's time we reach out to those sorcerers that have successfully graduated and train them specifically to train others."

"You want to train teenagers and young people to train others?" Nehanda sputtered in disbelief.

"Not teenagers. There would be a limitation to sorcerers at least my age and older, who've had a chance to be in the world and gain some wisdom and experiences of their own. Then, with our guidance, they could pass on that knowledge to others. I'm sure we can all agree that our experiences as members of the council are much different from other sorcerers. It could benefit the young ones to learn from people with different experiences than us."

"They're good points," Jabari said with a nod. "We can't afford to just turn young sorcerers away; too much of a chance that they get steered in the wrong direction."

"And what's to keep sorcerers from just claiming they have our approval?" Nehanda protested.

Adanya shifted in her seat, finding it increasingly difficult to ignore Nehanda's radiating ire.

"I think you're creating problems that aren't there," Kamaria said sharply. "Adanya has the magic to prevent that."

"I'm sure we can solve the issue of space by a simple conversation with the king," Adio added before Nehanda could speak again. "He's been very supportive of our efforts to find young sorcerers, and I'm sure he'll approve the funds to expand the Arena and grounds."

"It sounds like a perfect solution!" Naeemah said with a bright smile.

"I certainly don't see anything wrong with it," Gabir said. "I'll volunteer to help create the training criteria for the new trainers."

"I'll work with you!" Naeemah said.

"Shall we vote?" Adanya asked, inwardly grateful at the input from the other council members. "All in favor of creating a framework for magic trainers?"

Everyone but Nehanda raised their hands.

"All opposed?"

Nehanda raised her hand, glaring at the others.

"The ayes have it," Adanya said. "Let's get this set in motion. We're dismissed for the day."

Nehanda noisily pushed back her chair, stalking out of the room before anyone else could move.

"Don't let her bother you," Adio said comfortingly, patting Adanya's arm. "She'll come around when she realizes how much this plan aligns with her goals for the sorcerers."

"If you say so."

Jabari rose. "I'll try to talk to her."

She smiled and nodded gratefully as he left.

"It's an excellent plan," Naeemah assured her as she, too, rose to leave. "Don't doubt that!"

"She's just being contrary to prove a point," Kamaria laughed. "We Embers can't help it sometimes."

Before anyone else could speak, there was a cry from the hallway outside. "Fire! The garden is on fire!"

The remaining sorcerers ran from the room, joining the frantic servants running to see how they could help. They stopped as they reached the doorway to the garden, repelled by the heat from the flames that had already consumed most of the greenery.

"Stand back, now!" Kamaria commanded. She planted her feet so that she was facing the flames.

It looked as if an invisible funnel was extending from her body; the flames were sucked toward her, swirling in an incredible display that rose above the walls of the garden. Kamaria herself was a sight, cloak and hair billowing in the hot air caused by the fire. A subtle flare of her eyes and the flames disappeared, leaving everyone with spots dancing in their vision as they tried to readjust to the dimming light of late afternoon.

The king arrived just then. His face fell when he saw what was left of the garden. Wordlessly, he walked into the newly-made clearing, radiating a sadness that Adanya felt acutely.

"Kamaria, thank you for keeping the flames from spreading. What happened?" he asked quietly.

"We're not sure, Your Majesty," a servant responded. "It's possible that some of the mulch caught on fire."

Kamaria's eyes narrowed at the explanation, and she moved off to begin her investigation of the burned garden.

The king was silent, and Adanya could feel him trying to find words to say.

"I know that it won't be the same," Gabir said, stepping forward, "but I can regrow the garden for you. Will only take a couple of minutes."

Now she felt a spark of hope as the king turned questioning eyes upon the sorcerer. "You can?"

"If you'd like me to, Your Majesty."

"Please ... please."

Gabir nodded and turned to the ashes. Adanya shooed the servants back into the palace and gently pulled the king into the doorway so they were not in Gabir's way. With a practiced ease, Gabir knelt on the ground and placed a flat palm against it. A few moments passed, and nothing seemed to be happening. The garden fell into silence, the only sound the swish of Kamaria's robes as she continued her search.

Suddenly, plants shot up from beneath the ashes. Bushes flowered in minutes; trees took slightly longer, but they rose taller and stronger than before. The growth was so strong and rapid that many of the trees shook forth their leaves, carpeting the paths and hiding the ashes beneath them.

In ten minutes' time, the entire garden had regrown. Gabir rose, shaking leaves from his hair and shoulders as he turned to grin at the king. "Everything was still there, rooted beneath. The ashes just helped everything to grow stronger."

King Keon reached out to shake his hand, then seemed to change his mind and hugged him. "I cannot thank you enough, Gabir."

"I'm happy to help, Your Majesty. I know how much this garden meant to the queen, and what it means to you and the prince now."

Adanya smiled as the two men began walking through the garden together, feeling their connection and the king's joy radiating from them.

"It must be exhausting, feeling everyone's emotions all of the time," Kamaria said, coming back.

Adanya chuckled. "It's not *everyone's* emotions. Just the people I'm closest with."

"Or *used to* be close with."

Now she winced. "Am I that obvious?"

"No. But she is."

Adanya sighed again. "Did you find anything?"

Kamaria shook her head. "Nothing. It's strange ... it almost looks as if a trainee wasn't able to control their powers—there's nothing that would have started a fire here otherwise. But trainees aren't allowed this far into the palace."

"Do you imagine this was done purposefully?"

Kamaria started to answer, then hesitated. "I couldn't say without proof."

But you think you know.

The Ember sighed, nodding in response to Adanya's voice in her head. *It's possible that she was just letting off some steam and was careless.*

Adanya raised an eyebrow. *You sound like you're defending her.*

I know how our tempers can be. Again, I don't really have proof of it, just a hunch.

I'll keep that in mind.

Just then, Rashidi appeared in the doorway opposite them, his face filled with concern. "I heard there was a fire?"

Adanya smiled despite herself. "It's alright. Kamaria was able to keep it from spreading, and Gabir regrew the garden."

He studied her, realizing there was more to the story but reading her face and understanding she would explain later. "I'm glad to hear it. I shall return to my duties." He bowed to her and Kamaria and left.

Kamaria nudged her conspiratorially. "So. That's the mysterious guard who has your heart?"

Adanya blushed furiously, turning back inside to lead the way to the council room. "Yes. That is Rashidi."

"Mhmmm. I approve. Though I'm wondering how your shy self was able to hook him."

"Hook? Kamaria, I have no idea what you're talking about."

"We all know that being forthright doesn't come naturally to you. And while I'm proud of you for taking charge as Head of Council, I know that seducing a man isn't something you have much experience in."

Adanya laughed as she sat back in her chair, Kamaria sitting beside her. "Why did I have to seduce him? We just found that we had a connection and it grew."

"I'm glad you found him. I was about to convince Naeemah to give you man-catching lessons."

"Naeemah isn't even married!"

"Trust me. When she wants to, she'll find a man in no time."

"Is that how you found your husband?"

Now Kamaria laughed. "Ayomide? That man took one look at me and was instantly in love. I didn't have any use for love, I thought; I was too focused on learning to use my powers, and I was afraid that getting attached would give me something to lose. But he was determined to have me, and eventually he won me over."

As she spoke, Adanya could feel a slow, smothering heat, different from the wilting heat of Nehanda's anger. She smiled again, thinking how Kamaria's heat reminded her of how her love for Rashidi felt.

"And I can understand you wanting to keep him a secret. You've taken on leadership and visibility very well, but you're still a very private person. It makes sense that you'd want to keep your relationship more private."

"I've thought about introducing him, I really have. Especially since he doesn't care who sees us together. But ... it is nice, having something that's just mine."

"Love looks good on you," Kamaria concluded, chuckling at the dreamy smile on her face. "And I'm very happy for you. We all are."

"Most of you." Adanya's smile turned to a scowl as she glanced at Nehanda's empty chair. "What am I going to do about her, Kamaria?"

"Nothing much you can do, I suppose, short of kicking her off the council. Despite my like of the idea, we both know it would be impractical and unwise."

Do you think she's responsible for the garden?

I couldn't truthfully say. But it was definitely started by magic. Kamaria rose and placed a comforting hand on her shoulder. Aloud, she said, "I'm sure things will reveal themselves in time." With a smile, she turned and left Adanya sitting alone in the council room, her face troubled.

Chapter Thirty-Three

Adanya stared into the flames of the fireplace from where she sat in the cottage. She was tempted to use the fire to access her powers but decided against it; the chance of burning down their headquarters with her inexperience was far too high for her liking. Instead, she rose and slowly made her way outside, sitting on a bench against the cottage wall. She watched as Waed and Abiba sparred with sticks in the small clearing nearby.

She turned her attention to the small raspberry bush beside the bench. Since fall had taken its full effect, the branches were bare and brittle. Steeling herself against the inevitable, she focused on the bare branches, willing them to flower and bring forth fruit. Everything around her faded away; she could no longer hear the sticks clacking against each other, the rustling of clothes or grunts of the combatants. Suddenly she could *feel* the plant, in a way she had never been able to before. Whereas her Sage abilities would tell her where a plant was and what sort of condition it was in, this felt like ... *growing*.

She could feel the rush of energy and warmth from the sunlight; the damp earth on her feet, as if they were roots beneath the ground, soaking up the water; the slight breeze causing her to sway. She could even feel the plant changing the sunlight and water into energy, giving her energy as well. It suddenly sprouted leaves, looking as if it were the first of spring rather than a chilly fall day. Mere seconds later, the branches were weighed down by juicy red berries, which ripened almost instantly.

She pulled back her awareness to sense everything again. Abiba and Waed were staring at the bush, mouths open in astonishment. She gripped the edge of the bench with her good arm, bracing herself for the inevitable vision.

It came, though much gentler than the others. She stood in a forest, trees thick about her. A rustle nearby alerted her to the presence of a young man stooped among the underbrush, picking mushrooms from beside rocks and fallen logs. He stood up and stared right at her, his mouth open in surprise.

"Are ... are you Lady Adanya?" he stammered.

"Yes. You must be Gabir's great-great-grandson."

His eyes were still wide with shock as he managed to speak. "Yes, ma'am. My name is Idir."

"Do you live alone?"

"Yes."

"Do you know about the rebellion against Nehanda?"

"Of course!" Indignation laced his tone, but he quickly bowed his head apologetically.

"I'm at their headquarters now. I'm arranging a safe place for us to meet; we're gathering a council like the old days."

Even through her vision, she could feel his determination and excitement. "Tell me where and I'll go."

"I'll send word to you when we know for sure. Now that I can sense you, it won't take much."

He nodded firmly. "I've been preparing for this day for as long as I can remember. I'm ready."

"Good. Stay alert."

"Yes, ma'am."

She came out of her vision with a jolt, though nowhere near as violently as usual. Perhaps she was getting used to this.

"You found Gabir's?" Adio asked as he appeared in the doorway.

"How did you know what I was doing?" she asked with an amused smirk, shaking off the aftereffects of her vision.

"Felt you pulling me out of my sleep." He came over and readjusted her shoulder dressing. "You've got to be careful with this thing..." He trailed off as he worked, suddenly unwrapping all of her dressing to reveal her bare shoulder, now completely healed with only the traces of her old scar on her skin. "Well."

She craned her neck to look. "What?"

"It would seem that your connection to something growing healed you." He gently ran his hand over her shoulder. "Amazing. How do you feel?"

"Actually ... energized. I haven't come out of a vision feeling this strong before."

"You're building up to your full power," he said.

"Only one left." She paused as Adio helped her to rearrange her clothes. "I told Idir—Gabir's great great grandson—that I'll send word once we've found the safe meeting place." Turning to the others, she said decisively, "I'll find Jabari's family before Kamaria. I don't know what effect having all of the powers will have on me, and I'd rather have their powers with us first, in case I'm out for a bit."

"Makes sense," Adio agreed.

She settled herself and closed her eyes, turning her magical awareness to Fauna magic. Instantly she found herself on a boat with a young man and woman, their backs turned to her as they tended to a ripped sail. They were floating far from land, the sun beating down from the midafternoon sky and causing the water to reflect rippling patterns upon the boat's occupants. At her appearance, they stopped their work to look at her, mouths agape. They were clearly twins, and she could sense their Fauna powers.

"You're Jabari's great-great-grandchildren?" she asked, though she already could see the resemblance to him in their faces.

"Yes," the man said, dipping his head respectfully. "I'm Odeon, and this is my sister Nala."

"I'm sorry to tell you that your grandfather is gone," she said, her voice strained.

Their faces fell. "Nehanda?" Nala asked, her voice hardening.

Adanya nodded. "Yes. I'm gathering a council to defeat her; will you both come?"

"We will do whatever you ask," Odeon answered for them both.

"How far are you from Rydell?"

"Two days from land, then a two days' journey. Faster if we can find horses."

As Odeon spoke, Nala leaned over the side of the boat and trailed her hand through the water, making a series of clicking noises Adanya recognized as *pull us in*. Moments later, a green, scaled head broke through the surface. Nala tossed the enormous sea turtle a rope, which it caught in its mouth before disappearing back below. The boat began skimming over the surface as the turtle pulled it toward the shore.

"I'll reach out when I know the exact meeting place," Adanya said, nodding in approval at their speed.

Out of the vision and reoriented, she rose. "Do we have any word on our meeting place?" she asked.

"Not yet; we're still waiting on messengers to return," Sefu answered.

"Then I'll try and get some sleep."

Sleep, however, eluded her. Still feeling a flow of energy, she left the bedroom after an hour and went to sit before the fireplace. The living room was empty, everyone else either out scouting, sleeping, or training. It seemed the perfect time to try to access her fire powers, with everyone safely out of the way.

Taking a deep breath to settle herself, she focused on the flames, watching intently as they licked the wood and sent off heat. She imagined being able to take on that heat without being burned, possessing the same power—both constructive and destructive—the fire held. She tensed as a different magic flowed through her, and some of the fire leapt from the fireplace into her open hand. She allowed it to dance up and down her arm, marveling as it skimmed over her clothes and touched her braids without setting them alight, as if she had an invisible shield protecting her.

She felt herself slipping into her vision, so she hastily blew to extinguish the flames before her arm dropped to the chair.

"You're going to burn the cabin down at this rate." Kamaria grinned at her from her seat beside a fireplace in a small, otherwise dark room. "Took you long enough. I think I'm offended."

Adanya couldn't help but grin back. "How did you know that I was awake?"

"I've been feeling it, somehow. Feeling you getting stronger. I notice you waited to find me last, though."

"Did you consider that I was a little scared of fire?"

"Getting feisty in your old age, aren't you?" She lifted her hand and a tiny ring of flame danced around her palm. "Fire is just like anything else; it can be controlled, but can also be dangerous if left unchecked."

"Like Nehanda."

The flame grew, engulfing her entire hand. "Like Nehanda," she agreed grimly. "I've been waiting alone for all these years to make sure she paid for what she did."

Even through the distance, Adanya could feel Kamaria's deep sorrow.

"So where are you?" Kamaria asked.

"We're looking for a meeting place. I'll let you know when and where as soon as we know. The rest of the council and I are going to meet there as well."

"I'll be there. And Adanya," she added as Adanya began to release the vision, "I'm glad to see you. It's been a long wait."

This time, coming out of the vision had no side effects. She blinked in surprise to see everyone surrounding her, their eyes wide as they realized she had done it.

"I think you've finally fully come into your powers," Adio said wisely. "The ring in your eyes keeps changing colors."

She took a moment to be fully present, feeling her new powers swirling within her. "Time is short," she said. "There's a chance that Nehanda can sense me now, especially since we share all powers. We need to meet."

"Then we should get going," Sefu said. "The horses are saddled and ready to go. It's an abandoned town—I believe it was called Daria—about a day's journey from here."

"I'll let everyone know as we ride."

There was a flurry of motion as everyone gathered weapons and supplies. Within a few minutes, everyone was in the saddle and spurring their horses onward.

They spoke little, recognizing that Adanya's mind was churning. With all of her powers manifested, the different strands of energy flowed through her body, distinct and yet intertwined. She wondered how long it would take her to use them with ease, how long it must have taken Nehanda.

And she wondered what their confrontation would look like when it finally happened.

Chapter Thirty-Four

Adanya sat alone in the darkness of her room, not bothering to light the fireplace. In her hand was a crumpled letter, the latest report of a town being utterly destroyed by Harrun. She hadn't understood, initially, the crippling pain that would rip through her chest seemingly at random. Rashidi and the king were worried, and the other council members tried to keep a close eye on her. But soon she realized the cause.

The feelings coincided with the destruction of the different cities.

There had to be something she could do, some way she could sense the attacks coming and warn them—anything more than sitting and waiting for the pain to come.

She raised her head as a thought came to mind, her eyes catching the moonlight that filtered in through the curtains. Nehanda had always taught her to separate herself from the emotions of others, to protect herself from the intensity and overwhelm of always feeling others. But she had grown so much, surely she could focus her energy?

Without taking the time to talk herself out of it, Adanya began searching for the feelings of fear that would surely accompany an enemy attack. It did not take long to find them.

She found herself assaulted with a torrent of emotions and images. Soldiers on horseback and foot. The flash of weapons. The screams of those being cut down. The blood spattering through the air and turning the ground into dark, oozing mud. The fear of death, the fear for loved ones, the acute terror that paralyzed some and robbed others of their senses, sending them running to and fro with no real sense of direction.

It was all so incoherent and chaotic, it took her some time to realize she was truly experiencing it alongside the people at that very moment. But what made it worse was that she knew she was too late to save them.

Rashidi pulled out of her trance, wrapping his arms around her and rocking her as he shushed her gently. She looked around in bewilderment, realizing that at some point she'd fallen to the floor and was sobbing.

"I'm here," he assured her gently. "I'm here."

She tried to calm her breathing and stop her tears but couldn't. "It was so awful!" she wailed into his chest. "Everyone was dying around me and there was nothing that I could do!"

He continued to hold her until the sobs subsided.

"Their fear..." she whispered. "I've never felt anything like it."

"Why did you go searching for it?" There was no scolding accusation in his tone, simply an honest question.

For a moment, she didn't know how to answer. "I needed to know what was happening," she said finally. "Everything is so ... distant for me. I've never been in a battle; I've only ever seen a few people die. I needed to understand."

"If I have my way, you'll never have to be in a war," he said protectively.

"What kind of leader am I if I never see what's happening to the people? Never experience what they experience?"

"Not every leader has to be on the frontlines." He gently helped her to her feet, pulling her to her dresser and pouring water into the basin to begin gently washing her face. "Everyone has to use their strengths in battle. If everyone was a soldier, who would lead? Who would plan and strategize? Your magic can help, true enough, but on the front lines, you'd be more a liability than an asset."

"If you say so…"

He gently turned her head so he could look her in the eyes. "I say so," he said firmly. He finished washing her face, kissing her before hugging her again. "The king has called a war council. He wishes to see you and the other sorcerers in the throne room as soon as possible."

Adanya sighed heavily into his chest, attempting to marshal her thoughts and emotions to focus on the task at hand. "Will you come with me? I need your calming presence."

He chuckled, and she enjoyed feeling the rumbles in his chest. "If the Head of Council wishes it, who am I to say no?"

She leaned her head back for a kiss and then stepped away, rearranging her clothes and hair before grabbing her staff. She paused as she reached the door, closing her eyes and taking a deep breath to steady herself. A flash of the sights from before crossed her mind and her body tensed; before it could overtake her, however, she felt Rashidi's gentle but firm hand on the small of her back, pulling her back to the present. She walked out of the room with him directly behind her, using her magic to call the rest of the council.

King Keon was deep in thought, pacing back and forth before his throne with his arms crossed behind him and his head lowered. At Adanya's approach, he looked up and flashed her the briefest of smiles. Adanya could feel his familiar warmth, but it was overshadowed by the immense worry occupying him. "Not good news, I'm afraid," he said gravely. "Another village…"

She nodded. "I know. I … I saw it."

His eyes narrowed as he heard the tremor in her voice. He looked about to comment when the other members of the council began filing in, answering Adanya's summons in haste.

They stood in a semicircle around the king, Rashidi remaining slightly behind Adanya at the center.

King Keon looked at all of them in turn, his face grave. "Things are worse than we thought. It would appear that Harrun has declared war against us."

"Officially?" Adio asked.

"There have not been any formal messages sent, but five villages near the northern border have been destroyed. We have no choice but to respond. Therefore, I'm giving orders to muster our forces and send soldiers to protect the other villages, as well as create offensives to take back the land that has been overrun." He looked them each in the eye in turn. "I'm asking for your support."

"And you have it." Adanya spoke for them all, feeling wholehearted support from the rest of the council—except one. Pushing the feeling to the side, she continued, "Our magic can only do so much, and we will not be able to fight the war for the army. But we will do all that we can to strengthen and support them, in conjunction with Your Majesty's generals."

"That is all I could ask. I wished to see you all at once so there was no room for rumors to spread before everyone could be notified. We have to keep the people…"

The king continued speaking, but his voice was drowned out in Adanya's head as she felt the dissension coming from Nehanda, subtle but strong beneath her outward appearance of support. Was Nehanda objecting to the war? Or using magic in war? She wasn't sure, but the fact that she could sense these feelings in Nehanda troubled her.

She focused back on the king as Rashidi placed a gentle hand on her back, bringing her back into the present.

"…I hope that this will be resolved quickly," the king was saying. "The lives we have lost are already far too many."

"The council will meet to discuss the details of how we will support the army, as well as whether we can utilize some of the other sorcerers to help with the effort," Adanya said.

"Thank you."

She glanced left and right at the rest of the council, who bowed and turned toward the council room.

"Adanya…" The king's voice stopped her as she turned to follow them. "May I have a private word?"

Rashidi bowed as if to withdraw as well, but Keon stopped him. "You as well, Rashidi; perhaps your experience will be useful in this discussion."

Rashidi obediently returned, standing before Adanya and the king as they took their seats.

"This is scary for all of us," Adanya said softly, voicing the feelings she sensed from him.

Keon sighed heavily. "My father taught me how to wage war, but I hoped that I'd never have to use it. Strategies and plans are much different in practice than in study. Would you agree, Rashidi?"

Rashidi nodded. "True experience only comes in real-life situations."

"Do ... do you think this is the right decision?"

"Of course it is," Adanya said without hesitation. "I was able to see, to experience what our people experienced during these attacks. It's awful. Harrun's soldiers really are barbarians. We must stop them before the whole kingdom is destroyed."

He nodded. "It may seem trivial, Adanya, but I'm grateful I have you by my side as we do this. It's a new experience, but we can lean on each other's strengths."

"I'm honored that you think so, Your Majesty."

He squeezed her hand, then looked up at Rashidi. "Young man, I'll expect you to keep an extra close watch on your fiancée. She tends to overwork herself."

"I wouldn't dream of doing otherwise," Rashidi said.

"And who will look after you, Your Majesty?" she asked with a slight smile. "You have the same tendencies I do."

Now he chuckled. "I suppose we'll have to look out for each other. But I'm keeping you from your council, and I have councils of my own to hold." He kissed her hand before releasing it.

Adanya rose and bowed, then she and Rashidi left together.

As soon as they were alone, he took her hand and squeezed it tightly. "I don't have to be a Sage to see that you're nervous," he said quietly.

"This is ... big. But it's something we have to do."

"There's something else bothering you."

"There is. But I can't place my finger on what it is, exactly."

He raised an eyebrow. "You're not hiding something from me, are you?"

"No, I'm not. This is a very complex situation, with complex feelings and emotions around it."

She could tell he didn't quite believe her, but he stayed silent, continuing to walk her to the council room with their fingers intertwined.

He turned her hand slightly to see her engagement ring. "My love ... with everything going on, do you still want to do a wedding?"

Adanya turned her head to look at him as they continued to walk, noticing and appreciating his word choice of 'wedding' rather than 'get married.' "Why do you ask?"

He hesitated. "While I know that we planned on a bigger wedding so all of your friends could attend, I almost wonder if we should just have the king marry us, privately. We could have a larger celebration after Harrun is dealt with."

Now she stopped, turning to fully face him and searching his feelings before she could stop herself. What she found surprised her. "Are you ... afraid?"

His jaw tightened, and he looked away from her for a moment. "In a manner of speaking." He pulled her over to a bench that sat against a wall, looking down at her hands in his before he continued. "I have every confidence we'll be victorious in this war. There are so many things in our favor, despite how things look. But I've known too many of my comrades who went away to battle and never returned to the people who loved them. I suppose a part of me is afraid that the same thing will happen to me. That I'll get killed and we wouldn't have gotten the chance to be married."

Adanya was shocked by this admission of fear from him, this man she'd only known as a pillar of strength and confidence. She absorbed what he said, rubbing her thumbs over his. "If that's what you want, we can do that."

"Adanya, I don't want this to be just because you're trying to take my feelings into account. I want to know your thoughts." He caressed her cheek, smiling despite his feelings. "This is a partnership, after all. We should be able to communicate these things."

She leaned into his hand. Everything in her wanted to agree, to run back to the king and get married immediately. But underneath her longing, there was something stopping her. "Nothing would make me happier than to be married to you now," she said carefully.

"But?"

Now she smiled. He knew her so well. "But the part of me in leadership feels like it's not the right time. It would be selfish of us to go and get married when our people are being massacred. We wouldn't have to advertise it, but we'd know. And I feel like the knowledge would eat us alive and distract us from focusing on defending the kingdom."

He nodded, and she could feel his resignation.

"My love." She put her hands on either side of his face, making sure he was looking at her. "Thank you for sharing that with me. And thank you for giving me the space to be open with you."

He rested his forehead against hers, closing his eyes as she shared the warmth of her love with him. "I always want to know what your opinion is. We'll wait. And when this war is over, we'll have the biggest, most extravagant wedding you could ask for to celebrate us and our victory."

"I don't know about all that now."

They laughed together before rising and embracing.

His admission of fear made her feel closer to him. It reminded her that he was subject to the same feelings she was, despite not having magic. It also reminded her of how happy she was to have someone she could trust with every part of her.

She couldn't wait to spend the rest of her life with him.

Chapter Thirty-Five

The new council met in the woods just outside Daria, some two days from Ferandar, sitting on makeshift seats of stumps, fallen logs, or piles of blankets around the fire. Adanya struggled against a feeling of nostalgia, remembering her last time presiding over a council meeting—just before she'd lost everything. The mixture of new and old faces left her a little disoriented, trying to reconcile her past and present.

Adio seemed to sense her feelings and reached over to give her hand a reassuring squeeze. "We're all here for you."

She smiled at him, then raised her eyes to scan the assembled faces again. Adio to her left, then the twins, Abiba, Idir, Kamaria, and Sefu to her right. Waed stood slightly behind Sefu, warily scanning their surroundings but still attentive to the group. She took a deep breath, tightening her grip on her staff to ground herself.

"I'm happy that we all made it safely. And thank you all for coming. I know it hasn't been easy."

"No place we'd rather be," Kamaria said, drawing noises of assent from the others.

Adanya smiled gratefully, then continued. "As you all know by now, we've learned that Nehanda has been using powers pulled from other sorcerers to become a Sage Elemental—as I am now. We don't know if she can sense that I have accessed the rest of my powers, but we know from her diary that she at least suspected I was capable of doing so. I have no doubt she will begin an assault now that she knows we are actively standing against her. We were fortunate to take the palace in Ferandar without great loss, but further offensives will be suicidal now that she's expecting us. Our forces are strong"—she nodded at Sefu—"but they won't be able to stand against her without magic. And that's where this council comes in." She leaned forward. "The only way that this ends, that the people get their freedom back, is if we take out Nehanda. While I believe the final confrontation will be between her and me, we have to get to her first. I need ideas from all of you so we can decide our course of action moving forward. Adio and Kamaria, you knew Nehanda even longer than I did, so you may be able to provide some insight into her thoughts. Everyone else, you have a better knowledge of the world now and how she has moved in this time."

"She's known for not staying in one place, but we haven't seen any movement from her since we captured Ferandar," Sefu said. "My suggestion would be to draw her back there, rather than use troops and time trying to find her."

Adanya nodded. "Drawing her onto our territory would be ideal. Can we recall as many of our troops as possible?"

"It will take a little doing, but if this is our final offensive, we will make it happen." He glanced back at Waed, who nodded.

"So we lure her out," Adanya said. "How do we do that? What do we have that she wants?"

"Where has she been getting her powers from?" Abiba asked. "Since Kamaria and Adio are still here, we know it's not because she took them from council members."

"She must have found other natural-born sorcerers," Adio said with a scowl. "Wouldn't surprise me if she snatched their powers the way that she did with Jabari."

"Then that means *we* are what she'd want most," Adanya said. "So we spread the word that I've assembled a council at Ferandar. She'll have to come, if not to take our power, then to meet our threat to her rule."

"Will we all be there?" Abiba asked. "It seems like that would be dangerous."

"But we'll likely need everyone's powers to defeat her," Idir pointed out.

"Nearby, but not altogether," Adanya said. "We can't reveal our full strength all at once. But we'll have to have someone powerful enough to entice her."

"Me," Kamaria said without hesitation. "She always hated me anyways, and I'm sure she'd love to be rid of me."

"So we add that to the rumors. We'll have to find some way to get her where she won't be able to hurt anyone else, especially the non-magical folk. Then it will be up to me."

Everyone fell silent as they realized the gravity of her words; either she or Nehanda would not walk away from the fight.

"I'll leave you all to sort out the particulars." Adanya rose. "I need a bit of time to ... prepare."

They exchanged worried glances as she walked out of the clearing in which they sat and into the deserted streets, letting the firelight and warmth fade behind her as she melted into the darkness.

Things were nearing a head; she could feel it. And though she would be glad to be done with everything, she could not shake the unsettling feeling of dread in the pit of her stomach. Maybe it was the new powers flowing through her that unsettled her long-held status quo. Maybe it was the quickness with which she was forced to adapt to her new surroundings and circumstances, the extension of her leadership role to general, queen, and champion. Maybe it was because most of the people that loved and supported her were gone.

Maybe it was because the one who should have supported her the most was now her most powerful enemy.

"What did I tell you about holding your breath, little girl?"

She thought what she needed most was solitude, time to process everything, but at the sound of Adio's voice, she broke down into tears, dropping her staff and falling to her knees as Adio caught her.

He didn't shush her or scold her, instead simply held her and let her cry. There was a vague thought to control herself enough to not harm him as she had done the last time, but it was the only thought in her mind. She allowed herself to cry as she never had before, releasing all the confusion, frustration, and insecurity she was feeling. She cried until her eyes ran dry, leaning heavily into Adio's arms.

She did not know how long it was before she felt calm enough to sit back to look at his face.

"Is it normal to be this scared?" she asked.

She could see his broad smile even in the dark. "I don't know; I've never helped to overthrow a dictator before. But it seems appropriate."

Adanya could not help but smile at his infectious humor. "Glad to know I'm not completely off the rails."

"I know it's a lot to ask of one person. It would overwhelm anyone, and you've come to grips with everything in a few weeks. But you know that we're with you, little girl. Every step of the way. We'll support you and help you as much as we can. Don't be afraid to lean on us. Don't be afraid to ask for help." He kissed her forehead. "I'm prouder of you than you can ever know." With another loving squeeze, he rose and left her alone.

She sat in silence awhile longer, feeling the chill as she listened to the cold wind blowing around her and stirring her braids and robes. The faint murmurs of her companions' conversations around the fire drifted over her; even stronger was their determination and focus, their belief that she would be victorious.

She had to be victorious.

Gripping her staff, she rose and walked a little farther, where she could only barely see the light from the fire. Then she sat and began undoing her braids, intending to wash them and tie them back. But a thought struck her.

She'd worn braids since she was a child, too impatient to maintain other hairstyles and enjoying the ease with which she could care for them daily. They also served her shy nature, a way to hide her face when she was uncomfortable or embarrassed. But there was no place for that now; it was time to be bold and assertive, to carry herself with the power and authority she held.

It was time to display the courage and strength Rashidi had always seen in her but she didn't always see in herself.

Time for change.

Chapter Thirty-Six

The room was lit by the moonlight streaming through the curtains and the fire flickering in the hearth created a cozy atmosphere. Adanya sat taking down the last of her braids while Rashidi combed through the rest of her hair.

"You've never had anyone else do your hair?" he asked.

"I've never needed anyone to," she chuckled. "It's simple to just braid it."

He moved over to the bucket by the fire, testing the temperature before bringing it over to the basin sitting beside her on the side table. "Well, I'm happy that you're allowing me to help."

"Not like you aren't taking care of the rest of me," she chuckled, untangling the last few strands.

"Of course I am." He gave her ass an affectionate pat as she bent over the basin. Then he gently poured some of the water over her head, enough to wet it before pouring shampoo into his hands and beginning to massage it through her hair.

"I do have to admit that having someone else do my hair is nice," she said.

"Despite what your perfectionist tendencies tell you, you are allowed to ask for help."

"I know. I guess that there are times when I just feel like simple things I should be able to do myself, without bothering anyone."

He leaned around her so she could clearly see the frown on his face. "First of all, you're never bothering me when you ask for help. I love you, and I'm happy to help you whenever I can." He straightened and returned to washing her hair. "Secondly, I wouldn't exactly call taking care of your hair a simple thing."

She giggled, subconsciously leaning into the feel of his fingertips massaging her scalp. "I suppose you're right."

"I know that I am," he corrected. He worked in silence for a few minutes, then ventured, "Have you ever thought about styling your hair differently?"

"My hair? Why? Do you not like it?"

"That's not why at all; I love your hair. I just ... I feel like sometimes you use it to hide yourself."

"What do you mean?"

He finished rinsing the shampoo out of her hair and sat her back down so he could comb it through. "It's so long and beautiful, but it is rare for me to see you with it out of your face when you're in public."

"I don't like people looking at me, that's all."

"But that's just it, my love. You're in a position of leadership. Seeing your face shows your confidence and your command of your duties."

"Why do people need to see my face to know that I'm doing my job?"

Hearing the irritation in her voice, he stopped combing and came around to crouch down in front of her. "Truth be told, it's not so much how others view you that I'm concerned about. It's how you view yourself."

"What is that supposed to mean?"

"You always hide your face. I feel like it's a reflection of how you see yourself, your shyness, and your uncertainty about being able to be the Head of Council effectively. But you've proven that you can, and you've shown your wisdom in leaning on the strengths of others to support you. There isn't any reason to hide."

Adanya wanted to counter his argument, but deep down, she knew he was right. He saw her wheels turning and rose, gently kissing her forehead before returning to her hair.

"It's your hair, Adanya. Of course, I don't want you to change it if you don't want to. Just think about it, okay?"

"Okay."

They fell silent as he continued his work, detangling, moisturizing, and helping her to section it out into neat sections to braid.

Her hair finally done, she rose and flexed her shoulders. "This is always a bit of a workout. But your help made it go a lot faster."

"I'm glad. Do you usually leave it wet?"

"I go on a walk to let it air dry before bed, usually."

"Would you like some company?"

Adanya hesitated. "No, I ... I think that I need a little time to myself."

"Of course. I can go back to my rooms if you'd like."

She smiled, kissing him. "No, I'd like to spend a little more time with you when I get back."

"As my lady commands," he said with a dramatic bow.

Now she giggled. "Get some rest. You'll need your energy when I get back."

His smile turned devilish, and he turned back to warm up more water for his own washing up.

Adanya left the room with her staff in hand, treading a familiar path. This late at night, most of the palace was asleep, allowing her to lower her guard and let her mind wander without being assaulted by the thoughts and emotions of others. Ever since she became Head of Council, she'd found these late-night walks to be almost essential to her state of mind. Though no other threats had arisen since the Ugwe, dealings with other sorcerers and national matters almost always had her on edge.

She walked down the moonlit hallway, smiling as touches of people's dreams floated through her psyche. Occasionally she would see a guard and nod in response to their respectful salutes. But beyond that, all was still as she wandered through the hallways, down the stairs, and into the throne room.

Here she paused, looking down the long carpet leading to the throne. She never imagined she'd regularly sit in council with the king here, discussing affairs of state and making plans for the country.

Of course, she'd also never imagined that her mentor would have pulled away from her so much.

She bit her lip, feeling a twinge of sadness. Unwilling to give herself over to it, she walked down the carpet to sit in her chair, allowing the emptiness and silence of the great room to swallow her. She rested her staff against the arm of the chair, then leaned her head back and closed her eyes, listening to the sound of her breathing as it cast faint echoes throughout the room. She emptied her thoughts, her worries, her emotions, and just let herself focus on her breathing—almost entering her dissociative state but not fully reaching it.

After an unknown amount of time, she became aware of another presence approaching. One that she would rather not have to deal with.

Nehanda came striding into the room, engrossed in something she was reading by the light of the candle in her hand. It wasn't until Adanya straightened her back and lowered her head that Nehanda looked up from her journal.

"Oh," she said, unable to hide her unhappiness. "I thought you'd have been asleep. Since you're so worried about yourself nowadays."

Adanya's jaw tightened as she tried to control her emotions. "I'm allowed to spend time alone," she replied, careful to keep her tone measured and even. "Is there something that needs my attention?"

Nehanda stepped closer, studying Adanya from beneath her lowered brows. "Have you been noticing anything ... different about yourself, lately?"

Adanya immediately thought about her ability to see what the war was doing to villages, but Nehanda's energy toward her was ... off. Something told her to keep it to herself. She shook her head. "No."

Nehanda looked as if she were about to say more, even opening her mouth to speak. But Adanya watched as a thought passed behind her eyes, and she clamped her mouth shut before scowling at Adanya.

"Not like you would notice anything changing anyway."

Despite her wish to keep the peace between her former mentor and herself, she snapped. "What is it, Nehanda? What is bothering you so much that you can't just support me and help me grow?"

"You're a child! A child who knows nothing of the world, who somehow found herself the most powerful sorcerer in the world!"

"I didn't want this!" Adanya exclaimed, standing. "I would have been perfectly content to just stay on the council until I was old and gray, helping the people around me. But Ziyad and everyone else thought that I could do it. Everyone else but you! *You're* the person who was supposed to support me the most, to help me, but all you've done is be jealous and question me in front of the others like I was fresh out of training! The rest of the council shows unity, which is what we need now more than ever. But you insist upon being contrary!"

"The seat was mine!" Nehanda exploded. A wave of heat billowed outward from her as the flame on the candle in her hand flared. "I was supposed to be Head of Council! It was what I'd worked for my entire life! And it was taken away because some old fool showed preference to a Sage."

"I wanted you to have it!" Now that the dam had been released, Adanya let her feelings fly, her tumultuous emotions overflowing. "I wanted you to be Head of Council. I know how much you wanted it, how much you wanted to do good things for other sorcerers. But that's not how it worked. I want to use this power for good, but it's so hard when I'm constantly using so much of it to overcome you pulling me down!"

Nehanda fell silent, though the heat around her did not dissipate. "From now on," she said slowly, "I will do my best to hold my tongue in front of the others. But know this." She stepped closer until she was face-to-face with her former mentee. "You will never reach your full potential, because you fail to truly see what consequences will come from your actions."

"How can I learn when all you do is chastise me?" Adanya could not keep the quiver from her voice, tears brimming in her eyes. "You've changed, and not for the better."

Nehanda moved without hesitation, slapping Adanya across the face and sending her staggering with a stunned hand to her cheek. "You want a piece of advice?" she gritted through clenched teeth. "Watch your tone when you're speaking to those older and wiser than you."

She stalked from the room, leaving Adanya to sink back into her chair, feeling the literal and emotional heat from Nehanda's hand. Her tears flowed openly now. She knew her previous relationship with Nehanda was over; things would never be the same between them.

She would show her. She would show her she had grown, and would continue to grow without her help. She would prove herself to Nehanda, show her the good she could do as Head of Council.

She sat in the dark awhile, allowing her anger and sadness to dissipate along with the red mark on her cheek. It wouldn't do for Rashidi to see it. Or for him to know about it at all.

Finally, after a deep inhale and slow breath out, she retrieved her staff and walked back to her room.

Rashidi was asleep but woke as she closed the door softly behind her.

"Is everything alright?" Rashidi asked, sitting up on the bed and rubbing his eyes.

Smiling, she put aside her staff and began to take off her clothes. "I'd say so."

He tried to give her a stern glare but could not stop his eyes from traveling down her body as her clothes rapidly disappeared. "Are you trying to distract me?"

"Why would I do that? I told you I would need your energy once I got back." She finished undressing, standing naked for a moment to savor his reaction to her. Then she moved over and straddled him, planting a passionate kiss on his lips.

"Yes, ma'am," he murmured.

Chapter Thirty-Seven

The ride to the palace was silent, everyone lost in their own thoughts of the upcoming battle. Adio had raised his eyebrows at Adanya's haircut; her loose curls, barely touching the back of her neck, bounced as she rode, allowing her full face to be seen for the first time since she was a child. She did not have the time to be self-conscious about her decision, instead returning to the council and outlining everyone's responsibilities before they rode.

Now her brows were furrowed as they rode through the darkness, calculating and planning. They would have only one shot at defeating Nehanda. If she killed Adanya's new council, there was no guarantee there were other sorcerers skilled and trained enough to aid her. If Adanya herself were killed? Then all hope was lost.

Nervous energy wafted off the council, and she struggled to keep her anxiety in check. It wasn't about her now. She had to be the leader, to encourage and calm them, keep them focused on their goal. She did her best to radiate calm and confidence and was rewarded when she felt them responding.

The palace loomed before them in the darkness, the front gate illuminated with torches held by members of the resistance force. The rest was shrouded in shadows; Adanya had instructed them to make the castle appear abandoned until the council arrived and the rumors could be spread.

As they thundered into the courtyard, Waed came out to meet them at the top of the stairs. "Things are still a bit waterlogged," he reported. "We've got rooms ready for you on the second floor."

"Are we ready to start spreading the news?" Adanya asked as they followed him inside to a long hallway.

"Whenever you're ready."

They paused once they were inside, letting their eyes adjust to the darkness.

"Then let's begin." Adanya took a moment to look them all in the eye, sending feelings of confidence into each of them. "We all know the parts we have to play. I'm not going to pretend like this is going to be easy, or that everything will go perfectly to plan. But what I do know is that I'm surrounded by a group of people determined to stop Nehanda and free the people of this land from her control. And that is what we have to our advantage. Stay vigilant and be prepared for anything."

With those final words, everyone split to go to their positions: Odeon, Nala, and Idir to the woods; Waed and Abiba to the stream; and Sefu, Adio, Kamaria, and Adanya to the second floor of the castle.

The prepared rooms were dry and had been put back in order by Sefu's soldiers, all furnished with beds, tables and chairs for dining, and empty dressers.

"It didn't seem like anyone lived here besides the steward," Sefu explained as they gathered in Adanya's room for a final council. "The rooms were furnished but unused."

"I suppose that worked to our advantage," Adanya said.

"How are you feeling?" Adio asked.

She considered the question. "As confident as I can be going into the unknown," she answered finally. "I do seem to recall that waiting was always the worst part of anything."

Kamaria smiled. "At least for those of us who tend to be impatient."

"She won't wait long once she catches wind of our presence here."

"All the better. Waiting tends to set people's nerves on edge," Sefu said. "We don't want mistakes."

"There's so much riding on this," Adanya said. "All of these years, all of the lives that she's ruined. Or ended. If we can't stop her…"

"We will," Kamaria said confidently. "Like you said, we're determined to be rid of her."

"I'm counting on both of you, especially," Adanya said, looking at Adio and Kamaria. "You know her as well as I do; that gives us an advantage the others don't have."

"You know we've got your back," Adio said.

She nodded. "I know." Looking around at them again, she added, "We should get some rest while we can. I'll be able to sense if anything is amiss. I'll call if I need you."

Before they left for their rooms, Adio and Kamaria enveloped Adanya in a hug between them, squeezing her tightly. Sefu waited until they'd left, then took a step toward her.

"Adanya … thank you."

She chuckled. "I don't know what you're thanking me for. We haven't won yet."

"I don't think you understand how just your presence has invigorated the resistance. And you've adjusted to everything so quickly. I know that it's been a lot for you, but … thank you."

She hesitated before smiling. "If you hadn't found me, it might have been different. You deserve the credit. You're a wonderful leader, and the people are lucky to have you. You ... I know that Rashidi would be proud to know you're carrying all that he stood for."

"I'm honored that you think so." He smiled brightly at her, then left, closing the door behind him.

Adanya stood looking after him, tears brimming in her eyes at the truth in her words. Rashidi would have been proud. And though Sefu wasn't her true descendant, she was proud of him too, as if he were her son. Though their childhoods had been much different—she raised as a sorcerer, he raised fighting against a sworn enemy—their passion and love for the people around them bonded them.

As well as their hatred for Nehanda.

Adanya began to wash up in the small water basin on the bedside table, still fighting her tears. She'd thought she had no more after all that she'd been through in that week alone, but clearly that wasn't the case.

She thought back to seeing Nehanda in the woods; though there were remnants of the woman who had practically raised her, it was very clear she was altogether a different person. Her distrust for non-magical folk had grown into sincere hatred, bolstered by the magical powers stolen from others. What impact did taking their powers in such a violent manner have on her?

Knowing she wouldn't be able to sleep, at least not right away, she picked up her staff and left the room to wander the darkened hallways alone. At regular intervals, she would pass members of the rebellion standing guard; each would stand a little straighter as she passed and gave them a nod of acknowledgment. The ritual was comforting; though it had been years since she'd walked the palace at night, for her it felt like it had only been a few weeks.

Outwardly, she radiated calm and confidence, but inside she was a quivering mess, unsure of the plans she had made and worried about the hundreds—thousands—of lives at stake. It was always a weakness of hers, Nehanda had said. Caring about everyone and everything she came in contact with. That much emotional burden would lead to mistakes, things that could overwhelm her and keep her from thinking rationally.

But was that really the reason?

Or was it because that connection could make her stronger?

She stopped in her tracks. What if that was it? What if that was just one of the many tactics Nehanda had used to keep Adanya from fully coming into her own? All of the times Nehanda had belittled her, telling her that she didn't know what she was doing, questioning her in front of others ... it all had to have been her way of taking away Adanya's confidence so she wouldn't explore enough to learn the full extent of her powers. Though at first, her training may have come from a genuine want to help Adanya grow, it had slowly been eaten away by fear and ... jealousy.

Her hand squeezed her staff in anger so hard that it shook.

If only she had known what Nehanda truly was, then the people she loved would still be alive.

She started as she heard gasps of fear from the hallway ahead of her. She noticed a glow of light around her and realized in amazement that she was covered in flames from head to toe, heat radiating from her without feeling the heat of the flames themselves.

Eyes wide, she mentally dispersed the flames as she sent soothing feelings toward the frightened soldiers. The flames whooshed out as if someone had blown out a candle, returning the hallway to semi-darkness. She could feel the guards settling around her.

This wouldn't do. She wasn't fully in control of her powers; it could spell disaster for when Nehanda arrived.

Decisively, she turned and walked to the stairs that led back to the ground floor. After wandering around, she found what must have been the main meeting room: a wide open room with a raised dais at the end, similar to where Adanya had sat with King Keon to hear from those who sought an audience. This room reminded her of him, the man who, without knowing, had been a father to her in every sense of the word. Of Kayode, her little brother who never got to grow up. Of Rashidi, her love, the man who constantly supported her and pushed her to be her own person, standing on her own two feet.

Gripping her staff a little tighter, she set her jaw, rolled up her sleeves, and got to work.

Chapter Thirty-Eight

Adanya looked shyly up at Ziyad and the king, sitting at opposite ends of the table having dinner together. The young sorceress was so nervous, yet honored. The king had extended her the invitation to have dinner with them, without Nehanda's watchful eye. Nehanda had protested, but she couldn't deny the invitation for her pupil. So, dressed in her finest robes, Adanya found herself seated between two men of whom she was in awe.

"How is your training going, Adanya?" King Keon asked, smiling at her.

"It is hard, Your Majesty," she admitted, "but I'm learning a lot."

"You do have one of the more difficult skills to manage," Ziyad said sagely. "It's quite normal to be having some difficulty."

"Was ... was learning your skills difficult?" she ventured.

"Of course, child." Ziyad chuckled. "We Sages carry an immense amount of power. Telepathy itself can be difficult enough to understand and control, but being an empath? Using emotion and the energy of people's souls to create? That is another beast entirely."

"What do you mean?"

"Exercising your control over others can be easy. The hard part of it is learning when you're doing it so that you don't subconsciously influence others to fall in line with what you want. It is entirely dependent on your control over your abilities. But empathy? People emote without even thinking about it, and you just soak it all in. When I was younger, I struggled to separate the feelings I was sensing from others from my own. I ended up spending nearly a year living alone, trying to figure everything out."

Her eyes widened. "You lived alone for a year?"

He chuckled. "Indeed. It was an enlightening experience. I needed that time to make sure I was grounded enough in myself to keep my own identity when dealing with others. Knowing your background, I'd say that you've had a similar experience."

"I wouldn't say similar. I'm still struggling to control that part of my powers."

"Where do you go when you're feeling overwhelmed?"

"Back into the forest to be alone," she admitted. "Though Nehanda doesn't know that, and I'm sure she'd be mad at me for doing it."

"You have to do what is best for you sometimes. Nehanda means well, but we must remember her powers are very different from yours."

"Then ... may I ask ..."

"I chose her to train you because I feel there is a special connection between the two of you," he answered before she could get her question out. "Even I don't fully understand it, but I believe that you will bring something powerful out of each other." He reached over and patted her hand. "But don't ever feel that you can't come to me for advice or counsel. My door is always open to you, young lady."

She could not help but smile, feeling comforted by his words even if she knew that she and Nehanda would still butt heads at times.

"In the meantime," King Keon said, dabbing at his mouth with his napkin, "I'm thinking about organizing another trip into the city. The Harvest Festival begins tomorrow, and I'm sure that you haven't experienced anything like it."

Her eyes lit up. "A festival? I've heard wonderful things about them, but I haven't been to one since I was very little."

"It's settled, then! I'll make arrangements. You'll ride with the queen and I in the carriage and sit with us on our dais."

A pang of fear hit her gut, worried that she would somehow embarrass both herself and her mentor with her lack of control of her powers. "Oh ... Your Majesty, I don't know that you want me that visible."

"Nonsense. You deserve to be somewhere you can get a good view of everything. Besides, the queen and I will make sure no one presses you."

Adanya looked to Ziyad, unsure.

"I think it's a wonderful idea," he said. "You can't let your shy nature keep you from enjoying life. One day you won't have as much time to enjoy things like this; might as well do it now."

She grinned from ear to ear. "When do we go?"

Nehanda was waiting impatiently in the Arena after dinner ended. Adanya had purposefully taken her time changing into her everyday robes, not wanting to spoil her high from the plans she had made with the king and Ziyad. When she arrived, she could immediately sense Nehanda's irritation.

"We've got work to do," Nehanda said brusquely. "Let's get to it."

"Can we train a little extra today?" Adanya ventured, heart fluttering as her nerves picked up. "I'm going to the Harvest Festival tomorrow with the king and queen."

Nehanda's eyes flared instantly, and she appeared to be calming herself down with effort before speaking. "The Harvest Festival?" she repeated tightly. "I don't think that is such a good idea."

"Why? I went into town with the king before, and everything was fine."

"The Festival is much more chaotic than a normal day in town. I don't think you're ready for that kind of challenge."

Her excitement overcame her nerves about questioning Nehanda, and she said boldly, "Ziyad said it was a good idea. So I'm going."

The familiar wave of heat rolled off Nehanda. "I wonder what lesson he is trying to teach you."

Adanya tried to think of Ziyad's words, but a question was burning in her mind. "Nehanda ... do you *like* training me?"

Nehanda was clearly taken aback, blinking rapidly as she absorbed the question. Her heat abruptly dissipated. "What?"

"It's just ... there are times when I feel like you aren't happy that you're training me. Like you wish you could be anywhere else."

Nehanda paused, and Adanya could feel her gathering her thoughts and emotions. She didn't mean to bombard her with the question, but her own emotions and her need to feel wanted by her maternal figure overflowed seeing Nehanda's actions in comparison to Ziyad and the king.

"I will admit that I wasn't exactly pleased when Ziyad asked me to train you specifically," Nehanda finally said, speaking slowly. "But I've come to see how special and talented you are. Even if you don't see it yet. And … I know I'm hard on you, but it's because I can sense that you're capable of great things."

Now it was Adanya's turn to blink rapidly, surprised by Nehanda's confession. "Really?" she managed to say.

Nehanda nodded. "I know I haven't expressed that, and I'm sorry. I've never been very good at expressing any emotion but anger. I … I get angry with you about getting out of your routine because I worry about you. I suppose I could have communicated that to you better."

Adanya could feel the honesty radiating from Nehanda. "Oh. I … okay."

"Ziyad never does anything without a purpose. Whether it's putting us together or letting you go on these excursions. So. Go get some rest. You'll want to be ready for tomorrow."

Adanya wanted to hug her, but that seemed a step too far for the stoic Nehanda. Instead, she beamed a smile at her. "Thank you." She fought her urge to skip, so she settled for walking quickly back toward her quarters.

Though she knew she would never come close to a super emotional, super loving relationship with Nehanda, knowing that she thought she had potential and believed in her made quite a difference.

Chapter Thirty-Nine

Adanya sat cross-legged in the middle of the room, her staff laid across her lap as she reflected on how she had spent her night.

She'd spent hours exercising her new skills as best she could without drawing attention to herself or the castle. She found that her Sage skills came incredibly easy now; she was able to shield herself and the others while she explored without putting much thought into it. The practice made her feel more prepared, yet there was still something holding her back that she couldn't put her finger on.

She thought about all of the things she'd learned about Nehanda, all of the little things she'd said to her to keep her confidence in herself low—despite, at one point, still believing in her. What could she be missing?

"Why did I have a feeling that you wouldn't be sleeping?" Adio's voice roused her from her thoughts.

She twisted around to see him coming through the doorway behind her, stretching as he walked.

"Because you know that I like to be prepared?" she responded with a smile.

He chuckled. "I'm sure that's it."

"Did you get some rest?"

"Some. I admit I've got some of that anxious energy, too."

"At least I'm not alone." She looked over at the filtered, grayish light coming in through the window in the early morning hours. "That wouldn't be you, would it?"

He shook his head. "We never planned anything with the weather before she gets here."

"I guess it's natural, then." She paused, noticing the rain falling. "Is it strange that I want to feel it?"

"Not at all. Nothing like a fresh rain on your face." He extended a hand to help her to her feet.

They walked silently beside each other through the palace and up the two flights of stairs. At the end of the hall, a short staircase led to a wooden trap door that swung upwards, giving them access to the roof.

The roof was gently sloped to allow water to drain from it, with a waist-high wall to keep people from tumbling over the edge. The pair leaned against it as they looked out over the plain and the woods beyond.

The sky steadily brightened, though dark gray storm clouds filtered the sunlight, creating an orange-brown haze around them. Beyond the misty rain falling around them, they could see the rain collecting in clouds over the tops of the trees, drifting like gauzy curtains in the distance.

They stood together looking at the calming scene, letting the rain gradually soak them through. There was a peacefulness there, one that Adanya hadn't felt since she'd awakened. A peacefulness she needed for what lay ahead.

She glanced to her right, smiling a little at the raindrops beading on Adio's hair and eyelashes. His eyes carried a faraway look, like he too was escaping the stress of the moment and drifting away into memories. Shifting her staff to her left hand, she took his and squeezed.

"We'll have more moments like this," she said softly. "Moments where everything just ... is."

He opened his eyes and smiled at her. "You sounded like you believed that."

She smiled back. "Maybe I did."

He squeezed her hand back.

Adanya absently glanced at his other hand, resting on the wall. Then her eyes narrowed as she realized something was missing. "Adio? Have you ever carried a staff?"

He shrugged. "Never found a need to."

Her eyebrows lowered as she searched her memory. None of the other sorcerers on the council had carried staves. Nor had any of the sorcerers in training. In fact, the only other person she'd seen use a staff was Ziyad, and it was more to support his walking than to help focus his magic.

"That's it," she breathed.

"What?" Adio turned and watched her, puzzled, as she looked the staff up and down with a scowl.

"I've been struggling against something holding me back. I couldn't figure out what it was until now." Her hand shook with anger. "I didn't start carrying a staff until I was getting stronger with my training. Nehanda told me it was to help focus my power, but it must have been to keep my powers in check. Because she always knew how strong I was."

Adio's eyes grew wide. "That would make sense."

"She's always had so much control over me, but this?" She stared at the staff. "I should destroy it."

"Wait."

She looked at him, eyes flashing. "Wait? Why?"

He held up his hands defensively, backing a step away as a wave of heat radiated out from her. "Nehanda knows you've learned about all of your powers, but she doesn't know that you've learned about her control over you. If she sees you without your staff, she'll immediately put her guard up."

Adanya wanted nothing more than to burn the staff into ashes, but she forced herself to listen and consider Adio's words. She simmered down slowly, the heat around her dissipating. "You're right. Again." She rested the staff against the wall and backed away from it, flexing her hands as she tentatively attempted to change the weather.

Both of their eyes grew wide as the misty rain instantly turned into a downpour, obscuring their view of each other. A moment later, it returned to mist.

"I don't think Nehanda knows what she's gotten herself into," Adio said in breathless wonder.

Adanya was shaking, having scared herself with her own power. "Neither do I," she whispered.

They jumped as a loud crack of thunder echoed through the air, followed by a flash and crackle of lighting. The energy sizzled on their skin, and they both instantly knew it wasn't just a regular bolt of lightning.

Kamaria's head appeared through the trap door as she climbed up and joined them. "She's almost here," she said simply.

Adanya nodded and picked up her staff. They stood with their backs to the wall, muscles tight with anticipation and eyes searching.

There was another crash of thunder, and the wind picked up speed, whistling around them. A whirlwind, like the one that had appeared before Jabari's cave, formed in front of them.

As far as she knows, I haven't discovered all of my powers. Adanya thought to her companions. *Kamaria will take the lead.*

She saw them nodding out of the corners of her eyes as she kept her focus on the whirlwind.

The next few moments seemed like hours as they waited for Nehanda to appear. Adanya forced herself to keep her mind from spinning, knowing everything that happened next hinged on her ability to control all of her powers—and avoid revealing their strength until just the right moment.

Finally, Nehanda stepped out of the whirlwind and stood facing them, an appraising, searching look on her face as she studied them all.

This was it.

Chapter Forty

Adanya looked down from her perch in the fork of a tree at the tall, statuesque woman beneath her, staring back up at her.

"Who are you?" she asked, eyes narrowing in suspicion.

The woman attempted a smile; it was clear she didn't smile much by how forced it looked on her face. "My name is Nehanda. I'm one of the sorcerers on the council at the palace."

"What are you doing here?"

"I'm looking for you, Adanya."

Adanya tensed, her mind searching the stranger's to find answers.

Without breaking eye contact, the woman made her thoughts clear. *I know that you're a Sage. My job is finding sorcerers who haven't been trained and bringing them to a safe place to learn to control their powers.*

"Why would I want to go around other people?" Adanya asked, sneering despite herself. "They think I'm dangerous. Maybe I am. But I know I'm safer here, in the woods. It's worked so far."

"You're surviving, yes, but you could be thriving." The teenager sensed a sudden wave of sincerity as Nehanda ventured a step closer to the tree. "I know how you ended up out here alone," she said gently. "I'm not too different from you."

"What does that even mean?"

"When I was younger than you, I discovered my powers. I didn't know how to control them, and I ended up hurting people. They didn't understand me; I didn't understand myself. So they kicked me out, and I was forced to fend for myself."

Adanya relaxed ever so slightly. That was, essentially, her own story. While she was still suspicious of this woman's motives, knowing they shared similar experiences made her feel a kinship she had not felt with anyone before. "Why were you looking for me?" she asked in a softer tone.

"As I said, part of my mandate on the council is to find young sorcerers and train them to use their powers so they can protect themselves and others. I want you to come to the palace, learn in a safe place how to use your powers, and decide what you're going to do with your life."

"I don't know how I feel about that. I've been doing quite well out here by myself. And no one gets hurt." She knew the woman likely sensed her fear, but she couldn't control it.

Nehanda seemed sad, and Adanya felt the change in her attitude. "Adanya ... I understand. I understand wanting to stay alone, where things are simpler. But sorcerers have responsibilities just by being born with magic. It may not be what we want, but that's just the way things are. Besides, if the non-magical folk never see the good that sorcerers can do, they'll never learn to accept us. To *value* us. We deserve that."

Adanya considered. "What happens if I join your training and decide it's not for me?"

"Then you can return to your life here, and I won't bother you again. But I have a feeling you'll feel more connected with others if you come."

Though Adanya did enjoy the solitude being alone in the woods had afforded her, she could not help but feel an occasional pang of longing for connection with other humans that the animals around her could not fulfill. And learning from someone who understood where she was coming from didn't exactly sound like a bad idea.

After a few more moments of contemplation, she hopped down from the tree branch to stand before Nehanda. "Okay. On a trial basis."

Now a genuine, bright smile crossed Nehanda's face, and she gently placed a hand on Adanya's shoulder. "You won't regret it."

Chapter Forty-One

The smile on Nehanda's face was not the same smile of warmth and support from that day in the woods; this smile was haughty, smug, and mocking.

As Adanya stood between Adio and Kamaria, all that she could feel from Nehanda was immense hatred. And yet, beneath it she felt her own twinge of regret and sadness. Nehanda had utterly betrayed her and everything they were supposed to stand for; she'd even killed Jabari before her very eyes. But this was still the woman who had practically been her mother since she was a teenager, who'd taught her to survive among non-magical folk and learn the social etiquette she lacked from living in the woods.

"Well, well, well," Nehanda said, eyes scanning them all. "Isn't this a lovely trio?"

Adanya had to compose herself, to hide and guard her feelings from Nehanda's searching thoughts. But it took everything within her to follow the plan, not to burn the staff in her hands and lash out at Nehanda.

"Where's the rest of the merry little band?" Nehanda glanced around. "I would have thought you'd try a show of force. No matter. I'll deal with them after we've finished here."

Adanya fought the panic rising in her. Did Nehanda already know where the others were hidden? Had she guessed the plan? Suddenly she doubted everything she'd organized, wishing she'd spent more time planning before putting things into motion.

The others tensed beside her, wrestling with the same feelings.

Nehanda seemed to sense their inner turmoil, though none of them had spoken. Her smile grew wider. "Look at us. We four here, the last remaining members of the council. How poetic."

A wave of heat emanated from Kamaria. "Don't speak as if we're old friends, Nehanda. The things that you have done are unforgivable."

"All I have done is made this world a safer place for magical people."

"You can't actually believe that," Adio snorted. "Making the world safe for us didn't have to involve killing thousands of people."

"Didn't it? They may have pretended to accept us, but we all know they would have tired of us and tried to get rid of us in the end."

"You always did have a very dim view of non-magical folk," Adio said. "Wouldn't it have been easier to have some faith in them?"

Now Nehanda snorted. "Faith? Faith in people whose fears encompass what they don't understand, who refuse to learn and accept people who are different? That is high and mighty talk, especially coming from someone who never really experienced how cruel people could be." She turned her eyes to Adanya, who still hadn't spoken. Her gaze softened ever so slightly, as if she were remembering the connection they once shared. "Adanya ... seeing you here really takes me back. I did always say you'd do great things, didn't I?"

Adanya was unable to keep her voice from shaking as she responded, "A pity they came at the expense of everyone I ever cared about."

"Sweet girl. You always did have an idealized notion of people that I couldn't seem to dissuade you from. I tried so hard to make you the best that you could be..."

"How, by handicapping me? You took every opportunity to downplay my abilities! You would tell everyone else how you thought I'd soon be on the council, but you constantly made me feel inadequate and stupid!" She paused to take a breath as Adio placed a cautious hand on her shoulder, his touch reminding her of the plan and that revealing her full powers in her anger would put the others in danger.

Nehanda seemed unaffected by the emotion that Adanya was showing. "I was trying to keep you humble, child. We all know that pride can turn even the greatest person into something terrible."

"You were trying to keep me submissive. Keep me beneath you." She could feel Nehanda trying to break her shield, to see if she had manifested her other powers. She fought hard to keep her out.

"Children often misjudge the actions of their parents; you must know that. I wanted to keep you safe." Nehanda's voice held a caring tone, obviously feigned.

"Maybe that's how you started." Adanya loosened her grip on her staff, remembering to keep up the pretense that she didn't know its true purpose. "But keeping me safe wouldn't have involved keeping secrets. It wouldn't have involved lying to me. And it certainly wouldn't have involved killing everyone that I held dear."

Nehanda shook her head. "You would understand if you had children of your own."

"But you don't have a child. And since you separated me from my love, I never will, either." Her voice broke, a fresh wave of emotion threatening to overtake her.

"Enough," Kamaria said firmly, stepping out in front of Adanya. "This back and forth is getting us nowhere."

Adanya sent silent thanks to Kamaria, bracing herself.

"Nehanda, you have murdered thousands of people to make yourself the most powerful sorcerer in the world. But it's time that you pay for what you've done."

"Pay?" Nehanda repeated quizzically, a wave of heat coming from her. "You say it as if I owe something."

"The power you hold was gained by destroying and manipulating others."

"It's a dog-eat-dog world, Kamaria dear. Those who don't learn how to survive are the first ones to die. And since you all seem to think you can stand against me, I suppose you'll die, too."

Without further pretense, she whipped up her hand. A tongue of flame rolled down her arm and shot toward the trio. Kamaria was just as quick, raising both hands to absorb the flames without taking any damage. At the same time, Adio called forth heavy storm clouds that rolled in with frightening speed; they staggered as the wind and rain suddenly whipped around them. Just as the flames dissipated, a loud crack of thunder announced a lightning bolt that struck Nehanda.

To the other's surprise, the lightning seemed to have no effect on Nehanda. The electricity traveled around her body in little white shocks. They hissed and sent up steam when touched by raindrops, but they left her unaffected.

She chuckled dangerously. "You don't know what you've gotten yourself into."

All of the electricity moved down to her hands. Before the others realized what she was doing, she pointed both hands at the group. Lightning burst from her fingertips and struck them, slamming them against the roof's barrier wall and dropping them to the ground, writhing in pain.

Adanya was the first to recover. She staggered to her feet with the aid of her staff to face Nehanda again. The storm continued pouring rain down upon them, though Nehanda seemed unbothered. In fact, she seemed downright enthralled. She laughed, throwing her head back to the sky.

"You thought you could be rid of me that easily?" she asked, smiling at Adanya. "I'd expect you, of all people, to know better."

Adanya was torn. With all of their powers combined, it was possible to overwhelm and defeat her. But she had not bet on how powerful Nehanda truly was; if she could control lightning, what else could she control? Adanya couldn't put the others in danger—she was likely the only one powerful enough to truly face Nehanda—but was the timing right for her to reveal herself?

She pulled herself out of her thoughts as Nehanda drew a lightning bolt from the sky, preparing to fling lightning at them once more. Adio and Kamaria were only just coming to themselves, clearly unable to move out of the way. Without a second's hesitation, Adanya dove to shove them out of the way, taking the full brunt of the strike herself.

This strike was stronger, searing through her. Her hand clamped onto the staff like a vise as she tried to shake the pain from her mind.

Kamaria and Adio leapt up, moving to either side of Nehanda as they summoned their powers. Adio caused a whirlwind, the rain whipping around Nehanda in a cyclone. Into the cyclone, Kamaria threw twin tongues of fire, surrounding Nehanda with hot steam as the rain touched the flames.

As Adanya recovered, she thought to reach into Nehanda's mind and try to control her, but she feared that, if she entered Nehanda's mind, she would give her enemy access to hers—and that would destroy them all. Instead, she tried to pry her fingers off the staff so that if she did need to reveal her full powers, she could.

There was now a full cyclone of fire surrounding Nehanda, illuminating Adio and Kamaria with a bright orange light that could surely be seen for miles. Adanya sent a quick thought to the others hiding in the woods, alerting them to Nehanda's presence and reminding them to stay hidden until they received her call.

Then she asked Kamaria and Adio, *What do you need from me?*

An idea of what to do next would be helpful, Adio thought back, the strain on his face evident.

We can't hold fire too long, Kamaria thought. *She may have other powers now, but she's primarily an Ember.*

A surge of power drew into Nehanda, the sides of the cyclone pulling inwards as if being sucked in.

"Let it go!" Adanya cried in alarm.

They both reacted quickly, but not quickly enough. The cyclone disappeared, leaving Nehanda standing, seemingly, on fire. But it was clear she had drawn from Adio and Kamaria's powers enough to strengthen herself, because her smile grew more menacing.

Kamaria would likely be able to survive a fire attack, but Adio was in significant danger. Adanya focused on her Aqua powers, scooping a swath of rain from the sky to create a thick wall of water in front of her friends just as Nehanda released a blast of fire from her hands.

Adio and Kamaria ducked instinctively, but they were well protected by the water, which burst into steam as the flames met it but kept the fire from reaching them.

Nehanda's face changed as she lowered her hands. "Well, well, well. It would seem as though you have discovered what I tried to hide from you all these years."

Panic set in for the slightest moment as Adanya fully realized what she'd revealed. But then she accepted that what was done was done; now it was time to fully own her power. She tried to stand taller, subconsciously missing her longer hair as she faced Nehanda. The others stood respectfully to the side, understanding she was about to take the lead.

"It's far past time for us to end this," she said, trying to sound braver than she felt.

"It's already ended, Adanya."

A rush of wings sounded, as if thousands of birds were suddenly drawing near. They looked around to see a flock of crows winging toward them, seemingly heedless of the rain battering them. Some of them darted down into the trees, doubtlessly intercepted by Odeon and Nala, but most of them quickly formed a cyclone of black feathers and sharp talons and beaks that quickly set upon the trio, attacking them from all sides.

As they tried to cover their heads and faces from being torn to shreds, Adanya reached out to the twins. *What eats crows?*

The answer came quickly, their voices answering one after the other. *Red-tailed hawks or great owls!* Odeon said.

They don't travel together in numbers enough to overtake them, Nala countered. *But cats will attack them, too!*

Adanya managed to uncover her head long enough to change her power's focus, calling for any owls, hawks, or cats she could sense. The minutes passed with agonizing slowness as they tried to make themselves as small as possible, huddling against the barrier wall. She could sense the animals coming, but the madness of the moment made it impossible to know exactly where they were.

Crows scattered as larger birds came swooping into their midst, both large-eyed owls, their talons ripping out tail and wing feathers as they bowled into the fray, and beautiful red-tailed hawks, who stabbed at the crows with vicious tears of their beaks. A few moments later, all manner of stray cats scrabbled their way up over the barrier wall and fell upon any crows that had fallen to the rooftop, quickly finishing them off.

As their numbers thinned, Nehanda became visible again, her face flushed with fury. "It seems I'll need to deal with your little friends sooner rather than later," she growled.

In the blink of an eye, the wind changed, quickly blowing away the storm clouds and scalding them with the sudden heat of the morning sun. Any remaining birds scattered back into the trees, leaving behind gruesome carcasses strewn about the rooftop.

The remaining moisture evaporated in clouds of steam around them, partially obscuring their view of each other. Adio and Kamaria instinctively drew nearer to Adanya, protecting her sides as they kept their backs to the wall.

"Trying to sweat us out, disorient us," Adio murmured out of the side of his mouth, even as beads of sweat began to roll down his forehead.

There was nothing for it. Adanya stretched her mind, searching for Nehanda. When she found her, she physically staggered back; it felt like she'd run up against a brick wall. She was putting up a barrier.

"She knows!" Kamaria gasped, pointing down to the forest where the others were hiding.

Out of thin air, balls of flames rained down upon the trees, drying out the rain and setting them ablaze.

Abiba! Adanya sent, trying not to panic.

We're fine! The water from the lake is protecting us.

Get out of the trees as soon as you can. There's no use hiding anymore; she knows that you're there.

Should we come to you?

Adanya paused for the briefest moment. She could feel the fear setting in, threatening to overtake her and render her powerless. But the thought of the others being in danger snapped her into action.

No, go to the town and make sure the fire doesn't spread there. I'm sending Sefu to you. There's a good chance that she'll send soldiers to get you.

Understood.

"We've got to bring her attention back to us," Adio said.

"Kamaria, can you redirect those flames?"

"Difficult from this distance, but I'll certainly try." She turned toward the forest.

"Adio, can we get the cloud cover back?"

"On it." He turned to the sky.

Framed by the pair of them, she reached out to Sefu. *Sefu. Nehanda knows where the others are. Once the fire dies, they're going to the town to keep the people safe. I want you to meet them there; I have a feeling she'll be sending troops to bring them in.*

You don't need me here?

Trust me.

Understood.

She returned her focus to the rooftop. Nehanda became visible as the mist cleared, her eyes fixed on the forest. Kamaria was having an impact, some balls vanishing before reaching the trees, but it was clear that she was overwhelmed.

Decisively, she joined her efforts with Kamaria, keeping one eye on Nehanda while focusing on drawing the fire from the air. Adio slowly managed to draw some clouds into the moisture-starved air.

Her eyes widened with surprise as the flames all disappeared instantly. She felt the heat inside her bones, flushing her skin and energizing her.

Everyone's mouths fell open as they stared at her, awed by her power. Even Nehanda, who had to have known what she was capable of, seemed stunned.

Realizing she had a momentary advantage, she changed the energy to Flora. The decorative vines climbing the walls moved under her control, snaking out like extended limbs. They wrapped around Nehanda from head to toe, trapping her arms at her side.

Caught off guard, she lost her balance and fell hard on her back, banging her head.

Adanya felt Nehanda's mind block fall away as her consciousness left, and she seized the opportunity to enter her mind and paralyze her.

The tumult of emotions swirling inside of Nehanda froze Adanya. Anger, fear, sorrow, jealousy … sadness? Why would she be feeling that?

Then it hit her. Some part of Nehanda did love her despite the venomous hatred that poisoned everything else. It wasn't hatred of her; it was hatred of the non-magical people who had treated her cruelly, which had extended to all non-magical folk out of fear—and the betrayal of Adanya's allyship with those people.

As she tried to recover from the emotions and revelations, Nehanda's eyes flew open, looking into Adanya with sudden clarity. Her face tightened as they locked in a battle of wills, oblivious to the shadows overhead brought back by the clouds and the others on the rooftop.

Give up, Nehanda. I don't want to kill you.

As if you could! Even with all this newfound power, you're only half as powerful as I am. I will destroy you and anyone else who is a threat to magical people.

Magical people, or just you and your power? You can't tell me that all of the people in the world were a threat to you.

Everyone has the potential to be a threat.

The prince was a threat? He was a child; he wasn't even capable of hate yet!

He would have been! His father would have made him hate us, or he would have hated you because his father...

My father. You knew and you never told me.

Because I knew that if it came down to us, and you knew he was your father, you would side with him.

I wish that you would have had more faith in me. Yes, I loved him like a father without knowing he was mine. But I also loved you. The only reason I would have completely gone against you would have been if you wanted to hurt people. And even then, I would have tried to figure things out. You don't just abandon the people that you love. If you really loved me, you would have known that.

Nehanda did not respond, a tear brimming at the corner of her eye. Despite thoughts of making Nehanda pay for all she had done, Adanya could not help but feel a stab of pity for her one-time mentor. After all, she realized, no one had truly shown Nehanda what love was supposed to look like.

That slight hesitation proved to be too much.

Nehanda's tear sizzled and evaporated on her cheek. She clenched a fist and her entire body burst into flames, incinerating her plant bonds and sending waves of heat away from her.

Adanya was frozen in place, trying to fight Nehanda's control from within. Adio was knocked flat by the heat, attempting to shield his face. Unaffected, Kamaria quickly moved to protect the other two, her eyes flaming.

A smirk crossed Nehanda's face. "Yes, I think it's time that we finished this."

"We never got along, did we?" Kamaria replied coolly, allowing flames to roll down her arms. "I must have known your true nature all along."

"I'm glad you held on this long. It's going to be so much more satisfying to end you now."

There were no further words. Nehanda threw tongues of flames toward her. Kamaria blocked the flames, her hair billowing in the heated air. Nehanda's face was the picture of concentrated fury, eyebrows lowered as she pushed all of her power toward Kamaria, the fire steadily growing higher until the two of them were engulfed in the flames.

It was an awe-inspiring sight, the women channeling all of their energy and fury at one another and wrestling with the flames. Adio moved over to Adanya, trying to help her break from Nehanda's control.

"I don't understand," she gritted through her teeth. "She shouldn't have the focus to still be holding me."

"What can I do?"

"The staff. The lightning has fused my hand closed. It's got to be what's keeping her control over me."

He tried prying her fingers open one by one. "I'm sorry," he apologized. "I told you to keep the staff."

"I don't think we knew what we were up against. She's more powerful than I realized."

He glanced over his shoulder at the combatants. "Kamaria seems to be holding her own."

"Something's wrong." Adanya felt a strange sensation coming from Nehanda. She wasn't sure what it was, but she felt like something was about to change for the worse. "Hurry!"

Adio managed to get three of her fingers loose before the heat around them intensified. Nehanda now seemed to be made of flames herself, her skin, hair, and clothes tongues of flame in her shape. She released a focused yell as the flames burned white hot, singeing their hair and clothes.

Kamaria's yell was one of pure agony. The flames, once sitting on top of her body like a halo, began to truly eat at her.

The smell of burning flesh filled the air as she caught aflame, sending her to the ground and rolling around to smother the flames. Nehanda laughed maniacally.

Adanya could feel Adio's distress as he tried to pull clouds from the air to rain upon the horrifying scene and save her. But there was no moisture, and his efforts were in vain. He sank to his knees beside the still paralyzed Adanya, tears in his eyes.

A few moments more, and Kamaria stopped moving. Her body burned brightly, causing even the daylight to seem dull in comparison. Nehanda huffed a breath, and her body returned to its solid form. She slowly walked over to the burning corpse, eyes dancing with victory.

"I could have just taken your powers to strengthen my own," she said, "but this was so much more delicious."

Then she turned to Adio and Adanya. "It was a good try. Really, it was. But I think that playtime is over."

Adio stiffened beside Adanya, and she instinctively knew Nehanda had paralyzed him as well.

"A quick death is too good for you. No, I think that a public execution is the best way to remind everyone who holds the power here. They all think you'll save them? I'll put a decisive end to that delusion."

She came forward and paused in front of Adanya, who was shaking and straining against Nehanda's power, fury flowing through her body. She gently cupped her cheek for a moment, then grabbed her chin to force her to look directly into her eyes. "Go to sleep, little girl. It will be the last time I show you such kindness."

Adanya lost consciousness immediately, dropping into a dreamless sleep.

Chapter Forty-Two

Some of Adanya's favorite memories were waking up beside Rashidi. Her eyes fluttered open as a beam of sunlight crossed her face. She inhaled deeply, the smell of sandalwood filling her nostrils as she felt the weight of Rashidi's arm around her waist. She snuggled in closer to him, enjoying his warm body against her back.

He stirred at her movement, stretching before pulling her closer to him and burying his face in her neck. "Good morning, beautiful," he rumbled.

She giggled at the huskiness of his morning voice, which sent delicious shivers down her spine. "Good morning, my love."

"How did you sleep?"

"Like the dead." She chuckled. "But I always sleep like that when you're with me."

"Saying that you needed a burly man to help you get to sleep?"

"Something like that." She rolled over so she could see his face, gently tangling her fingers in his beard.

He stroked her cheek, pushing her braids from her eyes as he gazed lovingly at her.

"Why do you look at me like that?" she asked softly.

"Like what? Like you're my world? Like I would do anything to protect you? Like I'm willing to spend the rest of my life loving you and helping you love and value yourself? No idea."

She felt her face flush, and she ducked her head into his chest. "All that?"

He lifted her head and kissed her. "All that. Every word."

"I ... I never thought that someone could love me this much. That I could have feelings that are so intense."

Now he ran his hand over her side, lingering on her curves. "I don't know why. I have very intense feelings for you." Then he took her hand and moved it to his chest. "Do you feel that? Every time I look at you, my heart beats faster." Then he slid her hand down further, past his chiseled abs. "Something else happens, too."

She smiled again as she felt a familiar warmth in her hand. "We'll have to do something about that."

\#

When they finally got up for the day nearly an hour later, Adanya's mind was preoccupied.

"Where did you go, love?" Rashidi's voice brought her back as he parted her braids to oil her scalp for her, something he'd learned to do on his own after watching her a few times.

"Just thinking."

"About?"

"Something that you said to me once."

He raised an eyebrow. "Care to elaborate? I've said a lot of things to you."

She hesitated before reminding herself that she could literally tell him anything.

"How do you know that you love someone? I mean, not just like what you and I have, but people in your life."

She could feel him thinking as he continued his work, formulating his ideas.

It seemed a foolish question to ask; who didn't know what it meant to love others? But as her love for him grew stronger and deeper, and her other relationships changed and grew, she needed things to be clearly defined for her.

Besides, if there was anyone she could trust to give her clear answers without judgment, it was Rashidi.

"I think that there are a lot of layers to it," he said finally. "There are always going to be people n your life that you enjoy spending time with, that you can talk to and share experiences with. But you can like someone without loving them, and vice versa."

"Wait, loving someone without liking them? That doesn't make any sense."

He chuckled. "You'd think so. But I've lost count of people I know who love their spouses and create families with them, but they have absolutely nothing in common if it's not about their children. They're not friends."

"That sounds awful."

"It does. Which is why I was determined to be friends with whoever I decided to marry. My parents were a good example; they were always laughing with each other. I wanted to have someone that I could have fun with without always ... having fun." He tilted her head back to kiss her, raising his eyebrows suggestively before returning to his work.

"But the difference comes with the level of investment that you have with someone. For example, you'd be willing to help your friends to succeed, even though you may not extend yourself for them. But when you truly love someone, you're invested in helping them be the best that they can be. You are happy for them when things go well, and sad when they don't. You're willing to go the extra mile for them because your happiness is affected by them. Not in a bad way, like you're too connected, but enough that it's distinct enough from just being friends."

Adanya thought about that. "Like when Gabir lost his wife. I thought that my sadness just came from my magic, allowing me to feel what he was feeling."

"I can see it being more complicated for you since you're an empath. Especially since you didn't experience what real love was until you started working with the king."

"What? But I have Nehanda. I know that she loves me."

His silence, combined with the unspoken feeling of "Are you sure?" told her of his disbelief. Rather than pursue it, however, he paused to allow her to process further.

"I ... I never had anyone teach me what love means," she admitted. She felt a pang of sadness as she tried to remember her interactions with her mother. "My mother died when I was eight. Long before she could really teach me what love was. Though I always got the sense that she'd sacrificed something for me, to make sure I was alright. I remember thinking that even before my magic manifested."

"There's likely some truth to it. Sometimes love does require great sacrifice. But I can see how not being taught what love is would affect you now." He poured more oil on his hands and worked it through the length of her braids. "When it all comes down to it, you are the only one who can truly define if you love someone. Not only does love look different depending on who you're showing love to, but you will show love differently because of who you are as a person. For example, you're a very reserved person overall. It's hard to see what you're feeling unless someone knows you well. But for those that do, there are subtle differences, and you adjust depending on your relationship with the person. Kamaria wears her emotions on her sleeve, like Embers tend to do. So you're more open with your hugs and your smiles towards her, even if it seems to outsiders that you're all business. But someone like the king, who has to have a sense of restraint as our leader, isn't someone that you can laugh and joke with. So your affections towards him are more muted, though they're still there. He does like to see you smile, though, so he enjoys heaping compliments and support on you when you're in private."

She blushed, realizing how true his observations were. "Do you notice everything?" she asked with a smile.

"Almost. Comes with the job description." He finished with her hair and helped her to her feet, wrapping her in his arms as he kissed her forehead. "The most important thing to know is that the people you love will never hurt you intentionally. And if they do hurt you, they'll do what they can to make it right and not do the same thing again. I hope I've answered your question?"

"I think you have."

"Good." He squeezed her again, then went to pick up his sword belt from where it lay on the side table. "I'm off to work. Let me know if I need to remind you how I show you love." He kissed her deeply, then smacked her ass before heading out of the door.

Chapter Forty-Three

Adanya came to slowly, her head pounding and in a haze. There were lots of emotions swirling in the air; for a few moments, she couldn't tell if they were hers or someone else's.

"Adanya?" Adio's voice broke through the haze.

She opened her eyes, everything around her coming into focus. She was in a semi-dark room—the dungeon of the palace, she realized as she saw the iron bars across from where she was sitting. Some light filtered through through the barred window, but it was dull, as if the clouds were still in the sky. Time had passed, though she had no idea how long she'd been unconscious. Adio was in a cell to her left, separated by another row of iron bars. His hands were wrapped around them as he strained to see her better, his face filled with concern.

She attempted to turn but found her progress hampered by something. Looking down, she saw that her staff was no longer in her hand. Instead, it had been bent and wrapped around her like a coil, pinning her hands to her sides and preventing her from moving. Now she knew why everything felt hazy and confused; Nehanda had used the staff to keep her from using her magic to escape.

"Adanya, are you alright?"

"I'm ... here."

"I haven't seen anyone since we got here. I don't know if anything has happened to the others."

"She'll be down to gloat, I'm sure." Her voice was dull and lifeless. She'd given up.

Adio could tell. "Adanya, please. This isn't over. We're still alive; there's still a chance we can come out of this."

"There's nothing left!" she exploded, her rage and frustration pushing through the fog of Nehanda's magic to allow her to speak clearly. "We never had a chance. She's always been more powerful. I don't know why I ever allowed myself to think that I could be strong enough to defeat her."

"She's just gotten in your head. I don't think she's ever truly been *out* of your head. But you can't let her win." When she didn't answer, he kept pressing. "I saw what strength you have when you stop trying to control it. Nehanda has always known that you're more powerful than her; that's why she worked so hard on destroying your self-esteem. We all have faith in you…"

"Kamaria had faith in me," she said bleakly. "She stayed alive for all these years just to die a horrible death because I was too weak to save her."

"You made fireballs vanish into thin air!" he said firmly. "There is nothing about you that is weak. You have gone through more and grown so much in the past few weeks than some people do in a lifetime."

She finally turned her head to look at him, allowing him to see the bleakness and despair in her face. "I'm done fighting the inevitable."

He tried one more tactic. "So you're willing to just let everyone that cares about you die?"

She ignored him, closing her eyes and tilting her head back until it was resting on the cold stones. She allowed herself to return to the noise and chaos of her mind.

#

"Hello, my love."

Her eyes fluttered open at the familiar voice, rich and deep as the first time she'd heard it.

She looked around to find herself not bound in a cell but sitting in front of the fireplace in her room in the palace. Standing before her, a warm smile on his face, was Rashidi. Her heart leapt, but only for a moment. She knew that it was either Nehanda herself messing around in her head or just a result of Nehanda's magic; either way, it wasn't real.

"You're not here," she said sadly.

"I'm always a part of you, Adanya." He crouched before her and took her hand, looking up into her face. "Talk to me."

"There's nothing to talk about. It's over. Nehanda has won."

"And why do you think that?"

She looked at him in disbelief. "Everything! Kamaria, Jabari, everyone ... they're gone. No one is coming back."

"Why does that mean she's won?"

"If she so easily destroyed them, what is she going to do to me? She knows every move that I would make. She trained me. Raised me."

"But she didn't *make* you. Your heart for others, your strength, your ability to make it through remarkable odds? That all came from you."

"I don't believe that. If I did, I wouldn't be here."

"She tried to destroy you and disguised it as love. You survived that. You are continuing to push past her control." He put a finger on her lips, forestalling further argument. "She may have you physically and magically right now, but she doesn't have your mind. She tried, but she didn't succeed."

Tears brimmed in her eyes. "I have nothing left, Rashidi. I can't see anyone else die because I can't get control of my powers."

"That's the problem. You're trying to control it."

"What?"

"Control is what Nehanda drilled into you. Control your feelings, control how much of others you allow in, control how your magic works. But what if you stopped trying to control it all? Think about it. Did Ziyad have to think to use his powers?"

"I..." She thought back to the numerous times she'd seen him use magic. "No. It was effortless; he sensed what needed to be done and it just happened."

"Take from his example. You have so much magic swirling within you. Release it. Let it fully take you over."

He stood, pulling her to her feet so he could wrap his arms around her. "Stop doubting yourself, my love. I've always believed in you, and I'm not the only one. But now you need to believe in yourself."

She inhaled deeply, his familiar scent filling her nostrils. "Believe in myself..." she repeated quietly. Then again, a little louder. "Believe in myself."

Taking comfort in his arms, she closed her eyes and tried to center herself. Memories came flooding in like a hurricane, rushing past her mind's eye almost faster than she could process. But the face that she kept seeing was Nehanda's. Snatches of conversations, lessons where she had been taught to restrain herself, to hold back, to make herself smaller than she was. Everything boiled up inside of her—pain, rage, betrayal, sorrow—giving her the physical sensation that she was going to be sick. But she fought the urge to push everything back down, instead opening herself up to feel all of it, the emotions and the magic.

The sick sensation gradually eased, replaced by a sparkling feeling, as if she'd just drank a bubbly drink. Now she began to feel warm, like the fire she had captured from the sky was shut up in her bones and igniting her from within.

She felt ... powerful. A dam had broken loose within her, releasing the full force of all of the magic that she possessed.

Rashidi laughed proudly, squeezing her tight. "That's my girl."

#

Her eyes snapped open, everything suddenly crystal clear. Adio sat up from where he was watching her in his cell, noticing the change. Power surged through her, giving her a heady, swirling feeling that warmed her from head to toe.

She felt unstoppable. She knew not to get cocky, but she also knew that this power she felt would be what allowed her to defeat Nehanda once and for all.

"Adanya?" Adio said hesitantly.

She turned her head to look at him before he even spoke, feeling the pull of his magic. She smiled her brightest smile, rewarded by a matching one.

"Your eyes—they're glowing! I don't know where you were, but it seems to have done you some good," he said.

"I guess I was giving myself a pep talk." She rolled her shoulders, rewarded with a crack from the wood wrapped around her. Then she blinked several times until she couldn't see the reflection of her light on the metal bars and knew that her eyes weren't glowing as brightly anymore. "She's sending soldiers down to take us to the field to execute us; she wants to make us an example."

"How do you know that?"

She paused for a moment, considering. Before, she could only barely sense others around her unless she focused on them specifically. But now? She could distinctly feel every person for miles: soldiers, rebels, allies, townspeople. Nehanda. "I just … feel it."

She was surprised that he accepted her vague explanation. "Right. So, what's the plan? Does she have the others?"

"They're cornered in the town. They're holding their own, for now."

"Will they be able to help?"

"I think so. I'll tell them how to get out and have them join us."

She paused, closing her eyes and clearly seeing the section of the town where the young sorcerers, supported by Waed and Sefu, were defending themselves against nearly one hundred armed soldiers. The scene was controlled chaos, with various forms of magic at play: animals of all kinds attacking soldiers, water flooding in and sweeping soldiers off of their feet, plants seemingly coming to life and wrapping leafy limbs around ankles and arms, flinging soldiers hither and thither.

Waed and Sefu were a masterful team, directing their fighters while causing destruction of their own.

She spoke to them all at once. *Everyone, I'm going to tell you how to end this so that you can get to the field. Sefu, get your soldiers behind Abiba. Idir, once they're behind her, pull the grass up so it will stop the water from getting to them. Abiba, pull every ounce of water and flood them out. Odeon and Nala, have your animals take out any that escape.*

Their voices echoed in her head, overlapping each other with affirmative responses. It was only then that she considered she'd never been able to speak to more than one person at a time with her mind. She watched as they followed her directions with military precision, executing the plan in mere minutes.

Well done, she congratulated. *Get to the field, but stay hidden until I give you word.*

Understood.

She opened her eyes to Adio's expectant face. "Well?" he asked.

"They're on their way."

"So what's our plan?"

"Not that much different from before. I lay low, don't let her know that I've discovered my full strength and am free from her. We'll wait for the right moment. I'll have Sefu and the others handle the army, but she and I need to finish this alone."

Adio opened his mouth to protest, stopping short when he saw the determined, focused look on her face. "What do you need from me?"

"Once I'm gone, you'll be the ranking sorcerer. Root out the rest of her army; disarm and capture if you can, kill if you must. Whether I return or not, her control over this world is over." She paused for a moment as the weight of her own words hit her. Then she squared her jaw. "Keep your mind on me and wait for my signal. When the time is right, we end this."

Chapter Forty-Four

Moments later, as Adanya sensed the soldiers coming, she slumped her shoulders back and dropped her head, resuming her depressive countenance so it would appear that nothing was wrong. The soldiers seemed fearful of her, unlocking her cell and yanking her to her feet using only the branch wrapped around her. Then they shoved her ahead of them, spears pointing menacingly.

Adio was left unbound as his cell was unlocked and they pushed him roughly to walk between her and them as if he would be a buffer from her power.

They weren't exactly wrong, she thought.

Though she kept her eyes lowered, she used her magic to see their journey in her mind's eye, almost as if watching through a window like she had done with the others in town. The soldiers took them up two flights of stairs, then out through the courtyard and the front gate. The road leading to the palace was eerily deserted, without even the sounds of birds or insects. A little ways down, one of the soldiers pointed his spear at a smaller, less-used path that wound down through the woods and toward the field.

The early evening coolness surrounded them in the stillness of the woods. All of her senses, magical and physical, were sharpened to a height she had never experienced before. Adanya could sense her allies nearby; she could also sense the intense fear of the soldiers around them and those gathered in the field waiting for them. A sudden harsh wind blew through the trees, rustling the leaves and sending goosebumps across Adanya's skin, and she sensed Adio's nervous energy as they drew closer to their intended execution.

No fear, now, she thought.

Easy for you to say, he thought back, but she could feel his confidence in her.

As they left the cover of the wood, they saw the field was teeming with hundreds of soldiers. They stood in tight formation, leaving an aisle in the center for the prisoners to walk through them. At the center of the field stood Nehanda, an image of fierce barbarity in black robes atop a raised wooden platform. Adanya could feel the heat of her stare but was careful to shield herself from it.

They were pushed onto the platform and left alone with her, the guards retreating into the formation. Nehanda only gave Adio a cursory glance before turning to Adanya, looking her up and down with a smirk of victory.

"My little protege," she said condescendingly. "You thought that you'd be able to win, didn't you? And now look." She waved her hand at the soldiers. "Your end will be a glorious one, to be sure, but it will be an end. Now that the last threat to my rule is over, I can continue my work securing the safety of sorcerers all over the world. We will be the majority, and we will no longer have to fear the others for their ignorance and violence against us."

Adanya sent Adio a quick thought, which he voiced for her. "And what happens to the sorcerers who refuse to stand with you? Are we all to die like Jabari and Kamaria?"

"Die? Oh goodness, no. Your magic will simply be added to my own to support the sorcerers who have the sense enough to follow me."

"One person is not supposed to have that much power. Your mind and body won't be able to handle it."

"It's worked thus far." She nonchalantly flicked a finger, and a sudden gust of wind ripped through the tree branches, sending leaves falling and birds flying. "My powers come from hundreds of sorcerers whose magic I've taken over the years. They weren't nearly as powerful as the council was, since none of them had been trained. Still, the sorcerers I took powers from helped to strengthen me."

"And how many sorcerers have you found lately?"

Nehanda's mouth twitched, and Adanya already had her answer as she had Adio continue sharing her thoughts.

"Not many, hm? No wonder. If you're killing them all, how will they be able to have children or descendants of their own to inherit magic? If you had learned some manner of diplomacy, instead of threatening them to join you and showing them what would happen if they didn't, they might have listened to you."

"My methods," she said in a strained voice, as if struggling to control her anger, "clearly worked well enough for some." She sent a pointed glance toward Adanya, who still appeared to be lost in her mind. "But I'm not going to keep going back and forth with you. I've brought you both here so that anyone else who would try to rise against me—including that pathetic little resistance that's been aiding you—will see what happens when I decide to retaliate."

"I think that's quite enough," Adanya finally said.

Nehanda whirled to look at her in shock, eyes wide as Adanya raised her head to show that she had not been incapacitated by the staff wrapped around her. "What?" Her voice raised in anger.

"You're right. It's time to end this."

Adanya flexed her arms ever so slightly, and the wood around her burst into splinters. Adio ducked down to avoid being hit, while Nehanda ducked her head under her cloak. The soldiers in the first few rows weren't so lucky, splinters piercing through their armor into chests and faces, knocking them flat.

Everyone watched in awe as Adanya's eyes began to glow with a warm yellow light.

Before Nehanda could react fully, Adanya set her plan in motion. *Now,* she told her allies calmly.

Adio called forth a storm, dark clouds rolling in. A hailstorm of arrows came from the trees, followed by Sefu, Waed, the rest of the new council, and the resistance fighters. The soldiers turned to meet them in a panic, their surprise rendering them disorganized and scrambling.

Adanya nodded at Adio before turning her attention back to Nehanda. She could feel her adversary gathering her magical power to strike, so she struck first. Just as Nehanda's energy was almost focused, Adanya raised her hands and made a sudden snatching motion.

In the blink of an eye, the two women were standing in a clearing in the middle of the very woods in which Adanya had lived when she was young. The sudden stillness and calm jarred them, and it took a moment to reorient themselves. Birds chirped merrily in the trees and insects sang their songs. Beams of sunlight pierced through the trees, bathing the clearing in warm yellow and orange tones from the setting sun.

Adanya took a deep breath of the pine-scented air, taking comfort from being back in familiar surroundings. Her heart still raced for the battle ahead, but she knew that she was finally on equal footing with the woman who had tried to break her down to nothing.

Nehanda, by contrast, seemed to be struggling to breathe. She was shaking—with rage, Adanya could sense, not fear—and trying to send herself back to the field. But Adanya easily blocked her from doing so with no more than a thought, leaving the older woman struggling against her.

"Not as eager to destroy me when you know we're equally matched, are you?"

Nehanda gave up, scowling at Adanya. "Equally matched? Don't delude yourself. Even if you do have power, it's nothing without the experience I have."

"Sometimes experience isn't the only thing that can change an outcome."

Nehanda tried a different tack. "There are things about your powers that you haven't discovered yet. Things I don't even know. Think of how we can find and strengthen them together! Why, we'd be unstoppable."

Adanya scoffed quietly and shook her head. "You did everything you could to control my power. You even hid the fact that I had more powers because you knew I would be the only one who could stop you. And you want me to just ... trust you? To forget everything that you did to me?"

"I raised you when no one else would!"

"*Raising* someone implies that you do everything you can to give them their best chance, not smother them and make them doubt themselves at every turn. I won't forget that. I can't. And I can't forget how you murdered an entire kingdom of people to further your selfish agenda." She felt her anger rising, and struggled to keep it under control. "I'm done talking, Nehanda. I'm done bargaining. It's time for all of this to end."

Nehanda searched her eyes, as if trying to find the young woman who had been so pliable and impressionable. Adanya stared boldly back, preventing her from using her Sage power to seek deeper.

The older woman's whole energy changed, drawing herself up and bracing herself. "Fine."

They faced off, motionless as they each sized up their opponent. Adanya's hand twitched, used to the familiar feel of her staff. But she flexed it instead, refocusing herself. She would have a full spectrum of powers to contend with, so she braced herself for whatever the first attack might be, letting Nehanda lead the encounter to discover what she was thinking.

The attack was not long in coming. Nehanda's eyes flickered, and a shower of vines fell from the trees above, obscuring Adanya's view. Rather than use a different power, Adanya opted to use the same power to counter her. She tilted her head, the glow in her eyes turning green, and the vines twisted and curled until she could see Nehanda's furious face. Another twitch of Nehanda's head, and the vines suddenly sprouted sharp thorns, their tips glistening with poison.

Painfully aware that she was now surrounded by vines, Adanya changed tactics. She focused on her Clime energy as Adio had shown her, changing the air pressure and therefore the temperature in the woods to a scorching heat as her eyes glowed blue. Before Nehanda could send the vines curling around her, they withered away, the woods echoing with the crackling of the sudden loss of moisture. Another thought and a swift gust of wind blew the vines into dust that scattered into the trees.

Sweat glistened on both of their faces as Nehanda tried to consider a next move. Her eyes flashed, and Adanya became aware of a familiar rumble in the ground.

An Ugwe burst from the trees, heading straight for Adanya. Her eyes glowed a darker blue as she focused on it, ignoring the furious pounding of her heart and pushing past the blind, animalistic rage fueling the animal. She knew speaking to it would be a lost cause, so instead she tried to redirect its energy toward Nehanda, deeming her as the more important prey.

She was surprised at how quickly it worked. The monster skidded to a stop, its claws churning up chunks of the earth behind it so it could turn toward Nehanda.

Nehanda's face was white as she saw the monster running at her. In a split-second decision, she raised a new web of vines thicker than her waist to wrap around the Ugwe, stopping it in its tracks. As it wrestled and strained to get free, she sent several vines whipping around its throat. They got tighter and tighter, strangling the Ugwe until it stopped struggling; it dropped to the ground as its snarls ended and its body went limp. The ground thudded with the weight of it falling, and the calm quiet soon returned.

Nehanda shook her head slightly, and Adanya could sense she hadn't been sure that it would work. Skirting the corpse, she slightly closed the distance between them so she could see Adanya again.

Adanya watched her like a hawk, aware that Nehanda would move like lightning.

Little did she know that lighting would be her next move.

Nehanda called heavy storm clouds to come rolling in above their heads. The temperature cooled rapidly, and Adanya could again feel the zing of electricity in the air, giving her goosebumps. Her mind shot back to the palace rooftop, remembering how Nehanda had captured the lightning to use for herself.

Sure enough, there was a rumble of thunder in the air before a bolt of lightning zigzagged from the sky into Nehanda's waiting hands. As before, she allowed the lightning to dance across her body for a moment before directing the electrical energy toward Adanya.

This time she was prepared, raising her hands to reflect the strike. Nehanda was barely able to deflect the zigzags of lightning streaming back at her. They both strained against one another, lightning joining them at their fingertips and superheating the air around them. Their chests heaved and sweat poured from their foreheads as each woman tried to overpower the other.

Adanya winced, the strain causing the still-healing muscles in her shoulder to shake. She could feel herself tiring; a glance at Nehanda told her the older woman felt the same. There had to be something she could do to turn the tide. The problem was that she didn't know what would happen if she tried to use two elemental powers at once.

She suddenly became aware of a vision pricking at the outside edges of her psyche, something that looked familiar and yet not: a young woman in these very woods, looking down at a blurry figure. Nehanda's mental blocks must be fading with the strain of deflecting the lightning!

Adanya redoubled her efforts, releasing a grunt as she managed a step forward. Nehanda's eyes widened, her arms now visibly shaking. Getting into her mind would be the key to winning this battle. Nehanda sank to one knee, still trying to overpower Adanya even though she was failing.

With a primal yell, Adanya summoned all of her magic to send a burst of energy through the lightning tying them together. Both were flung backwards, Nehanda slamming her back into the trunk of a tree with a truncated cry of pain while Adanya tumbled through the underbrush. Relatively unharmed and feeling a surge of power through her body, she scrambled to her feet and ran in the direction she'd seen Nehanda go flying.

Back in the clearing, she stopped and searched for Nehanda's mind. She found it and immediately latched on to the memory she'd glimpsed moments before.

Chapter Forty-Five

Both women found themselves standing by a large house. Nehanda scowled as she tried to catch her bearings, but she stopped short when she saw a young girl standing in front of them. She stared at the younger version of herself, rendered speechless by the memory playing out in front of her.

The younger Nehanda was playing with tongues of flame, tossing them back and forth between her hands while she glared at the young boy talking to a woman and pointing an accusatory finger back at her. The charred remains of a stuffed animal were at her feet, and there was nothing approaching shame or regret at what she'd done in her attitude.

"Nehanda!" the woman snapped. She walked over to her with the boy hiding behind her skirts, stopping just short of her as if afraid to get too close. "Why did you burn his toy?"

She shrugged. "He wouldn't share. So now no one gets it." She spoke perfectly calmly, clearly not understanding why the woman seemed so angry. "It seems fair."

"Nehanda, this is my last straw. We took you in after ... the unfortunate incident that claimed your parents. We've tried to acclimate you. But you refuse to learn, refuse to adapt to living like a normal person..."

"Normal person?" Nehanda interrupted, a wave of heat flaring out from her.

The woman took another step back, pushing the boy farther behind her. "You know exactly what I mean. Go and gather your things. You can't stay."

Adanya winced, expecting Nehanda to immediately fly into a rage. But instead, the girl shrugged her shoulders and went inside. After a few moments, the boy and woman followed, she comforting him and telling him he'd have another toy.

Adanya looked at the older Nehanda and saw a look of passive understanding. A moment later, she knew why.

Screams ripped from within the house, followed by Nehanda running back outside and barring the door shut. With a touch, she sent it up in flames. Within moments the whole house was on fire, smoke pouring from windows and the cries of those trapped within echoing out into the road. The girl watched with grim satisfaction for a moment. Then she spat in the direction of the burning house and ran toward the woods on the outskirts of town before anyone could come and see that she had been responsible.

Adanya's face was full of horror. She'd known Nehanda had been thrown out of the orphanage where she'd been living, but she had no idea that Nehanda had murdered all of those people.

A moment later the scene changed. They were now further into the woods. Nehanda was sitting in the fork of a tree, looking up through the canopy of leaves. She was older than when she had been at the orphanage, starting to develop into a young woman. Adanya was stunned as an older man draped in flowing robes approached the tree, looking up at her just as Nehanda had found her.

"Hello, Nehanda." Adanya instantly recognized Ziyad's calm, even voice.

Nehanda was immediately alert, a tongue of flame in her hand as she turned to see the intruder.

He smiled calmly at her. Adanya could feel his calming energy all around them, and even she began to feel calmer. Young Nehanda slowly lowered her hand, the flame vanishing, though she still looked suspiciously at him.

"Who are you?" she demanded.

He spread his arms wide. "My name is Ziyad. I'm the Head of the Council of Sorcerers."

Her eyes widened at the realization. "What are you doing out here?"

"Looking for you, my child."

"Why..." She swallowed hard, clearly worried he'd come to punish her for what she'd done to the orphanage. "Why are you looking for me?"

His face turned serious. "So many young magical children have been forced to fend for themselves, and not always with the best outcomes. I've convinced the king that these young sorcerers need to be found and trained properly so they have a chance to survive in this world. And I decided to start with you."

She was still suspicious. "And what does this entail?"

"You'll come live in the palace. Myself and one of the other sorcerers will train you according to your magic. Then, once you're fully in control of your powers, you can decide what path you want to take, whether it be working for the kingdom or making your own way in the world. But you will have the skills and knowledge to do anything you wish."

"Who says that I'm not already in control of my powers?"

"When you allow your emotions to dictate your actions, you are not the one in control."

Nehanda froze, realizing that he knew her secret. But he didn't seem angry or judgmental; instead, he looked sad.

"You cannot blame a child who has not been taught for the negative things they do. I want to offer you a second chance."

"Non-magical folk hate me," she replied, her voice shaking. "They'll always be afraid of me."

"You can't know that. I know that people widely treat sorcerers with suspicion and distrust, but it is because they never truly get the opportunity to experience what good sorcerers can do. I seek to change that perception, but I can't do it alone." He reached a hand up toward her, palm upwards. "Trust me, Nehanda."

She hesitated, indecision flickering across her face. Then she reached down and took his hand, allowing him to help her down from the tree. He smiled brightly, squeezing her hand.

Chapter Forty-Six

Adanya chose this moment to bring them back to the present. Nehanda sank to her hands and knees as they left her mind, shaking uncontrollably.

"I don't understand," Adanya said, her eyebrows lowered as she tried to process what she'd just seen. "What changed?"

"What changed?" Nehanda repeated raspily, glaring up at Adanya.

"Ziyad gave you a second chance. How did you get to the point that working for the kingdom wasn't enough?"

"Stupid girl," Nehanda spat. "Ziyad may have wanted to change the world, but the world didn't want to change. No matter what we do, we're always going to be looked at with fear."

"Or respect!" Adanya protested. "Ziyad made it possible for sorcerers to be seen as more than just unknown powers that could destroy others. He made us visible in a way that allowed people to accept us."

"The only way to keep them from turning on us is to make them fear us. That is when we get the best results; that is when we are truly safe," Nehanda said.

"You think their fear wouldn't unite them against us?" Adanya asked.

"That is why I gathered all of this power. Even if they want to destroy us, they're not powerful enough to do it." She managed to stagger to her feet, though she was still unsteady, swaying like a tree in the wind. "I used Harrun's king to destroy everyone that could stand against me, and then I destroyed him. All of this time, I've been gathering power to ensure that I would never be cast out again, that I would be able to protect myself."

"So now you reveal your true mind. This was never about protecting magical folk; it was about protecting yourself," Adanya said slowly.

"Isn't that what I always taught you? To protect yourself above all else?"

Tears sprang to Adanya's eyes with the realization. "Even if you had truly wanted to help me, you couldn't. No matter what happened, who accepted you, who *forgave* you, you were still that little girl who was an outcast forced to protect herself because no one protected her."

"You speak like you're so different from me," she sneered. "You know what it's like to be kicked out because people were afraid of you."

"I do know that. But I also know that we can't allow our past to jade us to the possibilities of the future." Though Adanya knew this confrontation would soon end, she felt enormous pity for the woman standing before her. "If I didn't have people around me who saw through you and warned me, I would be just like you."

"I suppose it's a good thing that you aren't. Your bleeding heart is a liability."

Adanya cried out in agony as a tree root shot up from the ground, spearing her through her not-fully-healed shoulder and slamming her against the trunk of a tree at the edge of the clearing, effectively pinning her in place like a butterfly on a card.

Winded and in tremendous pain, Adanya struggled to control her breathing and calm her mind enough to retaliate. Nehanda stalked toward her like a lion circling its wounded prey, a smirk of victory on her lips.

"You really thought that you'd be able to defeat me by dancing around in my memories? My memories made me the strong woman I am today; you can't use them against me. And with you out of the way, I can finalize my takeover. No one will be able to hurt me ever again."

Adanya forced herself to take deep, shaky breaths. Blood flowed steadily from her shoulder, seeping through her white robes. Nehanda drew closer, her eyes calculating as she considered what magic to use to end her one-time protege.

Let go.

Rashidi's voice was as clear as day in her head. She could suddenly see him crouched in front of her, looking her dead in the eye. *Let go,* he repeated.

Suddenly, she flashed back to when she lost control after Jabari had been killed. Just the thought of it brought whispers of the voices in her mind. Rashidi disappeared as Nehanda reached both hands to grasp either side of Adanya's head, clearly intending to destroy her from the inside out.

The instant she felt Nehanda's fingertips on her skin, she did as Rashidi had advised. She let go.

Nehanda's mouth dropped in shock as Adanya's eyes flared wide, glowing a blinding white. A fierce wind whipped through the woods, tossing Nehanda to and fro. Her hands, however, were fused to Adanya's face. Adanya allowed every emotion, every memory, every ghost of the people she had lost to flow from her mind into Nehanda's, overwhelming her senses.

Nehanda struggled to fight back, trying to use all of her magic to free herself. First, she tried cutting through the voices to get into Adanya's mind but found them loud and unrelenting. Then she tried calling forth nearby animals to attack, but Adanya repelled her call with a single thought. Next, she tried water, managing to raise it from the nearby stream bed to flow over them both, but Adanya parted the water and froze it, leaving them surrounded by huge swaths of ice. When she tried to call the sun to melt the ice, Adanya summoned thick storm clouds to cover the sun and douse them both in torrents of rain. She turned her attention to the root in Adanya's shoulder, twisting it to cause more pain. Adanya winced, but her unblinking eyes still stared at Nehanda.

Finally, Nehanda turned back to her original power. She lit herself aflame, pressing her hands tighter to Adanya's face in an attempt to burn her to ashes the way she had Kamaria. She jumped in surprise as Adanya's hand reached up and clamped around her wrist, sending searing, burning pain through her skin. In an instant, both women were consumed by the flames. The voices in Nehanda's head grew louder, causing her to lose focus. That moment was all that was required. She caught on fire, the flames searing through flesh and bone and hair and anything else belonging to her.

Adanya was deaf to her screams of agony and pleas for mercy. Her glowing eyes watched impassively as Nehanda sank to her knees, hands finally released from her face, then fell to her side, the searing flames reducing her to nothing but ash and bone in a matter of minutes.

Adanya's face twitched, and as she blinked, her eyes slowly faded back to the calmer yellow glow. Unlike before, she was aware of everything that had happened. The rain continued to pelt her as she looked down at the remains of what had been her mentor, and tears flowed freely from her eyes.

"I'm sorry," she whispered.

She released a grunt of pain as she used her magic to remove the root from her shoulder, staggering forward until she fell onto her hands and knees. Shakily, she called forth her power to return her to the field.

Chapter Forty-Seven

Adio jumped in surprise as Adanya reappeared out of nowhere beside him on the platform. He was only just in time to catch her before she collapsed, easing her down to the ground.

"What happened?" he asked in concern, examining her. "Is she...?"

She nodded, wincing at the movement. "She's dead."

Sefu climbed the platform and came to kneel beside them. "It's done. All of the soldiers have either surrendered or been killed."

She looked around to see there were a few bodies scattered around the platform; for the most part, however, the field was empty.

Sefu directed Adio in carefully baring Adanya's shoulder so he could better see her wound. "No bones broken. Whatever pierced you was thin enough that it missed your major arteries as well."

"What was it?" Adio asked.

A half-smile cracked her face. "A tree root."

Sefu raised an eyebrow, then started tearing cloth from the hem of her robes to use as a bandage. "We'll need to cauterize it again."

"Wait, let me try something. Put me down, Adio."

"But..."

"Now who doesn't like to listen?"

He relented, helping her into a sitting position and backing away with Sefu.

She closed her eyes, summoning her Flora powers. The grass on the field around the platform suddenly burst into color, dandelions and other flowers sprouting as if they were late to greet the sun. As before, she could feel her wound pulling itself back together. She opened her eyes as the growth around them slowed, looking down to see a jagged scar on her shoulder.

Adio and Sefu's mouths had fallen open. "Well, then." Adio found his voice first. "I really can't call you little girl anymore."

She smiled and tried to get to her feet, the men catching her as she staggered.

"Healed or not," Sefu cautioned, "you still lost a lot of blood. Take some rest."

Adanya relented, calling the rest of the new council to her. When they were all gathered and she was assured of their safety, she gazed at them from her seated position at the edge of the platform.

"There's still much for us to do. The other kingdoms must be completely freed of Nehanda's influence, and we must help the people rebuild their monarchies and governments. It will take all of us to do this."

"With you as our leader, it should be an easy task," Idir said earnestly.

"I wouldn't say *easy*, but it will certainly be more manageable." She smiled at his enthusiasm. "Sefu, you, Waed, and I will work together to devise a plan to accomplish these goals. Adio, you and I will work together to determine where the council will be most needed in the rebuilding efforts."

"We will be proud to follow you as our queen," Sefu said.

She could not help but make a face. "For now, at least."

Adio noticed her discomfort and scooped her into his arms. "Alright, that's enough talk for now. You need some rest."

"I'll finish getting things cleaned up and organized here, and tomorrow we'll meet," Sefu said helpfully.

Adio carried her back up the path they had walked as prisoners only hours before. Adanya was silent, her brows creased as she thought.

Through everything that had happened, she had forgotten that she was queen by birthright—though there wasn't truly a kingdom to rule. But Sefu's reminder made her really consider if she could be a queen.

"Hey. I've got an idea of what you're thinking so hard in there," Adio said out of the blue. "Give it time. You did just save the world, after all; you're allowed some rest."

She smirked at him. "You know me too well." She paused as the weight of her words sank in. "You're the only one left who does."

"And I don't plan on going anywhere anytime soon. I'm sure those other council members will learn a lot from you, in time, and we'll all grow closer together. It won't be the same, of course, but it will all work out."

"Ever the soul of optimism, hm?"

"Always."

Chapter Forty-Eight

A year later...

Adanya and Adio stood looking up at the nearly completed palace. Memories flooded her mind, and she could feel Adio sharing them with her. Around them was a continual hustle and bustle: builders making finishing touches, carpenters bringing completed furniture into the palace, and the continuous bark of Waed training soldiers in the flatlands beyond the palace walls.

"My lady!" They were stirred from their reverie by Abiba's voice. She hurried over to them from the entrance to the palace, dipping her head respectfully. "Everything has been organized as you asked. Sefu and the others are waiting for you in the glade."

"Lead the way," Adanya said.

Adio offered his arm, and together they followed the young woman out of the palace grounds.

The glade was a tranquil spot, surrounded by flowers and serenaded by a gentle creek flowing nearby. Within the glade, a makeshift table had been erected, surrounded by carved stumps. The members of the new council rose as they approached, dipping their heads respectfully at Adanya. Adio saw her seated and then sat at her right hand. Sefu remained standing beside and behind her.

The Head of Council smiled, a twitch of sadness in her face as her glowing eyes passed over the empty space held for Kamaria while she searched for a worthy replacement. The young ones had grown in the space of a year, all given more responsibilities and proving themselves worthy replacements of their ancestors. In some ways, she felt like a proud mother. But there were other responsibilities to attend to.

"Thank you all for responding so quickly to my call," she said. "I was hoping to postpone this meeting until the palace was completed and we were able to convene in the council chambers, but I was reminded that a coronation will need to take place before the palace is fully restored.

"By now you all know of my claim to the throne. King Keon was my father, which makes the throne mine by birthright. I did consider the impact having a sorcerer on the throne would have, especially considering the throne's history. However, there is also the fact that we have been working so hard to regain the people's trust in sorcerers. All of these years under Nehanda's thumb have made the people wary, and it makes perfect sense that they are. It will take more than a year to rebuild that trust, but I know we are all committed to making it happen.

"With that being said ... my first duty is to the sorcerers and the people, not just of our kingdom. There is much work to be done, and I would be limited if I tried to do it while also ruling a country. Therefore, I have decided that I shall bestow the leadership of our country to someone who has more than proven themselves capable of caring for the people."

She rose and turned to Sefu, unable to hide a smile of pride. "Sefu. For years before I awakened, you fought for the people. You have all of the qualities that will make a good king. I name you King Sefu. Know that you shall always have me for counsel as you lead our country back to the greatness we once enjoyed."

He seemed initially surprised, awkwardly receiving her embrace and looking around him with wide eyes as the others applauded to show their approval.

"You're not doing this alone," she said into his ear. "No one expects you to be perfect. Everyone that you see around you is here to ensure you and the kingdom are successful." She stepped back, taking his face in both of her hands and looking deeply into his eyes. "Rashidi would have been proud to know how dedicated you have been to our people." She gently kissed his forehead, then stepped back. "Hail Sefu, our king."

"Hail!" everyone echoed.

Adanya stepped back to allow the others to congratulate him, watching as he grew in confidence. She raised an eyebrow as Abiba hugged him a bit longer than everyone else, sensing the deeper feelings there. *Something tells me that we won't be long without a queen,* she thought to Adio, a smirk on her lips.

A sorcerer in the royal family again? Can't be a bad idea. He turned to look at her. *What about you, little girl? Have you given any thought to finding someone?*

Now her smile was sad. *I think that ship has sailed. Everyone alive is some seventy years my junior; we wouldn't have a thing in common.*

You could always marry me, he quipped.

And ruin this friendship? Not a chance. She hugged him tightly, closing her eyes for a moment. *I'm glad that I still have you.*

He squeezed her back. *I wouldn't be anywhere else but by your side.*

They turned back to the rest of the new council and their king.

"Well, there is much to be done," she proclaimed. "A coronation, the celebration of the palace's completion, announcements to the people..."

"We'll take care of everything!" Nala exclaimed, clapping her hands together. "I love planning events!"

"The birds can help us to spread the word faster," Odeon said, matching her excitement.

The rest of the new council began chattering animatedly among themselves. Squeezing Adio's hand, Adanya moved back over to Sefu. "I'll be back in a few hours. There's someone I need to visit."

"Do you need a guard? I can get Waed to gather a few people..."

"It's fine, Your Majesty. This is something that I need to do alone."

"Of course, my lady."

Adanya winked back at Adio and then headed off into the woods alone, unnoticed by the excited new council.

#

Though she had found the location on the map, she had not had the chance to visit it. Full of contemplative silence, Adanya walked slowly through the woods and across the newly cleaned roads until she reached Rashidi's gravesite.

She sat down on the dusty road, crossing her legs and gently running a hand over his gravestone. "You would be so proud of me, my love."

"And why is that, my lady?"

She smiled as she saw him sitting across from her where the gravestone had been, a twinkle in his eye as he smiled at her. "I freed myself. I got past everything that had been placed on me to hold me down, and now I can be all I am supposed to be."

"Almost all, you mean."

"What?"

"There's still more for you to do. I think you know that. Just because Nehanda is gone doesn't mean her influence on you has vanished. There will be times that those old doubts come back; you'll have to be wary so you can deal with them when they arise."

"It was so much easier when I had your voice to remind me."

"What do you think is happening now, my love? I may be gone, but your power still allows you to speak with me."

"It's not really you, though," she said sadly. "It's just my mind speaking through you."

"Exactly. Which means that you've always had it in you to grow." He leaned forward and took her hand. "I've always had faith in you, Adanya. But I'm not the only one. You have so many people to love and support you, who need you to move forward. I have every confidence that you'll be just fine."

She ran her thumb over his knuckles, tracing the familiar calluses. "I miss you so much, Rashidi. Every moment of every day."

"I know. But that just means you carry a part of me in your heart." He reached up with his other hand to caress her cheek, brushing away her tears. "I love you, Adanya."

"I love you too," she whispered, closing her eyes and leaning into his touch. When she opened them again, he was gone, the gravestone in his place.

She took a few deep breaths, willing herself to be fully in the present. Then she stood and dusted herself off, preparing to head back to the palace. But before she did, she conjured up beautiful curling vines and golden flowers to surround his gravestone, protecting it from the elements. She kissed two fingers, then pressed them against his name on the stone.

Straightening her shoulders, she turned and went back to work.

Acknowledgements

Well, it finally happened.

I've wanted to be a published author since I was eleven. Now, at thirty-three, it's finally happening. After a previously disastrous first attempt at self-publishing and a couple of years of failed querying to publishers and agents, I'm back with a myriad of tools and resources that I didn't have before.

So many people have been instrumental in making my dream a reality, but I'd be here all day if I tried to name them all. So I'll just name a select few:

I first want to thank God, because I wouldn't be here in the first place without His gifts.

Thank you to my family for always being supportive and encouraging. Specifically, my brother Roman, who was always my first beta reader. (I think it still counts if I read it aloud to him, right?)

Thank you to the amazing writing community I've found online who have been a wealth of knowledge, encouragement, and connections. It wasn't until I took the plunge that I realized self-publishing was a viable pathway for getting my work out there.

Thank you to my beta readers, Kayla, Cara, and Aicilia. I was terrified to let others read my work, but I received not only helpful feedback but also reassurance that others would enjoy this story I've created.

Thank you to my girlfriends, Angie, Octavia, Constance, Hillary, and Michelle, for letting me ramble on about book things all of the time, and to Kris for talking bookshop with me.

Thank you to Kelly, the best editor I could have found – edits mixed with reader responses will now be my standard expectation.

And of course, thank you to Jack. I couldn't have written this from such an honest place without your support and love, and Rashidi wouldn't be the character he is without your example of what a good man is. I wouldn't have had the courage – nay, audacity – to just go for it and share my story with the world. I love you with all my heart.

About The Author

J. Ross has been chasing her dream of writing since she was eleven, when her dad first taught her to use a word processor to write down a dream she had. Twenty-two years later, she published her first novel, *Awakening*. When she's not writing, she is an avid reader and loves to do puzzles and complete annual rewatches of *The Lord of the Rings*.

Note From The
Author

Thank you so much for reading Awakening!

If you enjoyed this book, please leave a review! Indie authors live on word of mouth and reviews from readers like you to continue reaching their audience!

Please consider following me on social media to keep up with all things J. Ross!

Facebook: @jwritesfiction

Instagram/Threads: @jrossauthor

TikTok: @j.rossauthor
Website: @jrossauthor.net

Keep reading for a sneak peek at Book 2 in The Adanya Saga: Awoken!

Awoken: Chapter 1

I love you, Adanya.

Adanya awoke with a jolt, looking around in a panic, desperate to get a bearing on her surroundings. Was she back in the cabin where she'd awoken years later than she'd planned, alone and betrayed? Was she preparing to go to battle against the person she'd trusted most? Was she restrained in a dungeon, awaiting her fate?

No. No, she was in her room in the new palace, safe and secure.

She tossed aside the covers and wandered over to the standing mirror placed beside the window. No light was needed; the golden glow of her eyes illuminated the space around her, though she dimmed them to reduce the glare.

She stood in her sleeveless nightdress, staring at herself. She wasn't the same young woman she had been only a few years ago. Her loose black curls hung down to her shoulders, where she'd let them grow after cutting her braids. Faded scars peeked out from behind her shoulder straps. She still looked thirty-four, though now she was one hundred four. The magic that prolonged her life, however, did nothing to alleviate the bags under her eyes from lack of sleep.

A man's voice echoed through her head, and she rolled her eyes dramatically. *You do remember if you can't sleep, neither can I, right?*

I didn't call for you, she thought back.

You do remember you have less control over your magic when you're asleep, right? I'm coming over. His tone made it clear he wasn't arguing.

Adanya groaned, then raised a hand toward the fireplace. A tongue of flame appeared from thin air, dancing around her hand before zipping over to light the wood stacked within. The room was brightly lit in moments, and Adanya grabbed her robe from the foot of the bed, pushing her feet into her boots. As she moved, water floated from the basin on the bedside table. It vaporized above her head, wreathing her curls in steam as she quickly ran her fingers through them and tried to look presentable.

She turned as the door swung open to reveal her best friend Adio, dressed in linen pants and a shirt, looking much more rested than she. He plopped down into her armchair by the fire, grinning up at her with his signature twinkle of mischief in his teal-rimmed eye.

"Alright, little girl," he said fondly. "What's keeping you up tonight?"

"I have no idea what you're talking about." She sniffed, though her heart warmed from the care he radiated in her direction and the familiar nickname.

"Adanya. I know you haven't been sleeping well. And it's not because of the bags under your eyes."

She reflexively put a hand to her face, even though she'd been looking at those same bags only moments earlier. "I didn't need you to point that out."

He chuckled, then grabbed her hand. "Come on, now. Spill."

The sorceress took comfort in his grip, once again glad Adio had decided to stay around to support her when most of the original Council of Sorcerers had either died or been killed. "My dreams lately have been a jumble," she admitted. "The few peaceful ones I have are of Rashidi and our time together." She twisted the engagement ring she still wore, though her fiancé was long gone. "But there have been … voices. Like people crying out for help. Yet when I wake up and search, everything is as it should be."

Adio tilted his head. "Are you sure they're present voices? It could be people from before."

"No, these feel distinctly different. And … farther away, if that makes sense?"

"I don't know if it makes sense, but I think I understand. Do you think it has something to do with our search?"

"That's my best guess." She shrugged.

His eyebrows furrowed. "Do you think we should still go out tomorrow? If your magic is confused, it might make it harder for you to sense anything."

"We can't just put off the search," she said in frustration.

She could feel his intention to counter her, but he stopped himself and sighed. "There's still a lot about your magic that we still don't fully understand. Maybe hearing these voices is because being a Sage Elemental has amplified your powers."

Now Adanya paused, thinking. Four years after she defeated her mentor and became a Sage Elemental, the most powerful kind of sorcerer, there were still many things she had to discover. The basics, she understood; she could wield all six kinds of elemental magic—telepathy/empathic, fire, growth, animal communication, weather, and water. Sage, Ember, Flora, Fauna,

Clime, and Aqua. But she had yet to discover the full scope of her powers.

"Perhaps," she murmured. "Regardless, we still should go. Early, so we're back in plenty of time for the christening."

"You don't just want to *poof* us there?"

She glared at him. "That's not how it works. If we teleport, we might miss sensing any magic."

"I suppose." Adio rose and stretched, and a distant crack of thunder punctuated the weather sorcerer's movement.

"Show-off." She shoved him playfully. "We'll leave at dawn."

"Only gives me a few more hours of sleep. Guess I'd better head back to bed."

"Yes, leave me alone." She gave him a quick hug, then watched him walk out and close the door.

Returning to the chair he'd just vacated, she stared into the fireplace. Though she needed to learn more about her magic and discover the cause of her nightmares, there were more pressing matters. Her thoughts turned to the purpose of their journey for the next day. She needed to focus on finding new sorcerers in Rydell.

If she couldn't, then there was a good chance the council members would be the only magic users left in the world—and she didn't know what that meant. For anyone.